Surrender to Love

Julia Templeton

Hard Shell Word Factory

To my husband—
for modeling for the cover of this book,
and more importantly, for meaning it when you vowed
to love me in sickness and health. You got much more than
you bargained for, but have handled it in true hero fashion.
I love you!

© 2002 Julia Templeton
ISBN: 0-7599-0419-7
Trade Paperback
Published May 2002
ISBN-ebook: 0-7599-0416-2
Published April 2002

Hard Shell Word Factory
PO Box 161
Amherst Jct. WI 54407
books@hardshell.com
http://www.hardshell.com
Cover art © 2002 Julia Templeton
All electronic rights reserved.

Chapter 1

Richmond, Virginia
1850

SHE WOULD rather die.

It was a strange revelation, but Jordan realized she would rather die than become Marvin Johnson's wife. Glancing in the old man's direction, she cringed as he sat back in his chair, his bloated stomach straining the gold buttons of his waistcoat until it threatened to burst. Her gaze moved up to his face to find his black beady eyes watching her. His thin lips split into a smile, displaying a set of crooked, yellow teeth.

A shudder ran through her at the thought of sharing his name, and even worse, his bed.

Only three hours had passed since she'd learned the devastating news of her upcoming marriage to the deplorable man who was old enough to be her grandfather. Her uncle, with Marvin at his side, had said simply, "Jordan, Mr. Johnson has asked for your hand in marriage, and your aunt and I have given our consent."

Horrified at the sudden turn her life had taken, Jordan had watched them intently, hoping it was a joke.

Yet now, just hours after that fateful moment, a diamond ring secure on her finger, Jordan knew it was no joke and tried to find some positive qualities in her future husband. Yet all she saw was an old man with a double chin, hooked nose, thin lips, and gray receding hair, giving her little, if any, hope for the future.

"I can hardly wait to take you home to Carlisle," Marvin said, and to Jordan's dismay, she realized his voice irritated her as well.

Her lips trembled as she tried to smile, but failed. There was no way she was going anywhere with him, and it was on the tip of her tongue to tell him as much when her uncle abruptly cleared his throat. She glanced in his direction and read the subtle warning he sent her.

A small, ice-cold hand grabbed hers beneath the table. She glanced at her cousin, Kari, who sat next to her, staring down at her full plate. For eleven years they'd been inseparable, telling each other every secret, every fear...everything.

And now Jordan was sure that Kari was feeling the same revulsion over the news of her marriage, as though it were Kari herself who was going to be bound forever to the man sitting opposite them.

"Jordan, you were asked a question."

Jordan looked up with a start to find Patricia, Kari's stepmother, watching her with a forced smile. "Mr. Johnson asked if you would like to go to Europe for your honeymoon."

Lifting her chin, Jordan replied, "No, I wouldn't."

Patricia glared at her, her uncle shook his head, and Marvin smiled sardonically, as though he hadn't heard the venom in her voice.

As conversation resumed, Jordan continued holding Kari's hand, squeezing it tightly as Marvin, her uncle, and Patricia discussed the upcoming nuptials as though she wasn't present. Patricia's daughters, nine year-old twins, watched Jordan with sly smiles on their faces, obviously enjoying every moment. Ignoring them, Jordan kept her head down and picked at her food, wishing she were any where else—particularly at her ranch in Wyoming, far away from this life and these people.

Marvin slid his chair back abruptly, bringing her attention back to the present. "I hate to leave now, but it has been quite an eventful day and I have wedding arrangements to make."

Jordan stood slowly, trembling as Marvin came toward her, his gaze moving down her body before coming to rest on her bosom. A sinister smile played at his lips as he took her hand in his and brought it to his mouth. Jordan flinched as his cold, dry lips touched her. When she felt his tongue against her flesh, she instinctively ripped her hand from his.

"I will see you Wednesday," he said, his smile almost a sneer, before he turned and left.

Holding onto the back of the chair for support, Jordan could feel her uncle's gaze burning into her. When she glanced up, his smile was triumphant.

He raised a glass in salute. "Congratulations on a wonderful catch. Mr. Johnson is one of the wealthiest men in all of Virginia. You will have everything you want, Jordan." He drained the brandy in one swallow. "Now, don't look so down. Once you're living in that mansion in Carlisle, you will realize how lucky you are."

Seething with fury, she replied in a shaky voice, "Lucky? To be married to a man who is old enough to be my grandfather!"

"Jordan!" Patricia hissed.

"I don't want to marry Mr. Johnson," Jordan replied, hating how desperate she sounded. "I want to go home. Back to Fife, to my ranch. Please, I have never asked you for anything, but now I implore you—"

"Enough!" Her uncle slammed the glass down on the table. "You dear girl, will do no such thing. The taxes on the ranch far exceed your allowance. In fact, I have informed the bank to sell the property in order to pay them. If there is any money left over, you will receive it to do with as you please."

He was selling her ranch!

The blood roared in Jordan's ears. How dare he take away the one thing most precious to her! "My father built that ranch with his own two hands. It's all I have left of my parents, and the only thing I want in this world. Uncle Frederick, I'll pay you back every cent of those taxes...please don't sell it."

He closed his eyes and let out an unsteady breath. When he opened them a moment later, no kindness remained. "You are marrying Marvin Johnson. One day you will thank me for it." He stood, his gaze piercing into hers before he headed for the double doors.

The twins giggled and Jordan glared at them effectively silencing them, though their sly little smiles remained. They were enjoying her agony far too much. Jordan looked to their mother, who quickly schooled her features, trying in earnest to appear compassionate, but falling short of achieving it. "Tell me, Patricia, will you do the same to your daughters? Will you marry them off to old, perverted men?"

Patricia's mouth dropped open, then she quickly replied, "Go to your room, young lady. Right now!"

Before leaving the dining room, Jordan stared long and hard at Patricia, a woman who had never tolerated her, and who'd gone out of her way to make her life a living hell.

Leaving the room with her head held high, Jordan climbed the stairs. Prying the detested ring from her finger, her mind raced to find a solution.

Slamming her bedroom door behind her, she tossed the ring on the dresser, stripped off her dress and flung it over a nearby chair. If her parents were alive, she'd be back at their ranch nestled among the Rocky Mountains, no doubt living the kind of life for which she'd always yearned. How happy she'd been in those days. Her parents had been kind, loving people who cherished her. The only person who truly cared for her since their death was Kari, and now Jordan would be living fifty miles away from her dearest friend.

Icy fear twisted around her heart. All her dreams were fading away. Instead of moving back to Wyoming, she'd be in Carlisle with an ancient husband, attending endless social functions, of which she always abhorred. She was being forced to marry into a kind of life she'd always hated, and to a man she despised.

Blinking against an onslaught of tears, she took a deep breath as her gaze moved to the locked trunk. "I cannot marry him."

Going to the night stand, she lifted the lantern and grabbed the key beneath it. Her blood pumped wildly as she quickly opened the trunk and pulled out the gun. It would take a single bullet to end it—a simple solution. With trembling hand she brought the gun to her head and pressed it against her temple.

"Forgive me, Lord," she whispered. Closing her eyes, she gently began to squeeze the trigger, imagining what life would be like if she went through with the marriage.

Yet those images mingled with ones of her ranch, and her hand started to shake uncontrollably. "I can't!" she said in despair. Her shoulders slumped in defeat as she stared down at the small gun in her hand. She would just have to find another way to get out of marrying Marvin.

Hearing the door to her room open then close with a soft click, Jordan shoved the gun back in the trunk and quickly wiped the tears away. She turned to find Kari watching her, her eyes swimming with tears.

"Kari, I don't feel like company tonight. Maybe tomorrow morning—"

"I can't believe this is happening. Why would they do this to you? I never thought Daddy could be so cruel. Patricia, yes, but Daddy, never." She ran a hand down her pale face. "Will they do the same to me, I wonder? Oh, how I hate Patricia. She has always wanted us out of Daddy's life!"

Jordan had wondered if Kari also would meet the same fate and be married off. Although Frederick loved his daughter, Jordan believed he loved Patricia more and would do anything the woman wanted.

Taking her chemise off, Jordan swiftly pulled on a pair of breeches, a linen shirt, socks and Hessian boots. She didn't dare glance at her cousin, but by the time she sat at the vanity, Kari stood directly behind her with hands on hips.

"You're leaving, aren't you?"

Meeting her cousin's accusing stare in the mirror, Jordan nodded while plaiting her hair into a braid. "I have no choice."

"You cannot leave without me." Kari grabbed hold of her shoulders, nearly unseating her. "You cannot leave me," she repeated in a firm voice.

Pulling Kari's hands from her shoulders, Jordan held them within her own and smiled at the young woman who had been her saving grace since her parents' death. "I cannot go through with this marriage. I would be giving up my dream of returning to my ranch. I'll grow old before my time and turn into a bitter old woman."

"Then take me with you," Kari begged, dropping to her knees.

"I can't take you. Your father would hunt us down and when he found us, he'd bring us back and throw us in convents." She let out an unsteady breath. "When I get settled, I promise I'll send word. You can come see me as often as you like," she said, hoping to reassure her cousin, though she knew she'd have to wait a long time before contacting her— perhaps years.

Kari ripped her hands from Jordan's grasp and stood, her stance rigid as she turned her back on her. "You swore to me, Jordan Lee McGuire, that you would never leave me, yet here you are doing just that."

Guilt raced through Jordan, for she had promised Kari she would never leave her. Still, at that time she never imagined being in these circumstances. "I can't ask you to leave behind everything you've ever known and loved. You could never make it in the west. There are so many threats, so many things that could go wrong. The trip itself is far too dangerous, and once we get there, it will not be an easy life."

"I swear I could do it," Kari declared, turning to face Jordan again. "Please."

"I would never forgive myself if something happened to you. Understand that I want to, but I just—"

"If you don't take me, then I will tell them that you plan to leave this very night. In fact, right now."

Jordan stared at her cousin, wondering if she were bluffing. They had sworn long ago never to tell on the other, no matter what. Her eyes narrowed. "You wouldn't dare?"

Kari crossed her arms over her chest and took a step toward the door. "Either I go with you, or I tell Father and Patricia exactly what you have planned. And you know Patricia would have a guard stationed outside your door night and day until you and Mr. Johnson are wed."

Jordan stood so fast the chair hit the floor. Kari was already at the door, her hand on the knob, when Jordan grabbed her arm and spun her around. "I can't risk it! You would never make it, and why would you want to leave? You have but to ask for something and it is yours. I have nothing. What little money I do have will not last long, then I will have to get a job."

"I can work."

Jordan rolled her eyes, knowing her cousin hadn't lifted a finger in all her eighteen years. "Do you know how hard we would have to work to make enough money to pay off the taxes? I only have a couple hundred dollars stashed away as it is. It will cost at least that much to get to Fife, probably more."

"I have money," Kari said, her voice full of hope.

"What is going on in there?" Patricia called from out in the hallway. A second later she pounded on the door.

Jordan's breath caught in her throat.

"What is going on?" Patricia's voice became insistent.

Grabbing Kari by the wrist, Jordan whispered, "Swear to me that you will not say a word."

Kari met her stare with an uplifted brow. "Only if you take me with you."

Knowing that Kari had won the argument, Jordan released her wrist. "Fine, meet me in the stables in two hours...pack light."

Chapter 2

Wyoming Territory

The smell of death hung heavy in the air. Jordan tied her kerchief around her face. Swallowing the bile in her throat, she said a quick prayer for the unfortunate victims, hoping the murderer was not in the vicinity.

After three months on the trail, she'd been hardened by what she had seen, but nothing could have prepared her for this. This was beyond violent. She shuddered as her gaze fell on a woman, her naked body mutilated, her head bloodied where she had been scalped. Nearby was a corpse pinned to a tree by at least a dozen arrows.

Jordan turned away, tears stinging her eyes. She glanced at her cousin who looked ready to faint. "Kari, let's go," she said, her voice sounding as weak as her knees.

"This couldn't have happened too long ago. Jordan, you don't think that whoever did this is still around, do you?"

Thinking along the same line, Jordan replied, "Come on, let's get out of here."

"I'm not feeling—" Kari stopped in mid-sentence, her startled gaze fixed on something past Jordan's shoulder. As the color drained from her cousin's cheeks, the hair on the back of Jordan's neck stood on end. She went for her gun and muttered a curse, realizing she had left it in her saddlebag, which was on her horse, a good fifty yards away.

Having no recourse but to face the unknown demon unarmed, Jordan took a deep breath and turned.

Her heart slammed against her ribs to find an Indian watching them. His chiseled face was emotionless, giving her no clue to his thoughts or motives. Her gaze moved down his tall, lean form. The leather vest did little to cover his powerful chest and broad shoulders, or the stomach that rippled with muscle. Leather breeches hung low on his hips—and he was barefoot. A shiver ran down her spine. He was barbaric, right down to the gold band that encircled his muscular right bicep.

Sweat beaded her brow and her legs shook violently. Eleven years ago Jordan had seen another Indian who looked very much like him. She had been only seven years old at the time. It had been a gorgeous summer day in Fife. Warmer than usual, she had gone fishing in the stream behind the log home she shared with her parents. Then screams had pierced the serenity around her. By the time she reached the house, her parents lay dead in a pool of blood, their necks sliced open. In the distance, fleeing the scene, she counted four Indians on horseback.

A twig snapped. She looked up to find the Indian walking toward them. With every step that brought him closer, it took every bit of control Jordan possessed not to run.

He stopped a few feet from her. Now that he was near, she could see his eyes were not the brown she expected but silvery gray. A half-breed! Black hair, dark skin, and intense light eyes—that held no warmth whatsoever.

She and Kari had seen several Indians earlier in their journey, but those were civilized men who dressed and lived like the whites. There was nothing civilized looking about this man. He was just like the savages who had killed her parents and the two poor souls who had passed this way before them.

Her heart thumped wildly, and her mind scrambled knowing her next move could possibly be her last. "We were just leaving. We didn't do anything." Taking Kari's trembling hand in her own, she continued, "We just came upon them ourselves, just minutes ago."

He didn't so much as blink as an uncomfortable silence fell over the clearing.

Jordan jumped as he stepped around her, going down on his haunches beside the dead woman. His fingers lightly brushed the woman's face before he stood, his gaze then shifting to the other victim. The nerve in his jaw ticked and his fingers clenched into fists at his sides.

As she watched him, Jordan wondered if the woman was his wife or some other relation. A wave of compassion swept through her remembering the overwhelming agony when she'd found her parents slain. "Let's get out of here," she whispered, motioning for Kari to follow her.

She hadn't heard or seen the Indian move until it was too late. Strong, hard fingers encircled her wrist. She trembled as his gaze moved over her face, then slowly down her body, hesitating a moment on her heaving chest before meeting her gaze again. His face was void of any emotion, except the coldness of his eyes. With a jerk, she tried to pull free of his grasp, but his superior strength made it impossible.

Never in all her eighteen years had she stood face to face with such an ominous foe—one so intimidating, she didn't doubt he would kill her in the blink of an eye. When he picked up a lock of hair from her shoulder, Jordan tensed, concluding that he wanted to add her scalp to his collection. Unconsciously she pulled the hair from his fingers. Relief flooded her as he released her. "What do you want?" she asked, wincing when her voice broke. "We didn't kill them—you know that. We don't have bows and arrows."

Icy contempt flashed in his eyes before he turned to his mount that stood nearby. "Please leave," she whispered under her breath, watching and waiting as he walked to his horse. *Go! Leave us alone!* She yearned to scream the words, but instead stood silently, waiting. Then to her dismay, he turned and headed back toward them, a length of rawhide in his hand. Jordan's eyes widened in alarm as his intention became clear.

"Jordan?" Kari's voice was full of fear. "You don't think that he will—"

"Run!" Jordan yelled, bolting toward her horse as though the devil himself was after them. Her heart was pounding so loud she could hear nothing over it. Grabbing the pommel with both hands, she swung herself onto the horses back—only to be yanked off a second later.

Turning, she met the Indian's cold gray stare.

"Listen. We did not kill these people! We are innocent, do you hear me? We haven't done anything!" she screamed.

Ignoring her plea, he grabbed her hands roughly. She tried to pull free of his grasp, but his fingers were like steel bands. Fear overriding reason, Jordan kicked him in the shin. He only winced before tightening his hold and binding her wrists with the end of the rawhide. The leather bit into her skin as she twisted her hands in an attempt to loosen the rough binding.

Kari's ear-piercing scream startled Jordan, but the Indian ignored her and continued wrapping her wrists with the tough leather. Letting out some slack, he leaped on his horse with an ease Jordan had never seen, and some other time may have appreciated. But now she wanted nothing more than to stick a knife between those broad shoulders.

Kari's large blue eyes were wide with shock. Her mouth was open as she gazed down at her bound wrists, then back to the Indian. Jordan knew that look well—panic. Kari in a panic was not a pretty sight, and could very well prove to be disastrous for them. "Kari, everything is going to be just fine. There are two of us and only one of him. Besides, someone may come by—"

"Jordan, we are tied to one, if not the strongest Indian God ever made. If that's not enough, look around you. There is nothing for miles. We have not seen another human being for days now, except for the ones who are dead!" Kari's voice grew higher with every syllable.

"Kari, now is not the time to get hysterical."

"Would you like to tell me when the appropriate time might be?

Maybe when he ties us to a stake and burns us alive? Or maybe when his entire village rapes us? Or maybe he will—"

They were jerked forward, ending further argument. Jordan couldn't blame Kari for her anger, especially when minutes ago they were free and within days of her ranch. Now they were captives of an Indian, their fate unknown. She heard the stories of Indian captives, and knew they would be lucky to see the sun rise.

Her gaze returned to the Indian's back where strong muscle rippled beneath the taut dark skin of his broad shoulders. Knowing they needed a way out of this predicament, Jordan tried to think of some way to create a diversion and only one came to mind.

In stubborn desperation she stopped in mid-stride. The rope quickly tightened and she was jerked roughly to the ground. She heard Kari cry out. For what seemed an eternity, she was dragged over rock and across hard-packed ground. Dirt and grit filled her mouth, the rope rubbed her wrists raw, and her shoulders felt as though they were being ripped from the sockets. She nearly cried out in pain, but was saved from doing so when he finally stopped.

The next few minutes would seal their fate. She knew she had to plan her actions carefully so he wouldn't suspect her motives.

Eyes closed, keeping her breath shallow and even, she waited, listening as he slid from his horse and came toward her. A few moments later, the heat from his body told her he was right beside her. He pushed her onto her back, then a strong, calloused hand rested on her forehead as he raised her eyelid. For that split second she could swear she read concern in his eyes. Her chance came when he glanced over his shoulder at Kari.

Fear overriding reason, Jordan struck out. A well-aimed foot hit its mark and he fell to the ground in a heap, his hands instinctively clutching his groin.

Gray eyes flashed with rage and pain when he looked at her. But to her dismay, he slowly came to his feet, towering over her, his expression lethal. For a horrible instant Jordan was sure she was staring death in the face. Then she saw Kari standing behind him with a rock raised in her hand. Horror quickly turned to relief as a sickening thud sounded. A breath-stopping second passed before the Indian's eyes rolled back in his head and he fell to the ground at Jordan's feet.

JORDAN SAT at the base of a tree, exhausted, but unable to sleep, knowing that one angry Indian was out there somewhere. Kari sat beside her, looking like a terrified child as she stared into the darkness. As a lonely howl pierced the night, Jordan wondered if the full moon was a godsend or a curse.

Kari jumped at the sound, her hand lying flat over her heart. "Do you think he's all right? I mean, you don't think I killed him, do you?" she asked, biting her bottom lip nervously.

"Of course not. He's a big man. You probably just stunned him, that's all." Jordan hoped she sounded more confident than she felt. Kari had hit him hard, and head injuries could be serious, even fatal.

Since escaping the Indian hours ago, Jordan had been wondering where he was. Dead or alive, either way she and Kari were in a perilous situation. If he were alive, he would hunt them down and probably recapture them, maybe even kill them. And if he were already dead, his tribe would no doubt track them and kill them...slowly. Horrible visions raced through her mind and she shook her head to dispel them.

"It will do us no good to sit here and fret about it. Let's get going. The more space we can put between us and him, the better off we'll be." Jordan stood, stretched, then stopped, having seen a flash of movement from the corner of her eye. By the time she glanced over at her cousin, the half-breed had one arm around Kari's waist, the other clamped tightly over her mouth. "Let her—" Jordan was instantly silenced by his dark, angry expression.

Kari's gaze slipped to Jordan's waist, reminding her she had a gun tucked into the band of her breeches. Her heart beat triple time. Jordan didn't dare flinch, waiting for the Indian to make his move.

She didn't have long to wait as a few moments later, he started to bind Kari's wrists together. Knowing she may never have another opportunity, Jordan pulled the gun out and aimed it at his head. He was less than five feet away, point blank range, and she knew the damage it would do. He would die—they wouldn't.

His eyes narrowed dangerously. His hand flashed and in the blink of an eye, he held a knife at Kari's throat. Staring into his eyes, Jordan knew he had no intention of letting her win. Dropping the gun, she held her hands up in defeat.

"Do you have to bind us?" she asked, as he stepped toward her with rawhide in hand. She struck out at him, clipping his jaw with her fist. Her hand ached horribly, but his head barely moved at the contact, and if anything, it only served to fuel his anger. As he reached for her, she kicked him in the shin while landing a punch to his rock-hard stomach. Unfortunately, both tactics failed to stop him. He grabbed her wrists and tied them even tighter than before, his gray eyes flat and as unreadable as stone.

Releasing a short expanse of rope, he helped Kari onto the back of his mount, then quickly jumped on, leaving Jordan to walk behind them.

GRAY HAWK stared straight ahead, ignoring the redhead's curses as she tripped along behind them. The blonde woman sat silently before him, her back straight as an arrow, making every effort not to touch him. He glanced at the two horses, and again wondered why two women dressed in worn-out men's clothes would have such fine looking mounts. Unless they stole them, which from what little he knew of them, was probably the case.

When he'd come upon his aunt and her friend's bodies, Gray Hawk had been ready to kill the two at the scene, no questions asked. But that was before he'd seen the Crow's arrows.

He had masked his surprise when the two white women turned, proving they were not men at all, but young women. Their looks of horror confirmed they were shocked to see him as well.

His aunt had been a woman full of life and laughter. She was a valued member of their tribe, and now she was dead. He clenched his jaw. Death was becoming too much a way of life for so many who had been too young to die. Although he never agreed with the custom of taking white captives, he did now to replace the loss of the two who had been slain.

"What do you plan to do with us?" the red-haired hellion yelled at his back. "Do you hear me?"

A person would have to be deaf not to hear her. He glanced back at his captive, whose jaw was set in a rigid line, her green eyes shooting sparks of hatred. Although he'd known few white women in his life, he knew from the start how strong-willed this one was, and how very determined. She had very nearly escaped him twice. Had he not pulled the knife when he did, he would have been dead by now. He couldn't blame her for trying to escape—he would do the same if he were in her place.

He only hoped that once they reached the village, she would accept her fate. If she didn't, the consequences would be far worse.

Chapter 3

JORDAN COULDN'T remember a time she'd been so miserable. Her hair kept falling in her eyes, dirt clogged her nose and throat, and her feet were raw, bloodied and bruised. She'd give anything to stop, if even for a minute. Unfortunately for her, their captor seemed adamant on continuing at a grueling pace.

What was even more maddening was the fact he'd brought their horses along, but refused to let her mount up. No, instead he made her walk behind him the entire way, letting Kari ride in front of him, as though she hadn't been the one to knock him out in the first place. But what did she expect from a savage? A savage who was determined to torture them for murders they didn't commit.

Keeping her eyes on the ground, she tried to ignore her raw wrists that burned with every tug of the rawhide. Putting her physical distress aside, she instead focused on a new plan of escape, hoping time would allow another attempt.

But time proved to be her enemy rather than her friend a short while later when she heard the unmistakable sound of laughter. Her head jerked up and to her horror, she saw a group of dark-haired children running toward her. Her gaze darted around the valley to find at least six dozen teepees perched along the edge of a river, and Indians rushing her from all directions.

As tiny hands reached out and tugged on her hair and clothing, she tried to pull away, but they were insistent. "Stop it!" she screamed, but they seemed oblivious to her distress, and just kept poking and pulling. She was on the verge of hysterics when a sharp whistle rent the air, sending little brown bodies scurrying.

Blowing the hair out of her eyes, Jordan found their captor and Kari walking toward her. Her heart stilled when the half-breed pulled a knife from its sheath. He stopped before her. His light eyes seemed to pierce to the very depths of her soul, unnerving her. The temptation to turn away from that gaze was overwhelming. She was terrified, but she'd be damned if she'd allow him to see her fear.

He turned toward the group of children that mingled close by. He spoke in a rough, guttural language, and the children quickly scattered.

She glanced at Kari, who was obviously thinking the same thing by her confused expression...the half-breed didn't speak English. That knowledge gave her courage to tell him exactly what she felt and before Jordan could stop herself, she said in a harsh voice, "If you think for one minute mister, that we're going to be your squaws, then think again. I have no intention of living the rest of my days as some Indian's slave." Her gaze drifted to his weapon for an instant before returning again to meet his lethal stare. "When you least expect it, I'll take that knife you wear so proudly and stick it in your black heart."

Gray eyes clashed with green in silent battle, until a dangerous smile touched his lips. In one quick motion he cut the binds from Kari's wrists, then pulled Jordan so close his hot breath fanned her cheek. "Don't count on it," he said in perfect English. His voice, low and menacing, gave her little doubt he meant it. She let out the breath she'd been holding as he sheathed the knife.

Kari wavered on her feet. Gray Hawk abruptly released Jordan, grabbing her cousin before she fainted. With gentle hands he steadied her, then turned to Jordan with a scowl. "Be silent and follow me."

Her shoulders stiffened, her eyes narrowed. Never had she hated anyone the way she hated this man. Keeping her gaze on the ground, Jordan muttered obscenities under her breath, trying to ignore the crowd that stood waiting, which was impossible, their chanting and laughter was a roar that filled her ears. "Good-for-nothing son of a—"

The Indian stopped abruptly in mid-step. A second later she ran into his hard back that was more like a brick wall than flesh and blood.

He turned with a venomous glare. "Watch your tongue, or I'll cut it out."

She swallowed her retort and clamped her lips tight, her gaze riveted on his hand that was resting on the hilt of his knife.

As they made their way through the village, Jordan squared her shoulders and lifted her chin. Men, women and children stared at her and Kari with open curiosity. Some appeared angry, some confused, while others looked mildly amused, even laughing as they passed...all except one woman who caught Jordan's eye. Tall and slender, with black silky hair that fell to her slender waist, the woman's doe-like brown eyes were shooting sparks of hatred and jealousy as they approached the camp.

With a hair-raising cry the beautiful woman flew toward Jordan, sending her to the ground with a thud. Taken off guard, she struggled to protect herself, but her bound hands made defense useless. Long, slender fingers tightened around her throat, cutting off her air. Through blurred vision, she saw Kari come to her rescue and try to push the woman off, but the squaw only squeezed tighter until stars began to float through the darkness that was quickly descending upon her.

Her lungs were on fire and ready to explode when the weight on her chest was suddenly gone. Gasping for air, she looked up to find her captor standing above her. Even through the haze she could see he was not pleased.

Turning to the Indian woman, he spoke to her in his unfamiliar tongue, quick, slashing words that made the woman lower her head and walk away.

Jordan sat up, rubbing her bruised throat. Hauled roughly to her feet to meet her captor's searing gaze, she asked in a choked voice, "One of your wives?"

He remained silent as he cut her binds and pushed her and Kari toward a nearby teepee. The flap closed abruptly leaving she and Kari alone with a simple warning. "You leave, you die."

"God, why us?" came the muffled question.

Jordan turned to Kari who lay flat on her stomach, face down on a fur blanket.

"I have no idea. But I do know one thing...it won't be for long," Jordan replied, taking a quick look around the dwelling. It was much more spacious than it appeared from the outside. The floors were covered with furs, and in the center was a fire pit.

Kari sat up slowly. "Jordan, I'm scared. What if they...?" She let the question die as she choked on a sob.

A pang of guilt hit Jordan as she looked at her cousin. Kari's fragile wrists were raw from the bindings that cut into her tender flesh. Her blonde hair had long since come free of its braid and now hung past her shoulders in tangled disarray. Dirt smudges covered her face and arms. Jordan cursed herself again knowing it was her fault they were here. How many times since leaving Virginia had they been warned of the dangers in crossing Indian Territory? Early in their journey, she dismissed the notion that they would actually run into trouble, convincing herself that eleven years would have made a difference between white settlers and Indians. Apparently she'd been wrong. She was so intent on reaching her ranch, she had put their lives in jeopardy by trying to save some time and take a short cut.

Her thoughts scattered as sunlight streamed into the dim interior of the teepee and their captor entered, stopping to secure the flap behind him. Jordan tensed, her eyes moving to a wooden bowl that was more than three feet out of reach, then back to the silent man. If he tried anything, she could use the bowl to clobber him over the head.

Without acknowledging their presence, he lay down on the furs and closed his eyes. Jordan frowned. He was sleeping? With a start, she realized this could prove a good opportunity, or perhaps their only opportunity to escape.

As Kari watched him with a puzzled expression, Jordan knew if they could just wait for him to go to sleep, they could make their move. Crossing her arms over her knees, she stared at the man who lay on his back with one hand on his stomach, the other flung out to his side. As he lay motionless Jordan's gaze ran down the length of him. He was an impressive man; tall, lean, and muscular. The features of his face were so perfect they may as well be chiseled in stone, from high cheekbones, straight nose, and full lips, down to his long lashes. Her gaze shifted lower to his neck and the white line that ran up under his chin, as though someone had tried to slice his neck in one clean stroke, but failed. His vest had fallen open, exposing a chest that was broad and smooth. Two scars marred the surface, but unlike the one on his throat, these were precise marks, as though they'd been put there on purpose. A shiver ran down her spine, not only from knowing he was a dangerous man, but because she felt an attraction toward him—an awareness she'd never felt with anyone else.

She closed her eyes as though she could wish the thought away and him with it. Yet when she opened her eyes a second later, the half-breed was still there, reinforcing her desire to leave.

Within minutes his breathing slowed, becoming deep and even. Each breath became a number as she counted every time his chest rose.

From what little she recalled, Jordan knew the teepee lay on the outer edge of the village, which helped their chances of slipping out unnoticed and making a run for it. But what about their heavily guarded horses? She agonized over leaving Winnebe, but there was no way around it...they would have to take their chances on foot.

After watching the half-breed to the count of five hundred, Jordan couldn't stand it anymore and put a finger to her lips warning silence, then motioned for Kari to follow her. Taking a peek out the teepee, she saw several women off in the distance, busy cooking over a small fire, but no one standing guard. She motioned for Kari to follow while her gaze was riveted on the women outside, hoping they kept busy enough that they wouldn't see she and Kari trying to escape. "Kari." Glancing over her shoulder, she moaned inwardly, seeing the Indian was fully awake and holding onto Kari's wrist.

Letting the flap fall back into place, Jordan took a step toward their captor, who still held Kari. "We just need to relieve ourselves." Ignoring his look of disbelief, she let out a sigh. "Listen, we have to go...do natures calling. If you could release her, we'll go, then come right back."

He released Kari abruptly and took a step toward Jordan. "For future reference, I'm always aware of what's going on around me—always." His cold glare froze her to the spot. "You'll do well to remember that."

When she opened her mouth to speak, he held up a hand to stop her. "Don't say a word, I've heard enough from you."

Jordan planted her hands on her hips mocking him. "Good, then let us go."

Grabbing her by the arm, he pulled her out of the teepee.

"Where are you taking me?" Jordan snapped, trying to pull free of his iron-like grip.

"You said you needed to relieve yourself." He pushed her toward the brush. "Then do it."

She stared at him as he scowled at her, then looked toward the shrubs that could hardly be called cover. "I will not." She crossed her arms over her chest. "You cannot expect me to go in front of everyone."

His mouth quirked in annoyance. "Fine, then I'll take you."

"Take me? You don't mean what I think you mean—do you?" But even as the words left Jordan's mouth, she saw the look in his eye, and knew he meant to take her himself. As he came toward her, she held up her hand. "All right! We'll be right back," Jordan said between clenched teeth.

Grabbing Kari's arm, they marched past the shrubs toward the thicker brush. "I hate him so much, I could kill him with my bare hands."

"He'll probably kill us first," Kari said, sounding as tired as Jordan felt.

Jordan glanced over her shoulder to see the object of her hatred watching them. His gray eyes narrowed skeptically as though he knew she was talking about him. "No, he won't," she said, turning her attention back to the trail that headed into a forest of trees and brush. Her heart hammered as she kept going, ignoring twigs and limbs that pulled at her legs, arms and hair.

"Jordan, where are you going?"

"We're getting out of here."

"Now?"

"Can you think of a better time? I'm not about to become anyone's dinner. You've heard the stories."

Kari nodded, her eyes wide with terror.

"Start running," Jordan said without hesitation, as she broke into a run, Kari at her side. Darting through the trees, the voices from the village faded, and as they drew deeper into the woods, hope fueled her steps.

They were escaping!

Jordan hated to think where they would go from here. There was nothing but the vast plains all around them. Two women on foot with no supplies would definitely be vulnerable. The fact they had no money to bargain with made things even more dire. But it was better than the alternative.

A clearing was ahead, the sunshine streaming through the trees was like a beacon to freedom. Jordan smiled triumphantly at Kari as they raced toward it.

But her smile faded as the unmistakable sound of footsteps pounded behind them. Chancing a quick glance behind her, Jordan's eyes widened in alarm seeing the half-breed running toward them, his expression clearly determined. There was no way they could outrun him. He was like an animal, quick and powerful, but Jordan wasn't about to give up. "Run Kari!" she yelled, dropping her cousin's hand.

Picking up a rock, Jordan hurled it at the half-breed's head. It missed him completely, and he was close enough for her to see the whites of his eyes. The fury she read in the gray depths gave her pause.

"Jordan, stop! This won't work. We'll never get away," Kari said, coming up from behind her.

The Indian stopped a few feet away, close enough to reach out and grab Jordan, but he didn't.

"Let us go," Jordan begged, her voice cracking with the plea. "We've done nothing to you or your people."

He glanced down at her bruised wrists before meeting her gaze. For a moment she swore she saw remorse in his eyes, but it was gone a second later.

"I can't," he said, having the audacity to sound sorry.

Jordan took a step toward him and slapped him soundly across the cheek, her hand stinging from the contact. Annoyingly her captor hardly flinched. "You could if you wanted to," she said, before swinging again.

He grabbed her wrist before she could strike again. The nerve in his jaw beat double-time as he stared at her through cold eyes. "I'm Gray Hawk, War Chief of my people. You'll be safe as long as you're with me. But I can't say the same if you were to belong to another. Accept your fate, for I will not warn you again. One more time, just once," he said lifting a single finger for emphasis. "And you will find that I can be ruthless if pushed. There are others here who would give anything to teach you a lesson in obedience. If you keep it up, I may just let them."

Jordan kept her mouth shut, certain it would be a mistake to anger him further. But she did know one thing for sure—there was no way she would sit back and accept *her fate* as he called it. The Indians had changed her fate eleven years before when they'd killed her parents. They wouldn't ruin her life all over again. She and Kari were going to get out of the village alive and untouched.

"Go," he said, motioning for them to precede him back to the camp as he followed behind in silence. Jordan dug her fingernails into her palms as she watched Kari wipe away tears. She glanced back at the half-breed—Gray Hawk. Maybe he would listen to reason. What could it hurt? She turned and he stopped, watching her with suspicious eyes.

"What exactly do you intend to do with us?" she asked, lifting her chin a notch under his cool stare. "I have money if that's what you want. I'll give you anything."

One black brow lifted, his gaze moved slowly down her body and up again. "Anything. Are you sure about that?"

"Absolute—" The word died on her lips, suddenly realizing what he meant by anything. She bit her lip, sure that a response would only get her in more trouble.

She turned and kept marching. By the time they reached the teepee, her anger was like a volcano boiling inside of her.

He grabbed several bowls and handed them to her. "You will go with the other women and help prepare our meal."

She stared at the bowls, refusing to take them. He wanted her to serve him? Her self-imposed silence exploded a second later and she replied coolly, "I will *not* be your slave."

A nerve ticked in his jaw, and he pressed the bowls into her hands. "You *will* do as I say."

Jordan took the bowls from him with a curse. She followed behind Kari, then stopped in mid-step. Without considering the foolishness of her actions, Jordan turned and threw the bowls at his head.

He caught one in his hand, but a loud crack filled the air as the other hit its mark. Her eyes widened in alarm seeing the stream of blood run down the side of his face.

"Jordan!" Kari gasped in disbelief.

Jordan stood completely still, horrified at what she'd done, but was unable to do anything as Gray Hawk put a hand to his bleeding temple. His gaze moved from her to the bowl in his hand, then to the ones scattered at his feet before returning to her once again.

Jordan swallowed hard, watching with a sense of doom as his gray eyes darkened like angry thunderclouds.

Kari went to pick up the bowls, but Gray Hawk shook his head, giving her a silent order to leave them alone.

•

Do not be afraid. Do not be afraid, Jordan told herself over and over, hoping she appeared less terrified than she felt. Lifting her chin, she put her hands on her hips. "I told you I wasn't going to be your squaw."

He took a step toward her. She took one back.

"Pick up the bowl, Jordan."

Hearing her name from his lips was unsettling. Maybe it was because he sounded like any other white man, instead of a savage. Well, it didn't matter who he was...she wouldn't serve him. After all, she hadn't escaped one man only to become a slave to another. Glancing at the dish at his feet, she shook her head. "No, I will not."

"Yes, you will," he said through clenched teeth.

Her pulse began to beat erratically at the threatening tone in his deep voice. His dark face set in a vicious expression, he grabbed a length of rawhide, obviously intent on binding her again.

"Oh, all right," she hissed as she bent and picked up the bowls. "I'll cook your damn dinner!

Chapter 4

JORDAN GLARED at the brave whose duty it was to watch her and Kari while Gray Hawk was off hunting, or doing whatever it was he and all those other warriors did all day. It seemed to her that the women did all the work, while the men played.

"I hate this!" she shouted in frustration, scrubbing Gray Hawk's breeches with a vengeance. How she detested doing laundry, and having to do Gray Hawk's made her despise it that much more.

Although it was only the sixth day of their captivity, Jordan felt as though she and Kari had been in the village forever. Since coming to the camp, a good night's sleep had eluded her, and her mood was suffering because of it.

Things had been relatively easy for them the first few days when Gray Hawk had left to retrieve the bodies of his aunt and her friend. But upon his return, he worked them to the point of exhaustion.

"Things could be worse."

Jordan turned to Kari, her brow furrowed into a frown, wondering if she heard her correctly. "How in the world could it be any worse?"

"Well, he could have tortured us, raped us, or killed us by now. Plus, we've been here for almost a week, and you have to admit, he's treated us better than expected."

Kari did have a point, but the fact remained they were captives, slaving for a man they didn't know, and quite frankly, Jordan couldn't stand. It didn't matter that she found him strangely attractive. She hated his arrogance and the way his gray stare followed her wherever she went, as though she were his possession.

"If being tied to the ass-end of a horse isn't torture, I don't know what is," Jordan muttered, beating the leather against a rock. "Look at my wrists...I'm scarred for life!"

"Jordan, you'll destroy those pants if you keep doing that."

"Good," she replied with a satisfied smile, giving them another hard slap.

The brave watched her, his stone-cold expression still in place, his eyes narrowed in warning. He wasn't much older than her, and Jordan had considered using her feminine charms on him, but knew it was probably useless since he was loyal to Gray Hawk. The boy followed the older warrior around like a puppy.

"And you must admit that Gray Hawk seems like a well-respected member of the tribe," Kari said with something akin to pride in her voice. "From what Tawanka says, he is the bravest of all their warriors."

Jordan rolled her eyes. Obviously their captor had charmed Kari into believing he was something other than what he was. "Don't forget that my parents were killed by savages just like him. If you expect me to defend him, I won't. I want to get as far away from him as I possibly can."

Kari opened her mouth, but hesitated a moment before saying, "Tawanka says he took us to replace the loss of his aunt and her friend. Apparently the last white captive who was taken by the tribe was Gray Hawk's mother. She was just about our age, traveling with her husband when he died along the trail. Gray Hawk's father found her, brought her to the village, and in time they fell in love. He married her and they seemed happy. Yet after she had Gray Hawk, she missed the life she once led so much that one night she escaped. His father was completely devastated. I guess she didn't say goodbye to anyone, not even Gray Hawk."

"You'd think they would have found her?" Jordan said, fighting off the momentary sympathy she felt for her captor.

"I guess he didn't even go after her."

Although Jordan felt bad for the boy who had lost his mother, she could certainly understand why his mother had left. Being away from civilization all those years would be horrible. Jordan shivered at the thought. Days in captivity was bad enough, but years away was too much to even comprehend.

Surely Gray Hawk didn't intend to keep them here forever. But what did she really know about him? Their captor always kept her guessing. He was so mysterious, and if there was one thing that truly irritated her, it was his behavior toward Kari, versus his behavior with her. With Kari he smiled easily and seemed relaxed. But when it came to Jordan, she realized he hated her because he never smiled, and when he did talk to her, his voice was gruff and clipped as though he was constantly irritated with her.

She refused to think that the feeling consuming her might be jealousy, yet every time Gray Hawk flashed Kari one of his rare smiles, Jordan felt compelled to slap him. And even more frustrating was the fact that more and more she found herself looking for him, and then there was the way her heart raced and she felt all flushed when he was around. It was disconcerting to say the least—particularly since she'd never felt that way for anyone else, most of all, an Indian.

A splash of cold water hit Jordan in the face, bringing her out of her musings. "Come on, don't be so serious all the time."

Jordan wiped the water from her eyes and turned to Kari, who was grinning at her. "How can you be so content? I don't understand it?"

Kari shrugged. "What good does it do to be miserable?"

Her cousin was faring far better than she was. The people took to Kari's easy nature quickly, and conversed with her through the help of Gray Hawk, or Tawanka, the medicine woman. Not so with Jordan. As if she carried some deadly disease, they avoided her at all cost. Not that she cared. She didn't want anything from them since they were the source of all her despair.

"Oh no, here comes Running Deer."

Jordan glanced up to find Gray Hawk's woman, the one who attacked her, and two of her friends coming toward them, their expressions devious. Running Deer stopped to talk to the brave, flirting, giggling, her fingers toying with his braid before letting it go. A moment later the young man left.

"I don't like this," Kari said under her breath.

"It's all right," Jordan replied, hoping she sounded more confident than she felt. After all, Running Deer's friends were big women, and Kari would be useless when it came to fighting.

Running Deer approached Kari first, a sly smile on her lips. Jordan tensed as Running Deer touched Kari's hair, then suddenly the smile disappeared and she yanked so hard, she pulled Kari to the ground.

Jordan saw red.

With a lunge, she was on the woman, sending her crashing to the ground. Straddling Running Deer's hips, Jordan jerked her hair with one hand, while trying to hold off her claws with the other.

Running Deer's horrific cry pierced the air, making the hair on the back of Jordan's neck stand on end. Realizing too late the woman's intentions, Jordan couldn't duck away from the clasped fists that connected with her jaw in a bone-jarring crack.

Shaking her head to clear the fog and dizziness, Jordan swung at the woman, her fist slamming hard into the side of the Indian's face. She was elated with the stunning blow, but Running Deer was already swinging back in retaliation. Jordan turned just in time, avoiding the punch.

Jordan's eyes widened seeing Running Deer had a wicked looking knife. Screaming at the top of her lungs, Kari knocked the knife from her hand, giving Jordan the edge she needed. Her fingers enclosed around the woman's neck. As she pressed tighter, her anger controlled any and all reasoning. It seemed it was a stranger's hands and not her own strangling the woman. She could hear Kari's pleas for her to stop and as Running

Deer's dark skin began to turn purple and her eyes began rolling back in her head, Jordan's fingers relaxed slightly. Suddenly, just beyond the mass of Running Deer's black hair, there appeared a pair of large feet. She knew before glancing up who they belonged to.

GRAY HAWK let out an exasperated breath as Jordan glanced up at him with wild eyes. Why was it she was constantly finding trouble?

He reached out and lifted her abruptly to her feet. Instantly she lifted her chin and met his gaze without so much as blinking. Strangely he was impressed by her stubbornness, even though she was taking it to the extreme.

Running Deer came quickly to her feet, holding her jaw.

He knew the woman was jealous of Jordan and Kari. She had been from the moment he'd returned to the village, though she really had no reason to be. They had been lovers for a short while, but that's all they would ever be. When he went on long hunts, he knew she kept her body warm with another, and that thought never bothered him. But her behavior toward his captives did.

Jordan glanced over at Running Deer, her eyes narrowed, looking as though she'd love to take up where she'd left off.

When she took a step in that direction, Gray Hawk picked her up and threw her over his shoulder. With a curse, she jabbed her knee into his stomach. He caught his breath and landed a stiff hand to her rump. A smile came to his mouth when she didn't flinch, or even dare move after that.

"I hate you," she said through clenched teeth.

"The feeling's mutual."

"Put me down you bastard!"

He abruptly dropped her to her feet, and lifted her chin with his hand until she was forced to look directly into his eyes. "You have caused nothing but trouble since the day you came here. Do you want to belong to another? If that's what you want, it can be done. You have embarrassed and humiliated me more times than I can count. By acting this way, you are condemning yourself to a more agonizing fate than being my captive."

"I did nothing...she...that." She pointed in Running Deer's direction. "Forget it, I don't know why I even waste my breath. You never listen!"

"She was only protecting me, and for that we are to be given to another?" Kari asked, taking a step toward him. She touched his arm, then quickly dropped it back to her side.

"I never said I'd get rid of both of you," Gray Hawk replied.

Jordan gasped. "You would get rid of me and keep Kari?"

He did nothing more than lift a brow, making her come to her own conclusion.

She shook her head and bit into her bottom lip before blurting, "I hate you more than I've hated anyone. I never asked for this. You just took it upon yourself to snatch us up and take us away, stealing our dreams and aspirations...our freedom."

He didn't want to hear this, for he'd been struggling with the knowledge he'd taken away their freedom. Clenching his jaw tight, he remained silent.

"What do you expect of us? Do you think we should be thankful? Well, if you do, then think again. I live for the day I leave this horrible place and you along with it." When a single tear rolled down her cheek, he winced. All she'd ever shown was her strength, and now to see her vulnerable made him angry at himself.

"We just want to go home. We've done nothing to you or your people."

There was nothing he could say to make her feel better, so he said nothing, and instead motioned for them to head back to the village. "Go to the teepee and await my return."

She looked ready to run. He knew she would try to escape, and in a way, he almost wished she would. Yet for some reason that he couldn't even explain to himself, he wanted her with him.

With a final glare in his direction, she grabbed Kari's hand and they headed back toward the village. He turned to Running Deer who watched him intently.

He knew what she was thinking. It was what everyone thought—that he'd bought the women back for his pleasure. Yet he hadn't, at least that hadn't been his plan, even though at night he lay awake, finding it hard to find sleep with the red-haired hellion beside him, tossing and turning in her sleep, her hair fanned out over the furs, over her soft, white skin. How he yearned to take her beneath him and discover every inch of her body.

"Why do you not come to me?" Running Deer asked when they were finally alone.

"You are free to do as you please," he said in response, his gaze shifting to the running river behind her, not wanting her to read the truth in his eyes.

"You want her. You want the white woman. Which one, Gray Hawk? Or are you becoming like Iron Bear and want both?"

"Do not provoke them any more, Running Deer."

"Is that a threat?" she asked, her eyes narrowing.

"No, it's a promise."

Without another word, he walked away, ignoring her curses.

SLOWLY, JORDAN opened her eyes to darkness. The only light came from the fire burning low in the pit, and as she sat up on her elbows, she saw that she was alone. She stretched, glad to have napped for a few hours. A little rest did a lot for her attitude, and she needed as much of an adjustment as she could get before facing Gray Hawk again.

The sound of Kari's voice coming from outside the teepee brought her abruptly awake. Scrambling to her feet, Jordan threw back the flap to find her cousin sitting with the others in a circle around the fire. It struck Jordan how odd Kari looked sitting among all the dark-haired people, despite the fact that she laughed and talked with them as though she truly belonged.

Instantly Jordan's gaze darted around the camp, looking for one man in particular. Not seeing Gray Hawk among the others, she sat beside Kari and forced herself to relax and listen to the conversations around her. She told herself if she tried to learn the language, she would be giving into her captivity by trying to adapt. Yet, unconsciously she found she listened more intently these last few days, knowing it would be much easier, and perhaps even help them escape if she knew what they were saying.

A hush fell over the crowd as the flap to the chief's teepee opened, and the chief, Three Moons, stepped out, followed by his sons, Iron Bear and Gray Hawk.

Holding her breath, Jordan watched as Gray Hawk's gaze scanned the circle and came to rest on her, as though he'd been searching for her alone. To her distress, she couldn't look away. A strange awareness raced through her as she stared. Soft leather breeches clung to his strong legs like a second skin. His narrow hips accented a flat stomach that was hard and muscled. She swallowed as her gaze moved up his body to the bear-claw necklace that rested against his smooth chest, then up further to his face. The war bonnet of white feathers contrasted with his dark beauty, and the painted green stripes running along the base of his high cheekbones made the gray of his eyes brighter and more intense. He was compelling, his magnetism so potent, that the hair on her arms stood on end.

The haunting melody of a wooden flute floated on the breeze. The group around her clicked their tongues, and a few shrill cries rang out as the men of the tribe came together in the middle of the circle. As Jordan looked around the camp, she saw all the men were wearing masks or wore paint all over their bodies, which meant she was about to witness a ceremony of some type.

Her stomach clenched in a tight knot. Merciful heaven, was this it? Jordan wondered. Were she and Kari to be offered as a sacrifice? Had she been so difficult that Gray Hawk had decided to rid himself of them altogether? She jumped as warriors threw handfuls of powder into the fire, making it flare brightly into the night sky.

Jordan's heart matched the beat of the drums as she watched dark male bodies sway to the music. The men moved as one, so sensual, so exotic, so unlike anything she'd ever witnessed before.

Oddly enough, an emotion other than fear began to race through Jordan as she watched Gray Hawk. The way he danced was almost hypnotic, and at that moment, she felt as though she were under his spell. Her blood pumped wildly at the sight, filling her with a strange inner excitement as she sat riveted to the spot.

But as the dance continued and her excitement mounted, Jordan was ready to run from her thoughts and the man they were centered around. When the music stopped abruptly, the dancers went down on one knee, except for Gray Hawk who stood tall in the middle of the circle. A cry tore from his throat that was neither human nor primal. He raised his hands to the stars and silence fell over the group.

Jordan's pulse skittered, waiting for something, what exactly, she wasn't sure. Then the music started again, slower this time, each note romantic and stirring. Her heart beat faster as the momentum of the music gained speed and Gray Hawk's body moved to the pounding rhythm. With each motion his muscles flexed beneath his dark skin. "Oh my," she said under her breath at the sight he provoked, and the strange, disquieting thoughts that raced through her mind.

Kari leaned forward, not taking her eyes off the warriors. "What?"

Jordan's throat was so tight she couldn't reply. The dance continued, and with every second that passed, her skin grew warm, almost hot, as she watched the man she so hated. She ran a trembling hand down her face.

If she hated him, why then was she so aware of him?

He looked her way and her breath caught. His silver gaze burned into hers for an endless moment. Her skin tingled with an awareness so intense her body pulsed with it. The side of his mouth lifted the slightest bit in a smile she felt all the way to her toes. The simple gesture transformed him completely, from a man she feared, to one she desired with all her soul.

But too soon the magic was broken as Running Deer stepped into Jordan's line of vision to dance with Gray Hawk.

Raw jealousy ripped at Jordan's insides as she watched him move with the other woman in a dance, that from the looks of it, they'd known all their lives.

Perhaps it was for the best. She'd been letting her thoughts wander to places it had no business going.

"I'm going back to the teepee," Jordan said, coming to her feet when Iron Bear, Gray Hawk's half-brother approached her. His hand was outstretched, beckoning her to join him in the dance.

She glanced at Kari, who merely smiled and shrugged. At her side, Tawanka nodded encouragingly. Iron Bear was menacing with scars running down one side of his face. The claw marks were said to be from a grizzly, who in the end, Iron Bear had killed. He was also a man whose libido was proven by his twelve children and three pregnant wives. Although he was the last person she wanted to dance with, from the expectant looks of the crowd it appeared she had no choice.

What would it hurt? Maybe she would even gain a few friends tonight if she tried. After all, fighting with them was getting her nowhere. Perhaps if she gained their trust, it would be easier to escape them.

Surrounded by others, Jordan at first felt awkward, trying to mirror Iron Bear's movements, but soon she found the rhythm and began to relax and actually enjoy herself for the first time since being captured. Glancing up at Iron Bear, she returned his smile of approval, hoping he wouldn't misinterpret the look.

Feeling uneasy under his lustful stare, she quickly turned and looked toward Gray Hawk to find he was no longer dancing, but standing with the others watching her. His eyes shone like silver in the light of the fire. He was so tall, dark and handsome, his skin so smooth, that she wondered what it would feel like under her fingers. Her pulse beat madly in her throat as she continued to stare.

Chapter 5

GRAY HAWK watched Iron Bear's gaze move slowly over Jordan's body. It was obvious by the fire in his eyes that his brother wanted her. Though the knowledge angered him, he knew he couldn't blame his brother for desiring Jordan—especially when Gray Hawk wanted her himself.

Which was ridiculous, especially since she was becoming more difficult with every day that passed. He had little control over the woman who would just as soon plunge a knife in his back as look at him. But there was something about Jordan that also intrigued him. She was strong and independent...so much like Samantha.

Samantha—he would never forget her betrayal. It was like a wound that never healed, despite the fact that he had only been sixteen at the time.

He had traveled to Missouri, to a school that taught Indians English and the white ways. Having already learned the language from his mother, he'd been the prime candidate to go. Intent on his purpose, he left his people in order to serve them better. At first he took on his studies with vigor. But then he met Samantha Reeves, a young wife of a missionary who worked at the school, and his life changed overnight.

Samantha, a petite brunette with dark brown eyes had been kind to him from the start, and he had always liked her. For the first year he'd enjoyed flirting with her, but he never took her seriously, knowing she was married to a missionary, an older gentleman with a kind smile, but a firm hand when things didn't go his way.

One day while her husband was working out in the fields, Samantha asked Gray Hawk to help her move a dresser in her room. He agreed to help, not thinking anything of it. Knocking on the door, he waited. A few minutes passed without an answer. He almost left, but decided to try the door first. He found it unlocked, so he pushed it open. "Mrs. Stone?" he called, shutting the door behind him.

"In here, Gray."

He walked to her bedroom to find her lying on her bed, wearing nothing but a smile. Without thoughts of the implications, he took what she so graciously offered, and soon became oblivious to everything but her.

Samantha loved the power she had over him, and they took chances every day, meeting, making love in places where they could easily be caught. It was a dangerous game they played, but as a young man newly introduced to love, he would take any risk. His body craved the woman who constantly told him how much she loved him, and he in turn would tell her the same, sure it was love he was feeling. She always asked about his village and talked about the day they would leave together, saying she could hardly wait to become his true husband.

But that day never came. Instead, five months after their affair began, Samantha's husband discovered his wife's infidelity and told Gray Hawk to leave the school for good, or he would put a bullet between his eyes.

Gray Hawk packed, his mind racing, knowing there was no way he could leave Samantha behind. Believing she was also packing, he went to get her and found her crying. Her face was red and puffy from not only tears, but her husband's rage. Gray Hawk wanted more than anything to end the man's life right then and there when Samantha stopped him with words he would never forget. Her face was filled with self-loathing and disgust as she told him how much she hated him. The final insult came when she told him she couldn't believe she had allowed "a stinking savage" to touch her body.

Jordan's laughter brought his attention back to the present. His captive was a lot like Samantha in that both were strong-willed and usually said what was on their minds. But that's where their similarity ended. Jordan's auburn hair framed her perfect features. How different she looked now from the hostile captive he was used to seeing. Her rose-colored lips parted in a smile exposing small white teeth. Long lashes cast shadows against her tanned cheeks, making the green of her eyes that much more striking. Her slender neck led down to high, full breasts that molded against the soft doeskin of her dress. A man could span her tiny waist with his hands, and her long legs were meant to wrap around a lover's waist.

His body tightened. What was it with the woman? From the first time he saw her, he'd found her intriguing, and he had to wonder why, especially since she'd fought him at every turn. But despite the fact she was difficult, he still desired her, his body's reaction was evidence to that.

Her gyrating hips moved in perfect time with the music, making him wonder what kind of lover she would be. She was so beautiful it made his body turn hard with desire as her luscious bottom moved in a sensual motion. An unwanted wave of jealousy washed over him as Iron Bear's hand reached out to brush a wayward curl from her face. The fury he felt threatened to choke him.

As though sensing his perusal, Jordan abruptly met his stare. Her own smile vanished, but she didn't look away. Instead her gaze moved down to his lips, settling there for a heart-stopping moment before turning away.

"She is beautiful."

Gray Hawk nodded to his friend, Young Wolf, who was standing at his side watching the dancing. "Yes, she is," he agreed, noticing the younger man's smile of appreciation as he watched Jordan. Though Young Wolf took his responsibility to guard the women seriously, Gray Hawk wondered if it may have been unwise to entrust a lustful boy on the brink of manhood as guard for two equally young, desirable women.

"Do you want her?" Gray Hawk asked before he could stop himself.

Young Wolf's brows lifted in surprise. "They are both beautiful women."

"And?"

He shrugged. "I've no wish to anger you."

His question had been answered. Of course others would desire the white women—they were men after all. Now he wished he wouldn't have asked. He had known others would find the women attractive, but he hadn't planned on fighting his own emotions, never dreaming that he would become attracted to either one of the captives.

JORDAN TOSSED and turned on the fur blankets. Her body was on fire. Her breasts tingled against the smooth skin of her dress. Filled with a strange inner excitement she couldn't deny, she let out a heavy sigh and turned onto her side.

The more she tried to ignore the truth, the more obvious it became—she was completely infatuated with Gray Hawk, who was at that very moment making love to Running Deer. A picture of the two came unbidden to her thoughts and along with it came a rush of jealousy.

What was wrong with her? Gray Hawk was a half-breed for god's sake! An Indian...just like the ones who had killed her parents. It was wrong, she told herself over and over, but still the attraction was there, and she couldn't deny it.

Slamming her fist into the furs, she rolled to her back again, staring up at the starlit sky through the opening above her. She was completely demented, that's what she was. What kind of a civilized woman was attracted to a savage? To a man that ran around half-naked and who spent his days hunting, while his woman slaved for him.

Kari leaned up on her elbow, startling Jordan, who thought she'd been asleep.

"You know, I never would have admitted it before, but they are very interesting people, aren't they?"

"Yeah," Jordan replied, hoping her attraction to Gray Hawk hadn't been obvious to her cousin or anyone else.

Kari sighed. "Gray Hawk and Running Deer make a beautiful couple, but for some reason, I don't think he likes her as much as she likes him."

"What do you mean?" Jordan asked, ignoring the fist that crushed her insides at the thought of Gray Hawk and Running Deer together.

"I don't know, it's just the way he acts when he's around her. She's always touching him, and watching his every move. He just doesn't seem interested."

Gray Hawk and Running Deer made a striking couple. They were perfectly suited—two people from the same village, and the same way of life. Then why did the thought of them together make Jordan feel so empty inside? What was wrong with her anyway? Her jealousy was completely unfounded. Unexpectedly, an image came to mind, of little dark-haired children, and among them a lighter-skinned, lighter-haired child...a child that belonged to her and Gray Hawk.

"The dance was almost erotic in a way, wasn't it?" Kari asked. "And the music was haunting."

Jordan's eyes went wide, not only at her thoughts, but Kari's words. Maybe that was it! Maybe it was just the dance that had excited her. After all, it was by far the most sensual thing she'd ever seen. And it wasn't every day one saw half-naked men dancing to exotic music.

Before she could voice her thoughts out loud, Gray Hawk walked in, stopping further conversation. Jordan went completely still at his presence. Her pulse skittered realizing as he stretched out on his furs that he wasn't going to spend the night with Running Deer after all.

She smiled into the darkness.

Overly sensitized to his presence, Jordan's body tingled as she watched him from under lowered lids. As he stretched and closed his eyes, she took the opportunity to let her gaze wander down his long, lean frame, over his broad shoulders and well-defined chest. She glanced up quickly just to make sure he wasn't aware she was watching him. Seeing that his eyes were closed, her gaze wandered down where it shouldn't be—to his flat, muscled stomach, before shifting lower still to where his breeches cradled his manhood. What would it be like to make love to him? she wondered. No doubt he would be a wonderful lover, full of vitality and stamina. Similar to the virile men in the books Patricia hid under her mattress, completely unaware her step-daughter and niece were reading every passionate word.

Gray Hawk shifted abruptly, his gray eyes flashed in the darkness. Jordan closed her eyes, her heart racing, hoping he hadn't noticed where her gaze had been directed.

She released the breath she'd been unconsciously holding.

It was going to be a very long night.

Chapter 6

BEFORE LEAVING on the hunt, Gray Hawk had posted Young Wolf to guard Jordan and Kari again. Unfortunately for them, the young man appeared to have eyes in the back of his head, not to mention impeccable hearing.

Blowing a stray lock of hair out of her eyes, Jordan sat back on her haunches, looking up at the hills that rose around her on all four sides. Her stomach clenched in a tight knot. Escape was impossible.

Her fingernails bit into the dirt at her feet. She was exhausted from lack of sleep, and if she had to spend one more day in the village, she would go insane. Tossing a carrot into the basket, she glanced around at the other women in the garden who went about their task with pure abandon.

Jordan had heard a few of them talking this morning, and although she couldn't understand everything they said, she had picked up bits and pieces of conversation. Enough to know many were worried because the warriors were supposed to have arrived home by now.

In the past Jordan had often wished Gray Hawk would come upon harm, yet now she realized that like the others, she wanted him home safely. In fact, she found herself looking toward the hills wondering when he would come, anxious to see him, yet dreading when he did.

It had been impossible to get him out of her mind since that night when he'd danced and their eyes had met. Something had passed between them. Even his attitude toward her had changed. He no longer frowned at her, but watched her in a way that made the hair on her arms stand on end, and her pulse race with exhilaration. There was an attraction that neither one of them could deny, no matter how hard she tried.

Looking up, she saw Kari coming toward her, her basket brimming over with potatoes. "You're getting so dark, you look like a native," she said, dropping beside her.

Jordan looked down at her golden arms and legs in disgust. "Great. When a rescue party comes, I'm sure they'll take you away and kill me along with the locals." She dug her hands into the dirt and scooped up a glob of mud, packing it into a ball. The grim reality was that no matter how much she wished it, there was no rescue party coming to save them, and it was high time Kari realized that. "We've got to get out of here. I can't take it any more."

Kari closed her eyes briefly, as though she was dealing with a temperamental child. "Jordan, not again. We've tried. Plus, we could never get past Young Wolf."

Glancing up to find their personal guard watching them, Jordan glared at him with all the frustration she felt before turning her back on him. "Well, not hard enough. If the men don't return in a couple of days, they're going to send out a search party."

"How do you know?" Kari asked, her brows furrowed in a frown.

"Because I've heard them talk about it," Jordan said, ignoring Kari's surprised grin. Jordan had resisted picking up on the language, but in the end it was impossible not to. And actually, she was glad she had now—it would only serve to help her know what was going to happen, prior to it happening. "If they send a search party out, it will include all able-bodied men, including our shadow over there, leaving only old men, women and children."

Kari's silence made Jordan wonder if her cousin wanted to stay in the village. Granted, their lives had taken on a certain tranquility they hadn't had on the trail, but it was still a life of servitude. Kari had adapted easily, and had actually gained a lot of strength, physically and emotionally since they came to the village.

"Don't tell me you want to stay?" Jordan asked, making sure her voice remained calm when she felt closer to the edge than ever.

Kari bit her bottom lip, her gaze dropped to the ground by Jordan's feet. "Of course not...but even you have to admit things could be worse."

"I don't believe what I'm hearing!" Coming to her feet, Jordan threw the mud ball at Young Wolf's head, missing him by inches. The young brave flashed her a warning glare, but did no more. For once she almost wished he would—she was far too frustrated.

Jordan rested her hands on her hips and returned her attention to Kari. "You told them we were trying to leave, didn't you? That's why we've been caught every time."

"Jordan, you're being ridiculous. I never said a word," she replied, standing hesitantly.

Narrowing the space between them in two strides, Jordan whispered under her breath, "You're lying. I know you are."

"I can't believe you're accusing me," Kari said, pain evident in her voice. "You've been so mean lately. I don't like this any more than you do. I'm just not going to let it get to me."

As tears brimmed in Kari's blue eyes, Jordan felt regret and remorse, making her pull her cousin into her arms. She sighed heavily. "I'm sorry. I just want to get out of here. I didn't mean it. I don't want to be miserable when we can't change the circumstances."

Kari put her at arms length and dried her tears with the back of her hand. "We'll leave soon, Jordan. We just can't push it. When the time's right, we'll leave, and when we do, we'll never look back. You'll have your ranch—"

Jordan and Kari jumped simultaneously as a jubilant cry rang out over the camp. Realizing what it meant, Jordan's heart hammered wildly.

Gray Hawk had returned.

GRAY HAWK'S gaze moved over the familiar faces of women and children, looking for the woman he couldn't get out of his mind.

He acknowledged the greetings from his friends, but as the minutes ticked by and he didn't see Kari or Jordan, he began to worry. What if they had escaped despite his efforts to see otherwise? Or what if Running Deer and Jordan had gotten into another altercation and things had gone too far?

Certainly Young Wolf would have prevented that.

His gaze fell on Running Deer for a brief moment before they moved abruptly to Tawanka, the medicine woman, who nodded in the direction of the gardens. Seeing some of the women with baskets of vegetables, he smiled, knowing Jordan and Kari hadn't gone anywhere.

The days had been tolerable considering the raids took all his concentration and strength. But at night, when he lay alone under the stars, Jordan's face appeared, mocking him with her beauty as he imagined her soft body lying beneath him as she gave herself to him freely.

He'd had a lot of time to think. In all his twenty-six years, he always enjoyed the hunts and raids. Yet this time he found it no longer excited him the way it once did. He longed for something to fill this emptiness inside of him—this loneliness that threatened to eat him alive.

Iron Bear commented just that morning on how much Gray Hawk had changed, asking out loud, in front of the others, if his white blood wasn't stirring within his veins. He should have been furious, but instead Iron Bear's words triggered questions. Questions that neither his white or red blood would be happy hearing the answer.

As he entered the woods, he heard Jordan's excited voice mingling with Kari's. Relief flooded him at the sight of the two, carrying their baskets filled with vegetables to the teepee they shared. Young Wolf saw him first and nodded.

Gray Hawk raised his hand in greeting, unable to keep his eyes off Jordan, who if possible, had grown even more beautiful with the passing days. Her silky hair was worn loose, falling past her hips, swaying with each step. Both she and Kari appeared at ease, laughing and smiling. He wondered if the time away had made them think any more about being here. Perhaps in time they would even want to stay.

His thoughts were cut short when Jordan noticed him. The smile instantly disappeared from her face and she tripped, spilling the vegetables on the ground around her.

Gray Hawk strode toward her as she scurried to pick up the carrots. He noticed how Jordan's hands trembled, making him wonder if it was from fear, or something else.

Silence ensued for a few awkward moments. Young Wolf came to help, and Gray Hawk saw how the younger man's fingers brushed Jordan's, who didn't flinch or look uncomfortable by the contact. A horrible image crossed his thoughts. What if Young Wolf and Jordan had become lovers in his absence? They were closer in age than she and Gray Hawk, and Young Wolf was a good-looking man who had already caught the eye of many young maidens.

"Young Wolf, could you take Kari back to camp? I would like a moment alone with Jordan."

The younger man glanced up, and without a single word, walked with Kari back to the village.

Dropping the last of the carrots into the basket, Jordan stood and met his gaze with a forced smile. "I thought maybe something happened to you and the others when you didn't return. "Many feared for you."

"Did you fear for me?"

She swallowed hard, her gaze dropped to his chest. "A little."

The knowledge that she did care for him warmed him as much as her uncharacteristic shy smile.

The sweet smell of her filled his senses, and desire flooded him. Unable to resist, he reached out and touched her cheek, letting his thumb run over her lower lip. He felt her stiffen beneath his touch, but he continued, his fingers moving along her jaw, before weaving through her silky hair.

Her eyes were luminous as she stared at his mouth. It was as though her gaze pulled and invited him. He leaned forward. Encouraged even more when she made no move to stop him, his lips brushed lightly against hers.

"You didn't leave," he whispered against her lips.

Jordan's heart pumped furiously, wanting him to kiss her again, yet wanting him to walk away, to leave her alone to sort out her tangled emotions. She couldn't deny she enjoyed his touch. Her body tingled, wanting to experience these new sensations that rippled through her, making her forget who she was.

But as his hands moved up her arms, pulling her closer to his hard body, she knew this was wrong. They had no future together. All they had in common was lust, pure and simple.

She pushed against him, desperate to put some space between them. "I tried to escape but Young Wolf stopped us," she replied, instantly regretting the words when all softness left his features.

He released her hand abruptly, stepping away from her as though she'd burned him. She almost took the words back, but knew doing so would cost her more than her pride, and she refused to give anyone her heart. "You can't possibly think that I want to stay." Even as she said it, she hated herself for hurting him.

His eyes were dark with anger. "Do you hate me so much?" he asked.

"No, I don't hate you. I could never hate you," she whispered. *But I should*, she thought, knowing the attraction she felt for him was a dangerous thing, not to mention just plain wrong. Her parents were surely rolling over in their graves knowing that she was infatuated with an Indian of all people.

"Why can't you be happy? I've treated you well."

How could she tell him that perhaps she could be happy? That all she wanted when she looked at him was to love him. But she couldn't, because if she started something with him, she wasn't sure she would be able to leave him. He made her thoughts turn positively wicked, and just seeing him made her want him with a ferocity that terrified her. She'd never known such unbridled wanting in her life, and she doubted she ever would again. But how could she when he was an Indian, the people she hated with all her heart and soul? "Please release us, Gray Hawk. There can never be anything between us."

"I can't." He almost sounded sorry.

Her heart beat double-time, hoping she could change his mind. "Why not?"

"I don't want to," he said simply, his expression so intense, she thought he was going to kiss her again. For an uncomfortable moment he watched her, but when she dropped her gaze to his chest, he let out an exasperated breath, turned abruptly and walked away.

Closing her eyes, Jordan let out an unsteady breath. Deep inside she knew that she would never find another man like him...not if she looked for a hundred years.

Willing her heart to cease its pounding, she waited a few minutes to calm herself, then followed the path he had taken.

The moment she entered camp she saw him. Taller than the rest, his body lean and powerful, his looks commanded attention. He was so handsome it was impossible not to stare. Worse still, her traitorous body yearned for his touch. She pressed her lips together, remembering the light kiss they just shared, and to her chagrin, she wished for the moment back.

Why was life so unfair? For the first time in her life she felt true desire for a man, and he had to be an Indian. And not just any Indian, but the Indian who had taken her captive.

They would never be happy, she thought, blinking back the tears that threatened. He would never leave his people, and she would never be happy living in an Indian village for the rest of her life. It was an impossible situation.

Watching as Running Deer raced to Gray Hawk's side, Jordan's steps faltered. She felt an acute sense of emptiness and loss as the woman's hand moved up his powerful bicep, splaying against his hard muscles.

Jordan turned away and marched toward Kari, who was sitting beneath a cottonwood tree, working on a pair of moccasins. "I'm leaving tonight. You can stay, or you can come with me, but don't try and talk me out of it."

Kari lowered the moccasin to her lap, her brows furrowed into a frown. "We'll be caught. Especially now that he's back."

"I can't stay here a moment longer...I just can't." Running trembling fingers through her hair, Jordan watched as one of Gray Hawk's strong arms encircled Running Deer's slim waist. When he bent and whispered in the woman's ear, a wave of jealousy washed over Jordan, strengthening her resolve to leave.

"How long have you been attracted to him?"

Jordan turned abruptly. "I'm not attracted to him."

Kari smiled softly. "You could never lie to me, so don't start now. I saw you back there. The way he was looking at you, and the way you looked at him. He desires you, and if I'm not mistaken, I'd say you feel the same. That's why you've been so miserable. I'm surprised I didn't guess before."

"How can I be attracted to him? It's not right."

Kari stared past her to where Gray Hawk stood, her brow lifted. "Actually, I can see why. He is handsome. Definitely unlike any man I've ever met."

Gray Hawk was unlike any man Jordan had ever met, and he was more masculine than any man she'd ever known. She shook her head, trying to convince herself the attraction was purely physical, and therefore, far too dangerous to explore. Things could never work between us," Jordan said with firm resolve.

For some reason her mind was telling her differently as her gaze strayed to him yet again. His body was muscular and athletic. His strong back was turned to her, his long hair that was braided nearly fell to the band of his breeches. Her eyes moved lower to his tight buttocks. Her face began to burn when she realized Kari was watching her.

"Perhaps you're right. We should leave tonight," Kari said abruptly.

"I'll start getting things together," Jordan said, needing to get away from Gray Hawk and Running Deer.

Planning to check on Winnebe and Kari's horse, she hadn't gone far when a loud, shrill cry rang out in the valley. The hair on the back of her head stood on end when a band of fierce-looking Indians appeared from all directions, bearing down on the unsuspecting villagers. Men, women and children ran for cover and weapons.

Jordan watched with open-mouthed horror as a warrior with painted face and cropped off hair came bearing down on an elder of the tribe. She screamed as the warrior's spear pierced the man's chest.

She ran for the teepee, but before she could reach it, a strong arm wrapped around her waist and lifted her from the ground. Suddenly, she was flung through the air and landed with a grunt across a horse's back. All she could see were pounding hooves and dust stir. Lifting her head, she swallowed a scream as she found herself face to face with a menacing warrior. His face was painted bright red, with two angry black streaks beneath eyes so black they seemed fathomless as he glared at her with pure hatred.

Chapter 7

JORDAN CLAMPED her chattering teeth together.

Sitting cross-legged on the hard ground, her wrists bound behind her, she glared at the warrior who had tied the rope around her neck, and had pounded a stake into the ground to make sure she wouldn't be going anywhere.

She had stopped crying, realizing long ago, that tears only added to her captor's pleasure. They had traveled the better part of the day without stopping. When they finally reached the camp, the villagers had been hostile, spitting, hitting, pinching and taunting her. It was by far the most horrifying experience she'd ever endured.

The horses neighing in the makeshift corral caught her attention. Seeing her mare among the stolen mounts made her yearn for escape. If only there was a way to get out of her binds. But even if she did, escape would be difficult, and if she were caught, it would mean certain death. Plus, it seemed that every time she thought she was alone, she turned and there was someone watching her.

Her thoughts were in turmoil as she constantly wondered if her cousin and Gray Hawk had been killed in the raid. Refusing to believe they had, she chose to be grateful that at least Kari hadn't been taken captive, too.

Although Jordan wanted to remain positive, she had a horrible suspicion that her days were numbered. All she could hope for was a miracle—and his name was Gray Hawk.

How ironic it was that now, when it was too late, she finally realized how good the Cheyenne had been to her. Life with them had been simple in comparison to this. Gray Hawk had often warned her how bad things could be, and now she knew first hand that he was right.

Hopefully the Cheyenne would retaliate. Surprise attacks were obviously a way of life for the Indians. Already the Crows were waiting for their enemy. Guards were posted throughout the village, particularly around the anxious horses. Jordan prayed few Cheyenne had died in the surprise attack, and that they would have a force strong enough to rescue her. Yet a disquieting thought came to her, making her stomach clench. Would Gray Hawk want to rescue her? After the way she'd acted, she wouldn't be surprised if he looked upon her capture as a godsend.

Something wet hit Jordan's cheek. Glancing up she saw a white woman standing before her, hands on hips. The woman pursed her lips together and spat once more, this time hitting Jordan's arm. Adding insult to injury, the woman took a long, sharp stick and poked Jordan hard in the ribs. Shocked to find one of her own abusing her, Jordan could do little but try and shield herself. Lowering her head, she ignored the woman as she continued her attack. She bit her bottom lip until she tasted blood, trying to envision her ranch on a summer day—thinking of the horses she would breed and train. As Jordan had hoped, the woman, finally tired of the one-sided game, stopped and joined a group at the large fire who were laughing at her expense.

What a cold-hearted bunch, Jordan thought, her blurry gaze moving over the circle of people. Her body ached from the torture she'd endured. Every inch was covered with scrapes and bruises. She had never harmed one hair on their heads. So why then were they so determined to see her suffer?

She squinted. A young white girl sat among the savages. Jordan wondered if she belonged to one of the other white women, but seeing no white men among them, she had to wonder if she had been taken captive as well. The girl's small face was a solemn mask as though she was in a trance, and then as though sensing her scrutiny, she glanced up and met Jordan's stare.

Jordan tried to smile, though the slight movement split the cut on her lip. When the girl got up and came toward her, Jordan whispered, "No," fearing for the girl's safety, but she breathed a sigh of relief a moment later when no one seemed to notice her absence.

Dressed like the rest of the women in a doeskin dress with fringes running down the length of one side, the girl's tiny feet were encased in a pair of moccasins that went to mid-calf. As she came closer, Jordan saw how pretty she was. Her skin was pale, contrasting with the dark auburn color of her hair, and her eyes were hazel, framed by long, thick, dark lashes. Jordan guessed her to be no older than five or six.

The girl sat cross-legged in front of Jordan, watching her in silence. Her little head moved at an angle, staring at Jordan intently, as though she were admiring a toy through a glass window. A tiny hand reached out, taking a lock of Jordan's hair between dirty fingers.

Jordan steadied herself for the yank that was sure to come, and was surprised when instead the girl's touch was gentle as she pulled her braid up along side Jordan's. The color was nearly identical. A slight smile came to the child's face.

"What's your name?" Jordan asked, keeping her voice low.

"Rebecca." Her sweet little voice was tentative.

"Rebecca, that's a pretty name. I'm Jordan," she replied, noticing her captor watched them, his expression deadly. "How did you get here, Rebecca?"

The girl bit her lower lip and dropped Jordan's hair.

"Were you captured?"

"You look like her."

"Who?"

"My mama. She had hair like yours, but your eyes are different...a little. Hers are brown, not green."

"Is your mother here, too?"

The girl frowned. "No, she's dead. My papa, too."

Jordan's heart clenched at the girl's words, remembering far too well the pain of losing ones parents at a fragile age, and having to face the world alone and afraid. "I'm sorry about your parents. I know how much it hurts. My parents were killed when I was about your age."

Rebecca's brow furrowed into a skeptical frown. "They were?"

Jordan nodded. "Yes, and though I miss them, I just try to remember all the good times."

"I try to do that."

"How long have you been here?"

Fingering the fringes on her dress, Rebecca's teeth bit into her lower lip. "I don't know...a while."

The words hadn't left her mouth when her captor called out to her.

"You'd better go," Jordan urged reluctantly.

"I hope Lame Deer doesn't hurt you," Rebecca said with a sad smile. "He is so mean. I don't like him."

Lame Deer. The name was appropriate for the man who walked with a limp, his knee twisted inward.

Jordan watched helplessly as an older woman rushed over and grabbed Rebecca by the neck of her dress, pulling her to her feet and into a teepee. Her stern words vibrated throughout the camp. Although Jordan couldn't see what was happening, she heard the unmistakable sound of flesh hitting flesh. Holding her breath, Jordan waited for Rebecca to cry out, but there was only silence.

As the night wore on endlessly, Jordan watched as little by little the Crow villagers made their way to their teepees, until only Lame Deer remained. He stood next to the dying fire watching Jordan, his black eyes menacing even from a distance. Fear knotted her stomach until the bile rose in her throat. Jordan knew what he intended, and with her hands bound, she was helpless to do anything about it. So she did the only thing she could. Closing her eyes, she prayed.

Hearing her captor approach, she opened her eyes just as he went down on his haunches before her. His ugly face just inches away from her, he grabbed her chin roughly and smiled, displaying a row of rotten teeth. The smell of his breath and unwashed body gagged her. Trying not to breathe, she pulled away from his touch, but he grabbed a handful of hair and yanked her up against him, not caring that the rope was cutting off her air.

His gaze slipped to her lips and for a terrifying moment she thought he would kiss her. When his hand touched her breast, she tried to scream, but his other hand clamped over her mouth. Although her hands were bound behind her back, she struggled, kicking him, and biting the filthy hand covering her mouth. He cursed out loud, then snickered at her futile efforts to hurt him, pulling the rope tighter.

Kicking and screaming, her matted hair hanging in her eyes, she didn't see his fist until it was too late. Pain exploded in her jaw, and she could taste blood in her mouth. His expression was positively sinister, proving he was enjoying her agony far too much.

When he hit her again, this time harder, she could feel the blood run down the side of her face. "Why don't you untie these ropes," she hissed. "Maybe then it will be a fair fight, you coward."

Pulling the rope free of the post, he yanked her to her feet. A wave of dizziness washed through her as she stood on unsteady legs. His sinister laughter echoed throughout the village and she knew death was imminent...she actually welcomed it, preferring the end of her life to his assault.

His smile grew wide as he jerked the rope higher and her knees buckled. The breath left Jordan, the leather choking the air from her body as she struggled to get to her feet, only to have Lame Deer knock her back down, watching cruelly as she suffocated.

Images of her life flashed before her eyes; as a child living with her parents, going to live in Virginia, meeting Kari...and Gray Hawk. A wave of regret washed over her when she thought of the tall half-breed. If only they had time...if only she hadn't pushed him away.

Her dream took on reality as a low voice said from the darkness, "No one takes what belongs to me." A second later a large arm slithered around Lame Deer's throat and a knife sliced his neck wide open.

GRAY HAWK seethed with mounting rage as he untied the ropes from around Jordan's neck and wrists. Though it was dark, he clearly saw the purple bruises on her face. Guilt raced through him, knowing she should have never been taken in the first place. Who knew what else she had endured?

Gray Hawk had meant to prolong the man's death, to make it slow and painful, but when the bastard began beating Jordan, he couldn't control his rage.

"Let's go," he said, lifting her in his arms, knowing there was precious little time before others noticed the dead man's body and their prisoner missing.

He stopped abruptly when he saw a movement out of the corner of his eye. His body was rigid, ready to strike when he saw it was a young white girl. She stood outside a teepee watching them. He waited for her to yell, but instead she remained silent.

"We have to take her with us," Jordan whispered, motioning the girl over.

He could tell by the expression on Jordan's face that she wasn't about to leave the girl behind.

Chapter 8

SITTING ON the river's edge, enjoying the feel of the sun on her face, Jordan watched Rebecca splash in the water with one of Iron Bear's sons. In the weeks since they had escaped the Crow village, Gray Hawk's people had taken to Rebecca, especially the children, who seemed to be in awe of the little girl who acted much older than her tender years.

Each day Rebecca flourished. Her smile came quickly, her eyes now held a sparkle that had been missing, and her appetite was ravenous, filling out her thin frame. She was a different child from the one Jordan had met at the Crow village.

Rebecca had brought out a maternal streak in Jordan that she'd never known existed, making her think about having children of her own.

"Don't go out too far, Rebecca," Kari called from the log, where she was busy sewing yet another pair of moccasins, these for Rebecca. Jordan smiled knowing Kari had also become enamored of the little girl. She was constantly doting on her, which was odd in a way, since she'd never shown any interest toward her half-sisters. Yet Rebecca was far different from those two vile little creatures, who were as bad as their mother.

Rebecca's laughter filled the warm afternoon, sending a rush of joy through Jordan. Jordan believed in fate and knew that destiny had brought her and Rebecca together. The little girl turned to her with a smile. Her hair was slicked back off her face, making her hazel eyes appear enormous. Climbing from the water, her little body was goose-pimpled and her teeth chattered as she came to stand before Jordan shivering.

Wrapping a blanket around her, Jordan asked, "Did you have a nice swim?"

Rebecca frowned at Iron Bear's little boy, who still played in the water with his friends. "Yes, but he was splashing me," she said, sticking her tongue out at him. "I told him not to do it, or I won't play with him anymore."

Jordan tried not to smile. "And what did he say?"

"He said he didn't care. That he didn't like me any ways."

Jordan's humor died a quick death. She was instantly defensive. It was all she could do not to chastise the boy, but realized how silly she was being. Rebecca would have to learn things the hard way, just like everyone else. With a reassuring smile, she said, "Now, he doesn't mean it, love. Boys will say one thing, when they really mean another."

"Do they?"

Surprised to hear Gray Hawk's voice, Jordan turned just as he sat beside her. She was even more shocked when Rebecca threw herself into his arms and rested her head against his large chest. "Hi, Gray Hawk," she said, playing with the gold band on his upper arm. It seemed odd to Jordan that such a fierce warrior could take so easily to children. The two had become close in such a short period of time.

Gray Hawk grinned down at Rebecca. "Hello there, Miss."

Rebecca ran her fingers through his hair, then began braiding a strand. "Know what?"

Gray Hawk shook his head.

"Jordan says you're our hero, cause you saved us."

Jordan could feel his gaze burning into her, and when she glanced up, she clearly saw desire there. How could he possibly want her when she had been so mean to him? He still bore the scar from where she'd thrown the bowl at him.

Her stomach was in knots and she wondered if her thoughts were obvious to him and those around them. Uncomfortable, she dropped her gaze to Rebecca. Even then she could still feel him watching her.

When she glanced at him again, his eyes were like molten silver. Her pulse raced as his fingers moved to the yellow bruise on her cheek. His touch was gentle, just grazing her skin. "Does it hurt?" he asked, his voice barely above a whisper.

His touch is what hurt more than anything, not because it was on her bruised skin, but because she wanted him despite the fact she knew it could never be. "Not really," she whispered breathlessly, pressing her cheek into his hand, closing her eyes, needing his strength and his comfort. Lord help her, but she didn't care that there were others watching them. She wanted him to know how thankful she was that he'd saved her, and what he did to her every time she saw him—the way her heart missed a beat, or how she felt all tingly and light inside. And his touch—it was heaven and hell at the same time.

His fingers lightly cupped her chin, and she opened her eyes to find him watching her with a wanting that stole the breath from her lungs.

"You're a very brave woman, Jordan."

His compliment pleased her. "You risked your life to save me," she replied, swallowing past the lump in her throat as his thumb lightly grazed her bottom lip.

"You're not going to kiss, are you?" Rebecca asked, her voice mirroring her disgust.

Gray Hawk smiled and dropped his hand to his side, the moment forever ruined. Jordan bit her lip as she glanced down at Rebecca, who was occupied making faces at Iron Bear's son.

"Rebecca, let's get you dressed. I need some help gathering berries," Kari said, and Jordan was thankful for her cousin's quick thinking. She needed time alone with Gray Hawk.

Watching until Rebecca and Kari disappeared, Jordan turned to Gray Hawk. His expression was warm and inviting, causing her heart to skip a beat. He was so handsome. Those eyes, so light in his dark face held a person transfixed. Jordan had to keep herself from running her fingers along his strong jaw and high cheekbones. Her gaze fell to his mouth, staring at his full lips and his white teeth as he smiled softly.

There was so much she didn't know about him. So much she wanted to know, but had always feared asking—until now. "How did you learn to speak English so well?"

She saw something akin to pain flash in his eyes before he quickly masked it. "My mother taught me, and as I grew to manhood, my father felt it was important to have someone who could translate and teach the others. He sent me to school back east."

Hearing that he'd lived among the whites made hope flare within her. "Did you like it?" she asked, watching him closely. But as usual his expression revealed nothing.

"At first it was difficult, but as others like myself arrived, it became easier. I liked to work the land, and of course, I still hunted."

Would you do it again? She wanted desperately to know, but realized if he answered yes, it would only give her false hope that they could have a future together. He was a Cheyenne warrior, and from what Tawanka said, one day he would take his father's place at the council fire and lead his people.

"Where is your home?" he asked.

The question surprised her. For so long she had hidden her past from everyone they'd come into contact with—so much, she'd become an accomplished liar. A fact she wasn't proud of. When asked, she and Kari had never answered, but now she felt compelled to answer him truthfully. "Virginia."

He lifted his brow, looking at her uncertainly. "That's in the east by the Atlantic?"

She nodded.

"Why were you headed west then?"

"I wanted to return home. I left Wyoming eleven years ago when my parents were killed, and I was returning to claim my ranch."

"How were they killed?"

She hesitated only a moment, then before she lost her nerve, she blurted, "Indians. I was fortunate I was off fishing in the stream behind our home when it happened, or else I, too, would be dead."

His hand covered hers, and for a moment she almost pulled away, but instead she savored the feel of his long fingers as they moved over hers. "How difficult that must have been. I'm sorry for your loss."

He put an arm around her shoulder and pulled her close. She leaned into him, her head fitting perfectly between the hollow of his shoulder and his neck. Her skin prickled as his hand moved up and down her back. Even as she heard the children giggle, she couldn't pull away.

"I'll take the children and let you bathe," he said, his breath fanning against her cheek.

Before she could move, he was already standing and motioning for his nephews to get out of the water. Placing her change of clothes on a nearby rock, he smiled warmly.

As Gray Hawk and his nephews made their way back to camp, Jordan's heart swelled in her chest. Her gaze rested on his strong back, remembering the feel of those bunched muscles beneath her fingertips when he'd kissed her that day that felt like so long ago. A moment she wished she could have again and probably would have, if they ever had time alone.

What was she to do? Every day her attraction to him intensified to where she thought of him constantly. Wicked thoughts of them together, making love under the stars burned in her mind. Images of her hands moving down that strong back of his as he moved within her. Nights were the worst—having him so close, and not being able to touch him.

Suddenly, Gray Hawk turned to look back at her, one dark brow lifted, his eyes sparkling as though he could read her mind.

GRAY HAWK stared at his father from across the fire. Memories of the great warrior he had once been flashed through his mind as he handed him the pipe. How he wished he was still that strong, commanding presence he once was. Instead, he was a gaunt, fragile old man, who looked as though he was in his final days. The knowledge that his father was dying was unsettling, not only because he would miss his presence terribly but because Gray Hawk would become chief. He inhaled deeply of the smoke. Closing his eyes, he exhaled and handed the pipe back to his father.

"I feel the time has come for us to speak of the white woman."

Gray Hawk tensed, knowing that his father felt like many of the others in his tribe—that Jordan and Kari were a bad omen.

He knew his father well enough not to argue the point that the majority of the tribe had changed their minds. They had taken to the women, and he knew in his heart that they would hate to see them go.

"I know when you originally took the white women, you thought to replace the two of our tribe who were killed, yet in the meantime your heart has changed. When you look at fire hair, it is with lust in your eyes. You know far too well, my son, what I went through. I would not have the same for you."

"What would you have me do?"

His father remained silent for a moment, his eyes taking on a faraway look. "I think you should release them. I know that it will be the only way you will have peace."

Every muscle in Gray Hawk's body tensed. "It's not that easy."

His father nodded. "True, it won't be easy. Yet the price of not doing so now may be more than you can stand in the end if she were to leave you. I loved your mother, Gray Hawk. She meant everything to me. I was faithful and she was as well. I loved her and I thought she loved me, too, but that love wasn't enough. I tried to change her, to make her one of us when she never wanted anything but her freedom. Sure, for a time she was content, and when she gave birth to you, I thought she would stay with me forever. I never once dreamed she would leave us."

Yet she had. It had been devastating to both of them. At first his father had become intolerable to be around. It took him many months to accept she was not coming back, and then it seemed he was but a shadow of the man he once was. It was as though he had aged forty years in a few months time.

"I do not wish to release her."

"When you take a person away from what they are, it will ultimately kill them. It is a difficult decision, yet only your heart will tell you what is right. Listen to it, Gray Hawk, and listen well."

As he left his father's teepee, Gray Hawk knew that Jordan would leave the instant he said she could. Before she'd been taken by the Crow, she had once again asked for their release. Since it had only been a few weeks, her answer would no doubt be the same.

He found her sitting at the fire with the others, appearing content as she laughed and smiled at something Tawanka said. Lately she had seemed to belong to them, even doing her share of the work without complaint. Hope flared within him. Could that mean she would want to remain?

As Iron Bear sat next to Jordan, Gray Hawk tensed. Though he couldn't hear his brother, he could see by the frustration on Jordan's face that she didn't understand him. He realized she had learned some of their language, but not enough to hold a conversation.

When she glanced up and caught his gaze, Gray Hawk motioned for her to come to him. His brother glared, but Jordan was obedient as she followed him into the teepee.

Gray Hawk secured the flap. He motioned for her to sit, and though she looked hesitant, she did as he asked, facing him.

He sat down across from her, drinking in every detail. Already his body was responding to her. How could he possibly let her go? "I would ask what it is you want."

Her brows furrowed into a frown. "I don't understand what it is you're asking."

"I think you do."

Her face was impossible to read as she stared at him, and a few silent moments passed before she finally whispered, "I want to see my ranch again."

His hope faded, bringing a pain so vast it nearly took his breath. How could he have thought for even a second that she would want to stay with him? What a fool! Unable to say anything for fear he'd regret it, he nodded.

"Are you telling me that we can go?" There was no mistaking the excitement in her voice.

"No, but I will think on it."

"Thank you," she whispered, the corners of her mouth lifting in a smile. "It would mean everything to me."

Had he expected her to say that she wanted to stay with him and his people? He shook his head, knowing what a fool he must seem to all those around him. He had let his lust lead his head, and in the end, it would certainly cost him his heart.

The best thing he could do was to let her go. To take a wife and live the life he'd been born to—to be Chief.

Without another word, he left the teepee, feeling Jordan's eyes on him with every step. Taking Running Deer's hand, he led her to her teepee, determined to forget about Jordan and the pain it caused to let her go.

Chapter 9

SHANE CATALONO pulled the dusty hat from his head. His fingers moved through his thick, dark hair as he scanned the horizon. With every mile he was getting deeper into Indian Territory.

The last of his men, along with the Indian guide he'd hired to track, had disappeared over a ridge just an hour before. Now he wondered if he shouldn't do the same and head back to his ranch, the Triple T. He'd been on the trail for a month in hopes to find his niece, Rebecca, but with every passing day, he was beginning to lose hope of ever finding her.

As the sounds of night closed in around him, he felt uneasy about going it alone. It was quiet...too quiet. He stopped abruptly, listening. Hearing nothing, he continued on, then brought his horse to a halt and closed his eyes. It was then he heard it—the steady beat of a drum.

When he'd received word of his brother and sister-in-law's deaths, Shane had assumed his brother's stepdaughter had been killed as well, but her body was never found among the passengers of the ambushed coach.

It had taken him a lot of work and a lot of money to get to where he was now—hopefully within hours of getting his niece, and taking her home to Brogan...if she was still alive.

His stomach in a tight knot, he gripped the reins and headed south in the same direction. Laying his rifle across his lap, he would give just about anything if the guide and his men were with him now.

As the drums grew louder, Shane slid from his horse and tethered it to a tree. Running at a crouch until he reached the crest of the hill, he dropped to his belly and crawled through the long grass.

His pumping heart roared in his ears. Peering over the edge, his adrenaline raced through his veins as he looked down at the village alive with people. A bonfire lit the camp in a golden-orange glow as the villagers sat around the fire. His gaze scoured the camp, looking for his niece. Though he'd never met her, Shane had received a pretty good description of the girl, but he knew he needed to get a closer look. He was reluctant to get any closer in case he had the wrong camp.

He tried to remember everything the Indian guide had told him, mainly to stay calm, and before he did anything rash, to make sure Rebecca was in the camp before barging in.

He waited what seemed an eternity when he saw a young white girl with red hair sitting among the Indians. An invisible fist clenched his gut. At her side sat a white women, making him wonder if she had been on the coach as well. Or was she a captive who'd been living among the Indians for a while? What if the girl was not Rebecca? He shook his head. It didn't serve any purpose to be doubtful now. That *was* Rebecca down there.

Telling himself to worry about one thing at a time, he tried to relax, but even the relief of seeing his niece alive did little to ease his stress. The odds of getting her out were definitely not in his favor. After all, what good could one man do against a whole tribe? But he didn't want to take the chance to leave for help and return to find the village gone, which from what he heard, was common occurrence. No, he had to put this to rest here and now.

Cocking his rifle, he glanced at his horse that was busy chewing grass, oblivious of the impending danger. "See ya, Spook," he whispered, then taking a deep breath, he cautiously crept down the hill, hoping he lived to see his ranch again, and more importantly, his son.

JORDAN WATCHED Gray Hawk open her gift, a headband she had worked furiously on the days following her return to the village. Having used a lock of her hair, and under Kari's guidance, she had painstakingly braided it with multicolored beads. A feat in itself, since she hated sewing of any kind.

Gray Hawk smiled softly as his long, dark fingers ran across the strands. When he looked at her, his gaze was as soft as a caress, and Jordan quickly turned away. How dare he look at her like that when he had spent the night with Running Deer? Now she wished she hadn't even given him the headband. Yet, as Kari had pointed out, it would appear rude to the others if she gave him nothing, especially since he had saved her from the Crow village. She needed to show some gratitude, no matter how much she hated to.

Any way, it was irrational for her to be so upset just because he had been with Running Deer, but she was angry. Every time she even looked at him, she envisioned he and the Indian beauty together. He'd been so obvious, taking the woman's hand, leading her to her tipi.

"Do you like it?" Rebecca asked, breaking into her thoughts.

Gray Hawk's gaze shifted to Rebecca, and he smiled warmly. "Yes...very much."

Jordan watched him intently as he put the headband on, then moved to the next present. His long black lashes were lowered as he admired the arrows. Her gaze moved lower to his broad shoulders, over his well-defined chest, and then lower still to his muscled stomach. Her heart skittered. Oh, he was a powerful man all right. She was reminded of that every time she looked at him.

Rebecca nudged her side and she glanced up. "I think he likes it," she whispered, a wide smile on her face. "I knew he would."

Jordan nodded, not able to say what she wanted to. If only he would just let them go like he said he might. It was strange, because up to a few days ago, a part of her had actually wanted to stay with him. She had even envisioned being in his arms, making love to him. But now everything had changed. He was no longer the man who had saved her life. He was her enemy again.

And she wanted more than anything to leave.

A loud, sharp cry rang throughout the camp, bringing Jordan to her feet. Everywhere women, children and elders ran helter-skelter for the brush and their teepees as the warriors snatched up weapons to defend their village.

Jordan picked Rebecca up into her arms, the girl clutched her neck in a death-grip. "Don't let them take me," she cried, fear choking her voice.

Gray Hawk raced into the teepee right behind them, his expression intense. "Do not come out under any circumstances." Jordan looked at him and their gazes locked. She knew in that moment that he'd do anything to protect them, and she nodded to reassure him they would stay put.

Kari ran through the flap nearly colliding with Gray Hawk who was on his way out. "You don't think it's the Crow, do you?"

"I'm not sure," Gray Hawk said, stepping outside, throwing the flap down. "But don't move until I return."

Fear coursed through Jordan's veins. Surely it had to be the Crow coming to avenge Lame Deer's death. It only made sense that they would retaliate. They would take Rebecca back with them, perhaps herself as well, or worse, kill them both—or even the entire village. She closed her eyes against the horrible thought.

SHANE CLENCHED his teeth as his rifle was ripped from his grasp. With an Indian behind him and one in front, he had no choice but to enter the camp where only God knew what would happen to him.

Perhaps he'd gone about this all wrong, he thought, as a fierce-looking band of warriors circled him. Their dark gazes penetrating, their stances more than a little intimidating as they stood with weapons ready. Shane didn't doubt for a moment they would use them.

A sharp jab sent him stumbling toward a teepee. The flap lifted and he was shoved inside to an interior that was filled with a combination of fire and pipe smoke. An old man and two younger men watched him, their expressions set in stone. Shane guessed he was facing the chief, who stared at him with a look that made Shane wonder if he would have a chance to explain himself before they killed him. One of the younger men caught his stare and Shane was surprised to find himself looking into gray eyes. A half-breed...who didn't appear very happy to see him.

The old man motioned for him to sit and Shane immediately did as asked. The man spoke to the half-breed in hushed tones.

"Why do you come here?" the half-breed asked in perfect English.

Trying to wipe the surprise off his face, Shane replied, "You have my niece, Rebecca. I came to take her home with me."

Before the old man could utter another word, the half-breed's eyes became hard, pinning Shane to the spot. "She belongs to us now."

Shane shook his head. "I don't think so, partner. Her mother and father have been killed. I've been on the trail long enough to know it wasn't you who did the killing, so I'm not holding you accountable, but the fact of the matter is she doesn't belong to you. I'm going to take her home, and I want no trouble."

The half-breed told the others, then turned back to Shane. "Will she know you when she sees you?"

Shane cleared his throat. "No, she's never met me."

The half-breed's eyes narrowed dangerously.

"They were on their way to visit me when they were ambushed. She is my brother's daughter, and my only niece," he lied, knowing if he went into detail about her being his brother's stepdaughter, rather than his daughter by blood, the chances of having her returned wouldn't be as great. "I'm the only family she has."

Shane shifted under the half-breed's stare. It was obvious by his expression that he didn't like what he was hearing. "I own a large cattle ranch. I can offer her a good life. A life she deserves—"

He stopped in mid-sentence as the three men argued amongst themselves. The half-breed stood abruptly. "My father says that you will stay with us for a while. When you leave, if Rebecca wishes to go, then so be it. But *she* must make the choice." Anger was evident in his voice.

Shane nodded, completely relieved and pleasantly surprised things had gone his way so far. "All right, I agree," he said, though he knew there was no way in hell he would leave Rebecca behind.

"I'll go get her." The half-breed left and the chief signaled the meeting had ended. Shane was more than happy to get out of the cramped quarters. He waited patiently outside the teepee, ignoring the stares that were boring into him from all directions. At least he hadn't been shot on sight. And if he was real lucky, he and his niece would be leaving within a couple of days.

The half-breed returned with Rebecca, a little darling, just like her stepfather had said. She was holding the breed's hand, and seemed reluctant to let go.

Shane bent down to her height. "Hello, Rebecca, I'm your Uncle Shane."

Rebecca stared at him with eyes that held the wisdom of someone much older than five, and he wondered how much she had seen in her short life. "Have you come to take me away?" Even her voice was matter-of-fact.

"Your daddy was my brother, and you were coming to stay with me when you left Boston. I'd like very much if you'd come home with me."

Rebecca backed away from him, bumping into the white woman he'd seen earlier. His pulse skittered seeing her hair was the exact same color as Rebecca's. Could it be that his brother's wife was alive? His hopes were dashed, when she said, "I'm Jordan."

"Jordan was taken by the Crows, too." Rebecca smiled warmly at her. "She brought me back with her."

"It's nice to meet you, Jordan. I'm indebted to you for saving my niece. I hope you know how much it means to me to have finally found her."

Shane could see the maternal protectiveness in the woman's eyes as Jordan's grip on Rebecca tightened. He definitely had his work cut out for him.

"I'll give her a good life, I promise you that."

Rebecca took Jordan's hand, her eyes narrowing. "He wasn't even my daddy, so you're not even my real uncle."

The words stung, especially after he'd spent the last thirty-five days searching for her. The half-breed watched him skeptically, while the woman just looked plain wary. Shane cleared his throat. "Yes, I'm aware he wasn't your father, but he was your stepfather and he loved you very much." Shane hoped he didn't sound as irritated as he felt. From the letters his brother had sent him, he knew they had been close. Shane hadn't expected Rebecca to embrace him readily, but after all he'd endured, he had hoped for a little bit of gratitude. Captive life couldn't be that great, could it? "I'd like to get started back to my ranch in the next couple of days."

"I don't want to go," Rebecca said, looking up at Jordan with pleading eyes. "Please don't let him take me."

He stepped forward. "Oh pumpkin, I didn't mean—"

"Stop it!"

Shane looked up to find another white woman standing before him, wearing a doeskin dress just like the other. Her fair hair was plaited in two braids, her skin tanned to a golden hue making her blue eyes vibrant.

He glanced over at Rebecca only to find her crying. Jordan was trying to soothe her, and the half-breed was watching him with a lethal stare. Shane was at a loss for what to do. Could it get any worse? He had a feeling he was about to find out when the blonde said, "Could I please have a word with you?"

He nodded and followed her to a quiet spot away from the others. He leaned against the base of a tree, his gaze shifting over her. Never in his wildest dreams had he imagined a woman such as this being held captive in an Indian village, though he could certainly understand why someone would want her.

"Do you realize what she's been through?" The woman lowered her voice, though he could tell it was all she could do to contain her anger by the twitch in her jaw.

Shane lifted a brow. "No, but I'm sure you're about to tell me."

The blonde stepped closer. "She was a slave in the Crow village and treated horribly when she was rescued by Gray Hawk," she said motioning toward the half-breed. "Rebecca's time here has been good, and she has gotten to be good friends with us all. Now you, a virtual stranger come along and say you're taking her away. Perhaps you could give her some time to get used to the idea, rather than storm in here and just take her."

The woman was clearly agitated, and Shane wondered why. He wasn't any threat to her or Jordan. He simply wanted his niece and he'd leave. "I realize you've no doubt become close to Rebecca, and believe me, I sympathize with you and your friend for what you've had to endure."

She glared at him. "Jordan is my cousin."

Shane continued undaunted. "I'm sure you and your cousin have suffered, but the fact remains, Rebecca is *my* niece. I lost my brother, so I do understand her loss. But the fact remains that Rebecca deserves to be brought up with her own kind, not in an Indian village. I will not let her become a squaw." The moment the words left his mouth, he wished he could recant them, for he hadn't meant it as an insult to her.

But obviously she took it that way because a second later she slapped his face.

He blinked in surprise, his eyes narrowing as they focused on her. "I wasn't insinuating—"

"Oh yes, you were! You think just because I'm a captive that means

I'm sleeping with one of them, don't you?" she hissed between clenched teeth. "Not that I'd be ashamed of doing...that."

He truly hadn't meant to be offensive, yet as she continued her tirade, he found he couldn't keep the smile from coming to his lips as her cheeks turned a deeper shade of red.

Her nostrils flared as she took a deep breath. "What I am trying to say is that these are good people. Gray Hawk has treated Jordan and I with nothing but respect. I am not having...relations with anyone, but if I were, I wouldn't be ashamed. They are just like any other men. In fact, they are better than any I've known."

"And have you known many?" he asked, unable to keep the amusement he was feeling from his voice.

"Of cour—" The word died on her lips. Her eyes widened with sudden understanding. "No," she gasped, clearly outraged.

Her small, white teeth bit into her lower lip. Seeing her annoyance, his gaze dropped to her neck where her pulse beat erratically. "Well, I'd be more than obliged to help you out."

He wasn't sure who was more surprised at his blunt declaration, him or her—the way she looked at him with horror made him think the latter.

Before he could say anything else, she gasped, turned and walked away.

What was the matter with him? He never talked to a woman that way...ever. Why did this little filly ruffle his feathers? Where was his compassion?

Stifling the urge to follow her and apologize, he decided the best thing he could do was to let her cool off.

PULLING THE blanket up around Rebecca's chin, Jordan knew this would be one of last times she'd have with the little girl.

Tears burned the back of Jordan's eyes. She already missed her.

"You'll make a good mother."

Jordan looked up at the sound of Gray Hawk's voice. She tried to smile, but failed. "I love children."

"Do you mind?" he asked, motioning toward the fur beside her.

"Her uncle will stay for a while. He wants a chance to get to know her. Should she wish at that time to leave with him, then we will have to let her."

Jordan wrestled with her thoughts. She was happy for Rebecca, but at the same time she wished she would stay. The past week had been tolerable because of her presence, but once she was gone—what then?

His fingers touched her jaw softly, turning her to face him. "Tell me what it is that haunts you," he said, his eyes probing. "Tell me so I can help." His look was so intense and his fingers so gentle, she wanted to give him everything, yet at the same time she couldn't release the memory of him with Running Deer.

"I don't know what I want," she said hopelessly. "I mean I do, but I'm afraid."

"Afraid of me?"

She shook her head, meeting his stare. "I'm afraid of myself. My body betrays me every time you're near. Like now, my heart is pounding like a drum."

His gray eyes smoldered as he leaned toward her, his hand urging her closer. His warm breath fanned her cheek, sending an excited shiver down her spine. With feather lightness his lips touched hers. Heat filled her, coursing through every vein of her body, making her lean into him. His hand moved down her neck to her breast, cupping it, his thumb moving across her rigid nipple that strained against the soft doeskin. Pressing hard against his hand a moan escaped her lips. He tasted wonderful, his mouth exceedingly gentle, yet probing, wanting, demanding more.

Yet as the seconds ticked by, a nagging in the back of her mind brought her back to reality. Just last night he'd been with Running Deer, and now he expected her to forget? She pushed against his chest. "I—that was wrong." She shook her head. "This can't happen."

Eyes that had been soft before were now hard. He looked ready to say something, but then without a word, he stood and left.

A moment later the flap of the entrance was ripped open and Kari marched in. "Do you know what he said to me?"

Jordan shook her head, not trusting herself to speak.

"He thinks that I've...that I've." She stopped abruptly and took a deep breath. "That man actually thought I had...well that we are having relations with the Indians. Can you believe that?" Kari pulled the braids from her hair, then jerked a brush through it. "How dare he?"

"Why would he say that?" Jordan asked.

"I don't know," Kari said, looking perplexed and agitated. "He is such a...he's so arrogant."

"But it takes a brave man to face an entire village to save a niece he's never met."

Kari's shoulders slumped. "Yes, I suppose it does, but that doesn't change the fact that he's absolutely obnoxious." Lying down, she put her arms beneath her head. Silence ensued as they both became lost in their thoughts, then Kari went up on her elbows. "Sometimes I wonder how we ever got into this mess. To think there was a time we spent our days drinking tea and talking about boys. We didn't have a worry in the world...except Patricia."

It was the first time Kari had mentioned Virginia since they'd left, and it was odd considering all they'd been through that Jordan didn't regret leaving and had no wish to return. But did Kari feel the same? "Do you wish you would have stayed in Virginia?"

Kari shook her head. "This isn't exactly what I expected, but at least we're together." She let out a heavy sigh. "And you're not married to that awful Mr. Johnson."

"Amen," Jordan agreed.

"You'd probably even be pregnant by now."

"Kari!"

"I remember well the way he looked at you that night at dinner." Kari shuddered, sharing Jordan's sentiments. "I swear it even gave me the creeps to think of you sharing his bed."

"Luckily I don't have to worry about that. Even if Mr. Johnson and your father did find us, they certainly wouldn't have anything to do with us now."

Kari laughed. "Can you imagine Patricia? Once she heard we'd lived among the *savages* she'd faint. She would make up some grand story to tell all her friends, so that no one would know we had been taken captive by the Indians. Or perhaps she'd use it to her advantage by making sure we never set foot in her house again."

Jordan knew Kari was right. It hadn't taken her long to come to the conclusion that her step-aunt hated her from the moment they first met. She had no doubts that Patricia had been the one to plant the idea of marriage to Marvin in her uncle's head, and in time she would have seen Kari married off as well. Probably to a man who lived an ocean away. Patricia obviously didn't want any reminders of the life Frederick had before she and the twins came along.

"Do you think that someone is searching for us now?"

Jordan could hear the anxiety in her voice. Ironic that they should fear their only family more than the Indian that held them captive. "Knowing your father, I would have to say yes."

Kari's sigh filled the teepee. "I'll never go back...no matter what."

Chapter 10

SHANE WOKE to a pair of dark brown eyes staring upside down at him. He wasn't sure who was more startled, he or the child who went running from him as though he'd seen a bear.

Sitting up on his elbows, he was surprised he'd slept past sunrise. Actually, it was the latest he'd risen in weeks.

The village was alive with activity. Men, women, and children were filing out of teepees to start the day. His gaze moved to the one Rebecca shared with Jordan, her cousin, and the half-breed. He wondered not for the first time what the relationship was between them. Especially since some tribes were well known for marrying more than one woman. The blonde was adamant about not having "relations" with the Indian, but how could they all be living under the same roof and have nothing happen? If that was the case, then Shane had to give the man credit for his willpower. The women were attractive, particularly the blonde who'd confronted him yesterday.

Shane glanced over where several men were gathered, the half-breed among them. His appearance was striking. Tall, lean and strong, he didn't look the type to back down from a fight. It didn't surprise Shane that the man had gone into a camp full of his enemies and come out rescuing woman and child right under their noses.

As though sensing his perusal, the half-breed looked at him, his gunmetal eyes cold. Shane nodded in greeting. The man nodded in return before turning his attention back to the conversation.

Shane rolled up his bedroll and blankets then stuffed them in his saddlebag hoping Rebecca would wake soon. He was anxious to get home. Joining others at the fire, he ignored them as they did him. He had too much time on his hands, and as usual his thoughts turned to Lily, his wife. A petite woman, Lily had shared his excitement of ranching, and had a head full of dreams just like himself. Side by side they built their farm in the Wyoming countryside. A legacy they would pass onto their son.

Married only two short years, she had died giving birth to their son, Tanner.

He smiled at the thought of his boy. Tanner, a handsome young man with his mother's quick smile and deep dimples, not to mention an ornery streak that ran the length of Wyoming. Little girls from throughout the countryside blushed whenever his son went to town with him, making Shane dread the years to come.

He wondered how Tanner was doing without him. Though he was only fourteen years old, his son had grown up surrounded by males. Even now, Hank, Shane's foreman, watched over him like a mother hen.

When Shane had left in search of Rebecca, Tanner asked to come along. Feeling he was too young, and not wanting to put his son's life in danger, Shane had told him no, insisting he stay and help Hank and the other hands prepare a room for Rebecca. Shane knew Tanner tried to show some enthusiasm toward having his young cousin come live with them, but again the all male environment was about to be invaded. He could only hope things went well between them. He'd become accustomed to having just the two of them in their spacious home—a home built for he and Lily and the four children they had planned to have. It would be different to have a young girl underfoot, but they would manage.

Thoughts of his ranch slipped away when from the corner of his eye he saw the flap to the half-breed's teepee open and the white women step out. Jordan held Rebecca's hand in her own. Their hair was plaited identical, their dresses so alike, they could have passed as mother and daughter, or even sisters. Shane watched as Jordan glanced toward the group of men, her gaze lingering on the half-breed. It was the first time Shane had seen the man's face soften. But when she quickly looked away, all softness disappeared. Shane lifted a brow, curious.

Shane's glance instantly moved to the blonde who'd confronted him yesterday. The thin doeskin dress hug provocatively to her curves, stopping just below her knees. She wore moccasins, and Shane found himself staring at the expanse of skin that was exposed between the hem of her dress and the tops of her moccasins. Her calves were well-defined, much as he guessed her thighs would be. Her legs were long and she was taller than all of the Indian women in the village he had seen this far, though he doubted she'd reach to his collar bone.

Filling his mug with coffee, he smiled when he looked up to find her watching him. She was stirring something in a black kettle, her movements methodical, her look pure ice. She then poured a bowl full of the fare and surprised him when a moment later she walked toward him. Instinctively he readied himself to get a face full of whatever it was she held in her hands.

She smiled, though it appeared strained, and asked in a too-sweet voice, "Would you like something to eat, Mr. Catalono?" Her jaw was clenched so tight he wondered why her teeth didn't snap. It was obvious she had been asked to serve him, no doubt by the half-breed who watched their every move.

He raised a brow. "That depends, what's on the menu?"

Her eyes narrowed, obviously realizing his question held a double innuendo.

"I didn't ask. I usually don't, I just eat what's available."

He glanced down at the bowl in her hands. "Is that because you don't like knowing what's in your stew, Miss..."

Her eyes widened, and he could see the wheel turning in her mind.

"Well, are you going to tell me your name?"

"Hoffman," she blurted, pushing the bowl at him. Their fingers touched for a second and she jumped as though burned.

He smiled. "See, that wasn't so hard. Nice to meet you, Miss Hoffman."

Her mouth opened, but she quickly snapped it shut. Another few awkward moments passed before she blurted, "I'm sorry for yesterday. I had no right to speak to you as I did. I know that you came to get your niece, and it is a very noble thing indeed. I was just concerned—"

"Apology accepted," he said, smiling at the blush that raced up her neck. "Miss Hoffman, how is it you and your cousin came to be captives, and what exactly is expected of you?"

She appeared more relaxed now as she watched him tentatively. "We take care of Gray Hawk's needs."

He almost smiled, but refrained. "His needs?" he repeated, trying to keep the sarcasm out of his voice.

"Yes." Her eyes narrowed into suspicious slits. "But not in the way you're insinuating."

"The man is sharing his teepee with two beautiful women."

She shook her head. "Indeed, Mr. Catalono, it seems your mind is venturing somewhere it should not be...again."

And how right she was. He couldn't help think how soft her skin must be, how silky the texture of her hair was, and how wonderful it would be to kiss those rosy lips of hers. Her tiny nose was so delicate, her cheekbones so accentuated, she seemed as fragile as a china doll. Whether he wanted to admit it or not, Kari Hoffman was a lady and it was high time he started treating her as such.

"I'm afraid to even ask what you're thinking now, Mr. Catalono," she said, shifting on her feet, looking more uncomfortable with every second.

This time he did smile. "I'm thinking that I'd like very much to be your friend."

Her jaw slacked open in surprise before she quickly snapped it shut.

A tiny smile slowly came to her lips. "All right, Mr. Catalono, friends it is."

When she turned and marched away, he thought perhaps it wouldn't be so bad if they stayed around for a day or two.

JORDAN COULD still feel the touch of Gray Hawk's lips on her own. Who would have thought a man as strong and powerful as he could be so gentle? Her skin still tingled from where his hands touched her so intimately, and now she wished it had never happened. At least then she wouldn't have an idea of what it was like. But now that she did, it was almost impossible to get him out of her thoughts.

She glanced again at the men across in the clearing, practicing with their bows and arrows. Remembering his touch, her stomach tightened and a warmth filled her. A warmth that steadily worked its way downward as she watched Gray Hawk standing with a bow stretched tautly, every muscle in his body flexed as he aimed for the target. He released...and it hit dead center. She smiled, unable to help herself. The man was good at everything he did.

As though sensing her perusal, Gray Hawk glanced over at her. Their gazes met and held for a moment, before she quickly looked away.

She could feel his stare, but refused to look again. He would not hold any power over her. He had a woman to satisfy his needs. He only wanted her because she was his captive and he wanted to prove he owned her. Her hands clenched into fists at the same time her eyes were covered by a pair of hands and a small body pressed against her back. "Guess who?"

Glad to get her thoughts away from the man who disturbed her so much, Jordan asked, "Could it be a fairy princess?

The sweet sound of angelic laughter filled Jordan's ears as Rebecca let go. Jordan blinked a few times to find Rebecca standing in front of her. "Look at what my Uncle Shane gave me," she said, holding out a doll for Jordan's inspection.

"She's very pretty. What's her name?"

Rebecca cocked her head. "I was thinking Annabelle. What do you think I should call her?"

"I think Annabelle is a perfect name! I couldn't have thought of a better one myself." Jordan's heart melted when Rebecca put her arms around her neck. The girl had been affectionate these last weeks, but all day she'd been more so than normal. Looking down at her plaited hair, dressed in her Indian clothes, she wondered if Rebecca could once again live a normal life at her uncle's ranch. Jordan remembered the day she had first met her Uncle Frederick. He was nice at first, but as the years progressed he had become resentful to the point she dreaded seeing him. But she had a good feeling about Shane Catalono. She was confident he would give Rebecca a good life.

Even then Jordan was going to miss her.

"Why are you crying?"

Jordan wiped away the tears that had escaped down her face and forced a smile. Already she felt the loss. She knew her attachment to Rebecca came from their shared sorrow, being Crow captives and having both lost their parents when they were so young. "I just got some dust in my eyes."

Rebecca looked skeptical. "Oh, my Uncle Shane says he wants to talk to you as soon as possible."

"Good, I'd like to talk to him, too," she replied, grateful for an excuse to get away from her captor's piercing gaze.

"You'll like him," Rebecca said, grasping her hand. "He calls me Pumpkin. Isn't that a strange thing to call somebody?" Her expression was so serious, and she looked so grown up, Jordan couldn't help but laugh and suppress the urge to hug her close.

They found Shane standing off by himself, brushing down his horse. His strong back seemed more intimidating the closer they came, until Jordan considered waiting until she was more comfortable with the idea of Rebecca leaving before talking with him.

Hearing them approach, Shane turned, his hand still on the horse, then with a final pat to its side, he dropped the brush into a bag. "I was wondering when we'd get some time to talk." His tone was low and pleasant, making her relax instantly.

Rebecca looked up at Jordan with an endearing smile. "I told him all about you."

Jordan squeezed her hand. "Rebecca, why don't you go and see what Kari's doing."

"All right," she replied, skipping away as though she hadn't a care in the world.

"Miss Hoffman, I understand Rebecca's become very close to you."

Miss Hoffman? Jordan almost looked behind her to see if there was someone else he was addressing, but she knew by his direct stare that he meant her. She carefully schooled her features. Miss Hoffman—wasn't that the name of one of she and Kari's nanny's in Virginia...one of the many.

"I'm sorry, I thought you and your cousin shared the name—"

"We do. It's just been awhile since I've heard it. Go on."

"I was saying that you and Rebecca are quite close."

"Yes, we are. We share a common bond. We both lost our parents when we were young and I was also raised by my uncle."

Jordan relaxed knowing in her heart that Shane genuinely cared for his niece if he tracked her all this way to Indian Territory. It was a lot more than her uncle would have done for her. If Frederick did have people looking for them, they were probably Bounty Hunters who were promised a good sum to bring her back to Virginia so she could marry Mr. Johnson. A business transaction that would no doubt line his pockets with money.

"You'll miss her..."

Jordan nodded. "Yes, very much, but I also know she'll be happy with you."

He smiled widely. "I believe I have a solution. I've talked with Gray Hawk about you and your cousin. I asked him why he was keeping you here when its obvious you wish to be released. I asked him for your freedom, and he agreed to let you go. So, with that said, if you'd like, you could leave with Rebecca and I. Brogan is a small cattle town and there are plenty of opportunities for two young women like yourselves."

Shock caused any response to lodge in her throat. Gray Hawk had said he would think about letting them go, but she had never expected it to be this soon. A tumult of emotions swept through her, first and foremost, relief. She could leave—she would see her ranch again...and she would never see Gray Hawk again. The thought was sobering.

"I don't know where you and your cousin were headed when you were captured, but Brogan would be a great place to start over," Shane added, as though she needed assurance. "I'm not sure what you've been through—"

She heard every word he said, and knew he was giving her an opening to tell him where they were from and where they were going, but she didn't want to say anything just yet. Plus, she was having a difficult time registering the fact that she was free to leave and do as she pleased. They could go to Fife, but they didn't have enough money. In fact, they were damn near broke. They didn't have money for taxes, let alone food and other supplies they needed in order to survive the long winter ahead.

"I have a son who's waiting for me back home. We can make it in about a week." He lifted a cigarette from his shirt pocket, striking a match on his boot, he lit it and inhaled, the smoke circling his head as he exhaled. "I would really like to leave tomorrow."

Tomorrow? It was so soon! Before she could reply, Kari and Rebecca emerged from the trees and Shane waved them over.

"Should I tell her, or do you want to?" Shane asked, as Kari and Rebecca approached.

"Go ahead," Jordan said, her spirits lifting immediately realizing she was free at last. "And thank you." She knew this was for the best. They would all be leaving together and having a man along gave her more peace of mind. That way Jordan could see for herself how life would be for Rebecca, and she and Kari would just have to keep their plans about Fife a secret for now, until she felt it was safe to tell Shane the truth about them.

KARI'S BREATH caught in her throat realizing the cowboy looked better every time she saw him. She was almost irritated he was so attractive.

"Good afternoon, Kari," Shane said, her name rolling off his tongue like a caress, causing a shiver to work its way up her spine. It was a skill he no doubt used in luring women to his bed. And with his looks, it probably wasn't too difficult, she thought, her gaze moving down to the dark blue shirt he wore, the top buttons undone exposing a V of crisp black hair. His faded jeans rode low on his hips, an empty holster even lower. Kari heard herself swallow.

"What do you want?" she asked, hating how defensive she always sounded when talking to him.

An arched eyebrow indicated his humorous surprise at her question.

The man probably was married anyway. Her gaze instinctively strayed to his left hand. There was no ring, but that didn't mean anything. Men were notorious when it came to hiding the fact they were married. Well, not her husband, he'd wear his wedding ring like a flag. If he refused to wear one, well, so would she.

"I told your cousin that Rebecca and I will be leaving soon. You both are welcome to come with us. From there you can return to wherever it is you came from, or you can stay in Brogan."

"We're leaving?" she asked, not sure if that was good or bad news. No wonder Jordan had looked so stunned.

They were free! For a moment she couldn't quite grasp what she was feeling.

"Brogan is a good size town. I own a lot of businesses, and we have a real shortage of women."

She wondered exactly what it was he had in mind.

As though reading her thoughts, he smiled. "To work in the restaurant or mercantile. There are people who need help with their children, too, or housekeepers."

A relieved smile came to her lips. "I thought for a minute—"

"I know what you were thinking. It was written all over your face." Stomping the cigarette beneath his boot, he grinned boyishly. To her chagrin it made him even more attractive. "You don't have to go to

Brogan, but at least you'll have someone to travel with. Why don't you give me an answer by tomorrow."

What was there to think about? This is what she and Jordan had been hoping for from the very moment Gray Hawk had taken them. Not only would they be leaving with a man, a protector of sorts, but they would be going to a place where they could find work. A place they could put down some roots for a while. "All right," she said, hating the way her cheeks burned whenever he was around. "I'll talk it over with Jordan."

"Good, I'll be waiting for an answer."

Walking away she felt his gaze on her back the entire way to the teepee.

Chapter 11

GRAY HAWK met Jordan's gaze over the head of the young warrior he was teaching to use a bow and arrow. It was obvious that she had something on her mind by her serious expression, an expression he was getting used to since the day they'd argued and he'd gone to Running Deer.

What Jordan didn't know was that he'd regretted going to the other woman the moment he entered Running Deer's teepee, because all he could think about was Jordan. Before things progressed too far, he'd left, and spent the evening beneath the stars, thinking about what all the strange emotions he'd been feeling of late meant.

Telling the boy to practice on his own for a while, he walked toward her. She stared at him unblinking, not moving a muscle. "You wish to speak with me?" he asked, stopping a few feet away.

"Why didn't you tell me?"

He feigned surprise. "Tell you what?"

"That you're letting us go."

"Are you telling me the news doesn't make you happy?"

Instantly her gaze slipped from his to the ground. "Yes, I'm happy." Even though she said the words, he could hear the lack of conviction. His pulse skittered like a young boy's. Could it be she wasn't as happy to leave as she would have thought? Her reaction told him more than words ever could.

But he wouldn't get his hopes up. She would leave. Within days they would be gone, and he would never see her again. His eyes moved over her, memorizing every feature, every detail.

Though he had told Shane Jordan could go, the last thing Gray Hawk wanted to do was release her, especially since his every waking thought was consumed by her. Even in his dreams she was by his side, loving him, swearing she'd never leave him.

He didn't want her to go. How he wished he could take the words back.

Glancing over his shoulder, he saw the others had stopped practicing and were watching the two of them. Gray Hawk motioned for Jordan to follow him. When they were completely alone, he reached out and caressed the soft smooth skin of her cheek, before moving over her full lips. Her eyes turned dark, then drifted shut as his lips claimed hers.

Jordan was drawn up against his hard chest, her arms encircling his neck. His tongue played along the seam of her lips, nudging them apart. Her mind screamed what they were doing was wrong, but her body willed all negative thoughts away. She wanted this man, more than she ever wanted anything in her life, and she wasn't about to deny herself any longer, especially when she would be leaving soon.

A moan escaped her lips as she opened up to him, relaxing, knowing that what was about to happen had been a long time coming. Hypnotized by his touch, her body tingled where his fingertips stroked her skin. Inching her dress up, his hand splayed against her thigh. The breath caught in her throat as he came dangerously close to the core of all her passionate need.

Gray Hawk's entire body was hard as her fingers played along his back. Her breathing was coming in short gasps, and he knew at that moment the attraction had never been one sided. His heart rejoiced with the knowledge that she wanted him, too.

As Gray Hawk's fingers moved closer, Jordan's breath caught in her throat. No one ever touched her in such a way...and shouldn't be now. She gasped when a finger slipped inside her.

She couldn't deny it didn't feel good, and as his finger moved in and out of her, a warmth began to build, growing stronger with every second, penetrating her very soul, making her ache for something she didn't understand. As he continued the onslaught, she pressed her hips against his hand, wanting more of what he was doing, and then it happened. Her world shattered into a million tiny pieces...and nothing had ever felt so good.

His lips crashed down on hers, and as he pulled her up against him, his swollen manhood jutting against her belly, she somehow pulled out a thread of sanity. Dear lord what had she done? Did she have no shame?

Gray Hawk pulled her close, but when she stiffened and her arms dropped to her sides, he put her away from him with a heavy sigh. Her lips were swollen from his kisses, her eyes still bright with desire. She stepped away, her mouth open as though to say something, but she didn't, she just stared in disbelief.

He hated the condemnation in her eyes. Eyes that a moment ago had watched him in wonder as he'd brought her to climax. He remembered Samantha looking at him the same way before he'd left her. What exactly was she thinking? Maybe it was for the best that he didn't know.

"I...I can't do this," she said, and without another word, she ran.

As Jordan ran for the teepee it took every ounce of willpower Gray

Hawk possessed not to follow her, tie the flap down, and make long, leisurely love to her. She wanted him, even if she pretended she didn't. But he wasn't a fool. Her actions spoke louder than any words of protest. Even though he could tell her body yearned for his touch, her heart forbade it. Was it because he was an Indian—like the ones who killed her parents, or was it because she felt he'd betrayed her with Running Deer?

Maybe he should tell her the truth—that he hadn't been with Running Deer or anyone else since she'd come into his life. But would it matter? She was leaving and he would never see her again. They'd both be better off if they kept a distance.

"She's gotten under your skin."

Gray Hawk turned at the sound of his brother's voice, surprised he hadn't heard his approach.

"She has dulled your senses," Iron Bear said with a sly smile. "When you look at her, it is with lust in your eyes. Everyone can see it." He spit on the ground by Gray Hawk's feet. "You are making a fool of yourself, brother."

"Do you say this only because you're jealous, or because you feel it in your heart?" Gray Hawk asked, his eyes narrowing. Iron Bear said nothing. He didn't have to. The jealousy he felt was clearly written there for Gray Hawk to see. "Well, it doesn't matter anymore. She's leaving."

"What?"

"She's leaving with Rebecca and her uncle tomorrow."

Iron Bear's sardonic laughter pierced the air. "So she prefers the white eyes over you—just like your mother."

It was a taunt: one to anger him. Iron Bear never let him forget that his mother had willingly left the tribe. Although he didn't react to his brother's knowing smile, or the words that were barbed and direct, they hurt all the same. "Yes, all three will go with him."

"Two beautiful women—what a nice diversion for him."

"Shane Catalono is a trustworthy man. He will see no harm is done to them."

Iron Bear's smile widened.

"You are a fool. He will probably have both women in his bed the first night."

Before he could stop himself, Gray Hawk lashed out at Iron Bear with a solid right, and Iron Bear landed in the dust with a thud. Dropping one knee on his chest, Gray Hawk pressed his knife to his brother's throat. The entire village went quiet, but neither man took notice. Iron Bear grabbed his wrist in a quick viselike grip. Gray Hawk increased the pressure of his knee between Iron Bear's ribcage.

Gray Hawk ignored their father's stern voice as he yelled their names from a distance.

Iron Bear's grip on his wrist relaxed. A small rivulet of blood ran down the side of his neck to the dirt from where the knife punctured the tender skin of his throat. Gray Hawk lifted the knife high above his head, ready to thrust the blade home when their father's voice rang out again. Iron Bear's fathomless eyes stared into his, daring him to strike the fatal blow. Even now, those eyes were so full of hate and loathing. How easy it would be to end the continual smirks and taunts that reminded him constantly that he teetered between two worlds, belonging to neither one. A fact that had bothered him since he was old enough to understand that he was different.

With a curse, Gray Hawk threw the knife aside as though it burned his fingers and came to his feet, leaving Iron Bear to lie in the dirt. Ignoring everyone he marched toward his teepee and the woman he wanted more than anything...the woman he had just let go.

JORDAN HAD watched it all. She had seen the hatred between the brothers, and though she didn't understand completely what the fight was about, she had a feeling it had been about her.

From the moment she'd arrived in the camp, she knew many didn't want her or Kari there. One of those people had been Iron Bear. Despite his leering smiles and lewd glances, he despised her. Despised her because she was white.

A shiver ran down her spine.

Did he hate his brother because he was half-white? The thought was incomprehensible, yet it couldn't be ignored. Gray Hawk had gone to live with the white man. Did he have yearnings to be like them, or did he want only to serve his people? Her first instinct told her to comfort him, yet how could she?

Her gaze followed him to where he sat off by himself, sitting on the hard ground, staring at the fire. What had passed between them had shaken her to the core. Did he feel the same? Was he at this moment thinking about her?

How she yearned to go to him, wrap her arms around his waist and hold him tight.

"Did you see that?" Kari asked, coming up from behind her, nearly scaring her out of her skin.

Jordan nodded. "I did."

"What do you think it was about?"

Jordan turned to her cousin. "It was about us. We're leaving."

The sides of Kari's mouth turned up in a smile. "I know, Shane told me. Oh Jordan, we're leaving. We'll be gone and soon all of this will be behind us."

Her excitement was obvious, and Jordan knew thinking about Gray Hawk wouldn't help her now. He was part of her past, and that's where he would stay.

"Shane said he wanted an answer from us whether to go to Brogan or not. What do you think?"

"Well, since we have little money, it only makes sense to go with him. He said we could get work."

Kari's smile widened. "Just think, in a few months we'll be able to pay the taxes on the ranch."

Her ranch. That was the one thing that had to keep her going. And now Shane Catalono was escorting them out of Indian territory to a town where they could get jobs and work toward her goal of getting the ranch back.

With a final glance at Gray Hawk, she turned toward the teepee. "Come on, let's tell Shane we're ready to leave."

Chapter 12

JORDAN WOKE with a start. Today she was leaving. Last night she and Kari had gone to Shane and told him they were anxious to get started. His answer had come by way of a wide smile, and a promise that they leave at sun-up.

She glimpsed the first gray light of day through the smoke hole. Rebecca was curled up into a ball beside Kari. She turned to Gray Hawk, only to find his furs empty.

She wondered if he'd slept here at all last night, or if he'd spent the night with Running Deer. An image of the two lying together was like a poison inside her. "Stop it," she muttered under her breath, coming quickly to her feet. She had to stop these destructive thoughts. Gray Hawk could do whatever he wanted. After today he would be nothing but a memory anyway. Yet even as she tried to convince herself she didn't care, she knew it would be a long time before she could forget about him.

Heading toward the river, she was glad to see that only a few people were up. She needed the peace and solitude to mentally prepare herself for their departure.

Pulling the soft doeskin from her body, Jordan dove into the water. Making quick work of soaping her body and hair in case someone else had the same idea of an early morning bath, she tried not to think of Gray Hawk or the hours ahead of her, but it was useless. She closed her eyes, enjoying the feel of the cool water lapping against flesh that felt strangely alive, as though she were now aware of new sensations.

She swam for the riverbank when she heard a snap of a branch overhead. Twisting around, she looked up and her heart lurched madly seeing Gray Hawk stood on the ledge above her. The sight of him was everything she was trying so hard to forget. How tall, dark and handsome he was, standing there as though he owned the world. His lean body tense, every muscle flexed. For a moment she took pleasure in just staring at him, letting her gaze shift to where it shouldn't be, knowing she would never see another like him for as long as she lived. Her gaze slowly worked back up his length to find silvery eyes watching her with such intensity, she could feel his desire all the way to her soul.

Gray Hawk was both stunned and delighted to find the woman who plagued his dreams become a live vision as he stood on the rocks above the river. Jordan's eyes were huge, like a doe staring at a hunter. She stepped tentatively back into the water, depriving him of the view that he so hungrily devoured with his eyes. But he had seen enough, and his body was responding.

Knowing the river well, Gray Hawk gauged the distance it would take and without a second thought, jumped from his precarious position on the cliff into the cold water below. He heard her frightened yelp, and wondered if her fear was for his safety, or for herself. As he came out of the water, he watched as her face registered horror, then relief.

Although her body was submerged, Jordan wondered if he couldn't see right through the water, because his eyes were so dark with desire. "What are you doing?" she asked in a tight voice. When he said nothing, she took a step backward. Her teeth chattered, and it had nothing to do with the cold.

His gaze moved from her lips to her breasts. There was no doubt he could see through the water. Covering herself in a lame attempt at modesty, she quickly looked around, hoping someone would come and interrupt them, because right now she wasn't sure if she had the strength to resist him.

He moved so quickly, she didn't have a chance to react.

Pulling her against his chest, his lips crashed down on hers. Her hands pounded against his chest, but instead of releasing her, he held her tighter and nudged her mouth open, plunging his tongue inside.

Jordan tried not to respond to his passionate demands, but it was no use when every inch of her was pressed against his hard flesh, the desire that surged through her was more than she could fight. A second later all resistance fled as her tongue met his.

Fire raced through her veins. His hands seemed to be everywhere at once. When his hard arousal pressed against her stomach, her mind screamed for her to run, but her body refused to obey, wanting the release she craved.

Gentle fingers moved down her back, spanning her waist, then moved lower to cup her buttocks, raising her closer to the part of him that could end her torment. Suddenly he lifted her higher, his lips raining kisses over one breast, then the other. Holding onto him like a lifeline, Jordan tried to catch her breath and ease the mad pounding of her heart. His tongue flicked out, laving her nipple. A warmth flowed from her breasts, down to her belly and even lower. Her fingers wove through his hair, pressing his mouth closer.

He heard her groan low in her throat and it was his undoing. Ignoring the warning signals going off in his head, Gray Hawk continued his seduction. If this was all he could have of her, then he would take what she offered. The memory of this day would be all he would have left of her, and it would have to be enough.

Jordan's breath left her lungs as he continued his onslaught. As her head fell back, her body quivered with a need denied for far too long. Waves of pleasure washed over her, building an ache in that most private part of her.

His hand slid from her hip and moved between her thighs, achingly close to her throbbing center. Jordan's heart stilled when his fingers moved over the sensitive flesh of her womanhood. A delicious sensation began to grow in the pit of her stomach until it spread to every nerve ending.

Climbing higher and higher she reached for some unknown pinnacle. A part of her wanted him to stop, knowing what they were doing was wrong. Yet, his lips and fingers were working magic over her body, until she was sure she would burst.

Gray Hawk didn't know how much longer he could hold on. Her fingers clawed at his back as she found her release. Pulling her closer, he claimed her lips once more, swallowing her cry of passion.

With every intention of making love to her on the river's edge, he lifted her in his arms. Yet as he set her on her feet, he realized that if she gave herself to him, it would make separation more difficult. It wouldn't be fair to either one of them. A woman's maidenhead was a gift, and he had no right to take it, just as he'd had no right to take her captive.

She clung to him, her face pressed against his chest, her heart beating heavily. Gray Hawk fought the emotions that raced within him. He bent his head and kissed her slowly, knowing it would be for the last time.

It was the hardest thing he'd ever done, but he finally put her at arms length. Her brows were furrowed into a frown as she stared up at him.

He smiled softly as his fingers traced the outline of her jaw, and then her full pink lips as he memorized every detail. "I'll miss you," he said, watching as her desire cooled, turning quickly to rejection.

Unable to handle the hurt he saw in her eyes, he turned and left her, before he could change his mind.

KARI OPENED her eyes to find Shane Catalono standing at the entrance to the teepee, his hands planted on his hips. "Get up, sleepy head, it's time to go."

She sat up slowly, surprised to find Rebecca was wide awake and dressed in a pair of buckskin breeches, shirt, and moccasins.

"You have something other than that dress?" Shane asked, his gaze moving quickly over her. By the expression on his face, he obviously found her leather dress repulsive.

Kari threw the furs off and grabbed her worn pants and blouse that she'd put out for their ride to Brogan. Forcing a smile, she passed the cowboy, knowing she had to make an effort to be kind. After all, it was because of him they were leaving the village, and although he constantly taunted her, she mustn't let him nettle her. He was doing them a favor, and she owed him.

Heading toward the river for a bath, Kari kept her excitement in check. A small part of her was sad they were leaving, yet she could hardly wait to get to Brogan. Finally she and Jordan would have the independence they have craved for so long. If what Shane said was true, they would have jobs and make money in no time. Months ago she would have doubted she would like domestic work, but being in the village taught her she could do anything she set her mind to. In fact, she found she enjoyed the work, sewing especially.

Jordan passed by her, saying nothing more than, "You ready?" By the tone of her voice, it was obvious she was very ready to leave. A moment later Kari had her answer to Jordan's strange mood when she saw Gray Hawk coming toward her in long strides. His hair was wet, and water clung to his body. Kari smiled, but he did no more than nod.

Indeed, it was a good thing they were leaving today.

Kari didn't linger in the river, knowing if she didn't hurry, Shane would come looking for her. Bathing quickly, she put on the clothes she'd worn when Gray Hawk had captured her.

Shane was readying the horses, and when she approached he turned around. One dark brow lifted, and she swore she saw appreciation there. "Looks like they've seen better days."

Her shoulders slumped. "Believe it or not, these garments were new six months ago."

"A little testy this morning, Miss Hoffman?"

Folding her arms over her chest, she lifted her chin a notch. "Not at all, Mr. Catalono."

One side of his mouth lifted. "Could have fooled me?"

She'd been ready with a retort, but it died when she saw his gaze wandering down her body. To her horror, her skin tingled as though he touched her with his hands. Instinctively, she checked the buttons of her blouse to make sure they were fastened. Meeting his gaze again, his grin was so wicked, it suggested more than words ever could. "Don't worry, Miss Hoffman, I only take willing women to my bed."

His words brought an outraged gasp from her lips, loud enough to turn heads. The nerve of him to say such a thing!

"You think all women will just drop at your feet, don't you, Mr. Catalono?" Her voice was trembling, but that didn't stop her from voicing her thoughts out loud. "It's men like you who give all males a bad name."

He took the steps that separated them until she was forced to look up into his handsome face. "You wouldn't know how to handle a man like me, Miss Hoffman."

Was it her imagination or was he challenging her? "Don't flatter yourself," she replied through clenched teeth.

"Have I angered you, Miss Hoffman? Your color is a little high, considering the coolness of the morning."

She could feel the warmth of his breath against her face. The blue of his eyes were startling, so light, so full of—what exactly? Oh, but he was so sure of himself! No doubt he was used to women throwing themselves at him. Well, not her!

"We could be friends?" His voice was deceptively soft.

Kari took a step backwards. "Fine, friends then." His hand was extended, and it took her a minute to realize he expected a handshake. Although she didn't want to, neither did she want to look childish. She grabbed his extended hand. It was rough, callused, strong, and lingered longer than necessary.

"You've rough hands for a woman."

She ripped her hand from his grasp, leveling him with a hostile glare. "I'm a woman who's used to hard work, Mr. Catalono. Yes, my hands are rough from the work I've endured. I'm sure that even the best of women, who I'm sure you know personally, should they have been in the same situation would find their hands as dry, cracked, and rough as mine."

He regarded her with amusement. "I wasn't comparing."

"Oh, yes you were."

She was flustered...and he loved it. Even though he'd told her that he wanted to be friends, she had to wonder if he was serious. He was constantly sarcastic to her, and friends weren't that way.

Turning her back on him, she missed the appreciative stare as he took in the sight of her feminine curves in pants.

Shane's mocking smile died on his lips as he watched her. Gone were any traces of the woman who lived among Indians and survived it...perhaps except for her work worn hands. He truly hadn't intended to criticize her, but when they were together, he couldn't help himself, and all his good intentions were buried in the dust.

He watched as she walked around the camp, talking and laughing with the Indians as though they were friends, and not the people who captured her. She shook each of their hands, her smile serene and peaceful by the time she returned to her horse ready to leave.

"Well, it looks like all we have to do now is wait for Jordan," she said, as she walked toward Rebecca. His gaze lingered on her derriere that was so clearly defined in her pants. A coincidence because his pants had grown uncomfortably tight in the last few minutes. He shifted on his feet, wondering why in the world he hadn't just offered to buy them tickets on the next stage out of the territory once they reached Brogan, instead of inviting them to stay with him.

AS JORDAN prepared to leave, a few friends came by to wish her well, while others showed their obvious delight she was leaving—none more so than Running Deer.

Having learned her nemesis would soon be out of the way, Running Deer was pleasant, almost taunting, and although Jordan tried not to be jealous, she was.

The woman would have Gray Hawk to herself, and Jordan would never see him again.

The thought ripped at her insides. It was crazy to want a future with him—impossible. But in her dreams lately she'd done just that. They'd been together and were so happy, living at the ranch, raising horses, having children. How happy and at peace she was in those dreams. Despite their differences, she and Gray Hawk had made things work between them.

But this was harsh reality.

There would never be anything between them, and she would never see him again. She told herself that she should thank her lucky stars that he hadn't taken her virginity, especially when she'd been so willing to give it.

Yet what frightened her more than anything was the fact that she wasn't thankful. She'd wanted Gray Hawk with a ferocity that scared her. And worse still was the fact she still wanted him.

Taking a deep breath, she headed toward the corral where Kari and Shane were on their horses packed and ready to go. Jordan helped Rebecca up, then looked around at the villagers who came to say goodbye. Not so very long ago she feared these people and now she was sad knowing she'd never see them again.

Gray Hawk wasn't among those who came to say farewell as they mounted up, and it hurt, especially with all they'd been through. She was hoping for at least one last look, to memorize his features, although they were already etched in her memory.

Certain she'd seen the last of him, she was surprised when he came out of the teepee and headed straight toward them. With heart in throat, she watched as he went to Rebecca, who was saddled up before Shane.

"Goodbye Little One," he said, his hand cupping the side of her face. "You take care of yourself."

Rebecca threw her arms around Gray Hawk's neck, clinging to him before finally letting go.

Shane shook Gray Hawk's hand, and she didn't miss the gunmetal stare that spoke volumes where words couldn't.

"Don't worry, I'll take care of them," Shane said in response to the unasked question.

Jordan could see the tears swimming in Kari's eyes as she took the hand he offered. Her own throat growing tighter by the minute, she waited for him to say goodbye to her, all the while trying to convince herself this was the way it should be.

But her defenses crumbled when he stood before her, his gray eyes staring into hers. They'd come so far together. To think she hated him not so very long ago, and now her heart was aching knowing this was to be their last goodbye. She wondered if he too was feeling the pain. He was always so good at masking his emotions, and she was curious what it was he was thinking now.

"Gray Hawk..." She hesitated, closing her mouth, taking in every feature and the familiar proud stance. "I'll miss you," she said, her voice breaking.

For a moment she thought he would touch her as his hand lifted toward her, but just as quickly, he dropped it to his side. "Take care, Jordan" he said, taking a step away. "I hope you get everything you want."

Jordan was tempted to tell him that all she wanted was for him to come with them; that perhaps together they could make a future together. Yet her gaze shifted past his shoulder to his people. She swallowed hard. This was his life. These were his people, and he would never pick her over them. Her gaze returned to him and she smiled softly. "I'll never forget you—not ever." Her voice cracked, and before she said something she would surely regret, she turned her mount toward the hills.

AS GRAY HAWK watched Jordan's back, his mind was telling him that her leaving was for the best, but his heart was telling a different story.

Once the four disappeared out of sight, the others in the village went about their normal routine, most of them relieved to have them gone, but Gray Hawk felt their absence all the way to his soul until a sense of panic came over him. He wanted Jordan desperately, with a need he never experienced before. If she would have stayed, she would be his, but he had been the one to send her away. It had been he who had given her the freedom she so craved.

"Your heart is sad."

Gray Hawk looked down at Tawanka, a woman who he loved and respected, and who had taken Jordan and Kari under her wing, showing them the ways of the Cheyenne. He nodded. "Yes."

"Perhaps you should have gone with her."

Those were not the words he expected from Tawanka, or any one of his tribe. He was a Cheyenne warrior, their war chief, a defender of his people, and they should come first always. "But this is my home."

She didn't reply, but there was something in the way she looked at him that made him wonder if she couldn't see into the future as she so often claimed.

"All will be right one day. All will be right." Without another word, she left him to his thoughts.

But the day was far too long and torturous. He tried in vain to put Jordan from his thoughts, yet the more he fought it, the more embedded she became in his memory. That night he barely ate, and went to bed early. As he lay in the teepee alone, he closed his eyes, envisioning Jordan laying there beside him, her sweet smile as she looked at him, the taste of her lips on his own, the feel of her body pressing against him in need.

Why hadn't he taken her? Why hadn't he slated his lust? Perhaps if he had, then it would have been enough.

What he needed more than anything was a woman. He should visit Running Deer, satisfy his craving, and hope that Jordan would be just a memory. Yet as he came to his feet, he couldn't get the vision of Jordan out of his mind. Would she so easily go into the arms of another? Right now would she be sleeping with the cowboy, while trying to get him out of her mind?

He knew she wouldn't.

Laying back down on the furs, he closed his eyes, hoping he would find peace.

Chapter 13

TRAVELING WITH three females, one under the age of six, was proving to be easier than Shane originally thought it would be.

The first day they traveled in silence, each person in their own thoughts. Now on the second day of their journey home, they were making better time than he could have possibly hoped for.

The anticipation of seeing his son after being parted for over a month was enough to make him push the group even harder. They were all exhausted, and he could tell by the dark circles under their eyes that the four hours of sleep the night before hadn't been near enough, but he had no desire to stop. They could rest all they wanted once they reached the Triple T.

After long hours in the saddle, Kari rode up beside him. He was surprised since she'd been avoiding him the entire trip, and he could tell by her angry expression that she was not happy.

"Don't you think we could stop now?"

He ignored the sharpness in her voice, knowing she was tired. Hell, they were all tired. He looked past her to where his niece rested against Jordan, who stared blankly ahead. A pang of regret and guilt assaulted him. But why should he feel bad? He had done the right thing by bringing the women with him now, although this one beside him was surely getting under his skin. "I suppose we can stop for a spell."

"I meant for the night."

He looked up at the sun before turning back toward her. "Got a good hour or so of daylight left."

"Mr. Catalono, we are past the point of exhausted. I have blisters on my derriere from the rubbing of the saddle, and if I don't get something to eat soon, I'm going to scream."

His gaze moved to where her dainty little rear made contact with the saddle. A mistake he found as his body hardened. "You're irritated with me, aren't you?" he asked in a low, smooth voice that seemed to anger her even more.

"Trust me, I passed irritated miles ago," she replied with a sneer. "Are we going to stop?"

His gaze lingered on her face for a long moment. He loved the way she looked when she was agitated. The way her eyes shot sparks, the way her color heightened, and the pulse at the base of her neck throbbed. She'd be one hell of a lover, he thought, his gaze drifting to where her shirt opened exposing the swell of her breasts. A sheen of perspiration glittered along the line of her collar bone. When his gaze returned to her face, her eyes were narrowed to suspicious slits.

"Don't even think about it," she said, and turning from him, rode over to Jordan to announce they were stopping.

From Jordan's relieved expression, he knew Kari was right—it was for the best that they stop. He was used to long hours in the saddle, the women weren't. Seeing a nice clearing in which to camp, he reined in and went over to help Rebecca and Jordan down.

Kari was already off her horse by the time he came to help her. He didn't miss the glare she threw his way.

"Are you happy, Miss Hoffman?" he asked mockingly.

She planted both hands on her narrow hips. "Happy about what, Mr. Catalono?" she hissed.

"Happy that we've stopped for you."

With an exasperated sigh, Kari turned her back on him, knowing he was just waiting for her retort so he could continue to harass her. He loved to annoy her. Even now, when he was pushing them all to the extreme, he just couldn't resist and place all the blame on her shoulders. As her hands moved over her sore rear end, a strangled intake of breath came from his direction. The sound brought a smile to her lips as she lay a blanket out for Rebecca who was fighting sleep.

"Miss Hoffman—Kari, could you help me with the horses?" Shane asked from behind her. Having just tucked the blanket under the girls chin, she turned to find Shane trying to hold all four thirsty horses in check. "Come on." He held two sets of reins out to her.

Seeing that Jordan was already getting ready to prepare their dinner, Kari knew she was stuck. "Oh, all right," before ripping the reins from his grasp.

He moved ahead of her through the brush, swearing when his hand made contact with a prickly branch. He looked back as though sensing her delight, but she masked her smile by biting the inside of her cheek.

The horses were trying to rush forward long before Kari heard the sound of water over rocks. Once the animals had their fill, she tied them to a branch and went to her knees on the bank, cupping the water, letting it run down her face, neck, and arms. She wanted more than anything to get out of her dusty clothes and scrub herself until her skin tingled.

She looked up and her pulse skittered to find Shane had thrown aside his shirt and stood naked to the waist. Muscular biceps moved as he soaped the hard planes of his well-defined chest. Sinew moved under his tanned skin, and Kari licked her dry lips as the water slid toward his flat abdomen and the dark path of hair that disappeared beneath the band of his pants. Her heart pounded in her ears. Why did the man have to be so virile and good-looking? Turning away from the sight, Kari willed her blood to cool.

Sitting on the bank, she took off her boots, and rolled her pant legs to her knees. She unbuttoned her shirt until she was dangerously close to exposing her breasts. A wicked thought drifted through her mind. If seeing him unclothed did strange things to her, what if the tables were turned? She undid another button, then another for good measure.

She knew the moment he noticed her. He went completely still. Not daring to look in his direction, she stepped into the cool water letting it lap at her calves. Cupping the water, she brought it to her face and closed her eyes as the water slid down her throat and trickled between her near naked breasts.

"Want some soap?" His voice sounded forced, and when she turned, his gaze slipped from her chin to her breasts. Her nipples were already hard from the cold, and under his gaze they tightened more. The heat in his eyes made her pulse skip double time, and for once she felt like the one in control. She held out her hand.

His brow arched in question, before he mumbled, "Oh, yeah, the soap." He handed her the bar that was forgotten only seconds before.

"Thank you," she replied, trying to ignore the delicious feel of his fingers against hers as she took the bar from him.

Shane watched her for the next ten minutes as she washed and re-washed her hair. Sure it was dirty, but that dirty? Of course, he enjoyed watching her—what hot-blooded man wouldn't? He could clearly see her rose-colored nipples through her shirt, pebble hard, straining against the white linen. She bent over, stretching the material of her breeches against her firm bottom that he ached to take within his hands, pulling her up against the length of his hard—

"Mr. Catalono?"

Hearing her soft voice, Shane forced his thoughts away from their dangerous wanderings. Despite the innocent look on her beautiful face, it was obvious to him she knew exactly what he was thinking by the little smirk on her lips.

"I asked how long it would take before we reached the ranch?" she asked, one delicate brow lifted in question as she twisted the water out of her long hair. His gaze moved to her now soaked shirt. He could barely think, let alone breathe. Shaking her head, she flipped her hair forward, then quickly back again, where it hit her back with a slap.

He swallowed so hard he was surprised she couldn't hear him gulp. She may as well be naked for all that the transparent shirt covered. "About four more days, maybe more, maybe less," he said in a strained voice. Clearing his throat, he tried to keep his eyes averted from the fetching sight, but it was impossible. He was like a man starved.

She looked like a water nymph standing before him with her firm breasts exposed to his all-consuming gaze, and her pants clinging to shapely legs. With her wet hair slicked back off her forehead, her delicate features were even more accented. Her blue eyes appeared huge in her face as she stared at him. When she combed her fingers through her hair, she arched her back, thrusting her breasts out. He groaned inwardly.

It was all he could do to keep his gaze from slipping past her chin as he watched her, watching him. Dark lashes were spiked from the water, her lips full and pink, and as she smiled, he caught a glimpse of straight, tiny white teeth. He'd seen the smile so rarely that the magnitude of it took his breath away.

Kari shifted under his intense gaze. His very presence made her uneasy. He was so close she could smell his manly scent and feel the warmth of his strong body.

"I understand Gray Hawk found you and Jordan alone on the prairie," Shane asked, sitting down on the bank, lighting a cigarette. He stared at her under long, dark lashes. "And what may I ask were the two of you doing out in the middle of this God forsaken country alone?"

Kari squirmed under his stare. If she told him the truth, quite possibly he wouldn't take them with him to Brogan, or worse, he could wire her father thinking he was doing the right thing, when actually it would be the worst. They had never told a soul about where they truly came from. She knew from the pounding of her heart that now was not the time either.

"Well?"

"We were traveling west—"

"By yourselves?" he asked, the tone of his voice saying he found it hard to believe.

"No...with—my husband."

His brow shot up. "Your husband?"

Kari nodded, looking at her feet as she continued the lie. "Yes...he died."

Shane blew a ring of smoke above his head. "I'm sorry," he said, his voice softer than she'd ever heard it. "How did he die?"

She'd never been any good at fabricating stories, and when she looked up, she saw the rolling water and blurted, "He drowned." Meeting his gaze again, she noticed he watched her intently, his look somewhat skeptical, but she saw a hint of sympathy there too. To her chagrin, she realized she would have preferred his scowl for once.

"I know how tough it is to lose a spouse. A part of you dies in a way..."

His words had the same effect as a blow to the stomach, and before she could stop herself, she asked, "Your wife?"

All he did was nod in response. It appeared he had nothing else to say on the subject, which disappointed her. She wondered what kind of a woman Shane Catalono had married. Had she been beautiful? Certainly, she would have to be. A man like him could get anyone. Uncomfortable under his searching gaze, she waded through the water toward a large, flat rock where she stretched out.

Shane's heart hammered mercilessly. The blood soared through his veins as Kari sat on the rock, kicked her feet in the water, then leaned back on her elbows, her face lifting to the sun as though worshiping its warmth. Her breasts strained against the shirt until he swore it would burst open. A coincidence, since he felt he would explode at any moment so tight were the pants on his crotch.

He glanced at the water, then back at Kari, who still had her eyes closed. Slowly her lips parted looking like she was waiting for her lover. For a moment he envisioned he was that lover...the blood coursed through his veins straight to his groin.

He ground the cigarette into the ground and dove into the frigid water.

NO MATTER how hard Jordan tried, she couldn't keep her thoughts from Gray Hawk. In the days since she'd left his village, she thought of nothing but him. Sure, for a few minutes here and there she could focus enough on the landscape, letting her mind go blank, but then she would see something that would remind her of him and she had to fight the urge to cry.

If her thoughts were traitorous, her dreams were downright cruel. Last night she'd dreamt of him again—his hands on her, bringing her body to life.

"You're thinking of him again, aren't you?"

Jordan jumped at the sound of Kari's voice. She turned to her cousin with a half-hearted smile.

"You'll see Gray Hawk again."

"How can you be so sure?"

Kari shrugged. "I just believe it, that's all. Everything will be all right once we reach Brogan. I can't wait to see it. I just know things are going to work out for us. Like Shane said, we'll find jobs, and we'll start saving our money, and before you know it, we'll have the ranch."

Kari's enthusiasm was catching, and Jordan decided the best thing to do was focus on the future and forget the past. After all, this is what they'd come west for. She wanted her ranch more than anything, and now she had to fight to keep it. She wouldn't spend her days pining away for a man that wasn't meant to be hers. He probably was with Running Deer anyway. It would do her good to put him from her mind.

"There it is. Do you see it?"

Both Jordan and Kari stared past Shane to the ranch in the distance. An enormous log house with a wrap around porch sat among numerous outbuildings', corrals and stables. Men who had been working stopped what they were doing, and began waving their arms in welcome.

"Oh my gosh," Kari said under her breath, unable to help the smile that came readily to her lips. "This is huge!"

Jordan couldn't help but grin. The Triple T was far grander than she imagined. The house itself was built of honey-colored logs, rising three stories, with a wraparound porch, and a balcony off the top level.

If Jordan thought the outside was impressive, then the inside was everything her dreams for her own ranch were made of.

Two enormous couches dominated the living room. A touch of culture was evident with bookcases filled with classic literature. She traced her fingers across one of the two oak side tables adorned with oil lamps. With a sigh, she settled into the folds of the only chair and admired the large stone fireplace that was set and ready for the chilly night. With an impressive glance around the room again, Jordan knew she was meant for this kind of life.

An older gentleman with silver hair and a quick smile came into the room. Shane introduced him as Hank, the foreman of the Triple T. Hank was friendly and went out of his way to make them feel welcome.

A minute after they sat down, a thunderous pounding came up the porch steps and a proud, beaming smile came to Shane's face as the door flew open.

"Dad!" A boy on the brink of manhood bounded through the door. With a smile identical to Shane's, he hugged his dad. "What took you so long? I've been waiting for weeks to hear from you."

Jordan glanced at Kari with a smile.

"I'm sorry, Tanner, but you know I couldn't come home without Rebecca, but I'm back now, and I have another surprise."

Noticing their presence for the first time, Tanner stepped back from his father, looking embarrassed at his display of affection. His smile faltered as he looked from Kari to Jordan, then back to Shane.

"This is Miss Hoffman, and...Miss Hoffman, but I bet they wouldn't mind if you called them Kari and Jordan. It's a long story, but let's just suffice it to say they helped me get Rebecca out of the Indian camp, and until they get back on their feet, they'll be staying here?"

"Miss Kari—Miss Jordan," Tanner said, taking his hat from his head. "Nice to meet you."

Tanner Catalono was the spitting image of his father: dark skin, dark hair, light eyes framed by long, dark lashes any girl would kill to have.

"Sit down," Shane said, pulling his son down next to him. He flung an arm around his neck, pulling him up against him and kissing the top of his head. Jordan's heart constricted, smiling as Tanner's cheeks flamed red.

Tanner cleared his throat, pulling away. "I'm going to get some of those cookies Hank is baking." He was halfway to the kitchen when he turned. "I'm glad you're home, Dad," he said, before disappearing into the kitchen.

Jordan watched Shane as he watched his son leave. "You must be very proud."

He nodded. "I couldn't have asked for a better son."

"His mother?" They were only two words, but the reaction was unforeseen. For an instant pain crossed his features before he quickly hid it beneath that tough exterior she'd become accustomed to this past week.

"She died giving birth to Tanner. He's a lot like she was; caring, kind, loving." The last was said with a longing that surprised Jordan.

He looked up. "Sorry, I can drag on at times. I'm sure you know what that's like," he said, glancing over at Kari.

Jordan was feeling awful for having brought up his wife, but as she glanced at Kari, she was even more perplexed when her cousin sank down into the cushions, her face turning white.

She nodded at Shane. "Yes, I suppose I do."

Feeling like she was on the outside looking in, Jordan sat back and waited to be let-in on what appeared to be a private conversation.

"How old was your husband when he was killed?"

Jordan barely concealed her gasp of disbelief with an exaggerated cough. She turned to Kari, anxious to hear a response.

Kari cleared her throat. "Uhmm...forty-one."

He nodded, his face soft with understanding as he sat back and ran a hand down his face.

Kari finally met her gaze, her expression pleading.

"Were you traveling with your husband as well, or were you with Kari—"

"I'm not married," Jordan said quickly, stepping on Kari's foot for the lie she was making her tell.

"It must have been so difficult for the both of you to survive after he drowned."

Jordan bit the inside of her lip and nodded. Unable to continue looking Shane in the eye while lying through her teeth, considering everything he'd done for them, she stood abruptly. "You know, I'm really tired, and I think it would be a good time for us to take a nap, don't you?" she asked, turning to Kari who quickly agreed.

"Hope you ladies don't mind sharing a room."

Jordan smiled. "Not at all. It's perfect and we're grateful to have a place to stay."

"Don't think anything of it. You've gone through a lot, and you deserve a chance to get back on your feet. Don't worry about anything."

Jordan's hand slid along the slick log banister as she walked up the steps to the second story where the bedrooms were. Once they were safely on the other side of their bedroom door, she cornered Kari. "Your dead husband? Where did that come from? What else haven't you told me, Miss *Hoffman?* How did you explain that we both have the same last name if you're married? Or am I your dead husband's sister, instead of your cousin?"

Kari shifted on her feet, looking like a guilty child. "Well...he was asking me where we were going, and why we were alone when Gray Hawk took us, and I just thought it up. I didn't know that his wife died. If I had, I would have been more—"

"Creative?"

She shrugged. "Well, what would you have done?"

Jordan sighed. "You could have at least prepared me. What if he would have questioned me when you weren't around?"

"I completely forgot about it. I guess I was hoping that he would forget, too."

Jordan sighed heavily. "Well, it appears he hasn't."

GRAY HAWK rode beside his brother and Young Wolf. Iron Bear pointed to the sea of buffalo that grazed in the valley below. "Letting the women go was what the Great Spirit wanted. It has brought back our buffalo."

Avoiding his brother's gaze, Gray Hawk looked over the land he'd spent his entire life defending against other tribes. With every day more whites came, a force he feared would not be overtaken.

"The herd heads North. Let's move our village this night."

Gray Hawk heard his brother's words, but didn't comment. He for one had no desire to move their village, but for a selfish reason. He wanted to believe that Jordan, having realized she loved him, would make her way back to him one day. If they moved, she would never be able to find him.

Why was he thinking this way? She was where she wanted to be, living in the white world again. She was probably trying to forget her stay in his village—and forget him. The best thing he could do was move on and try to forget her. "We will speak with father when we return."

Without another word Gray Hawk took off for the village alone, letting his mind drift and as always, they turned to Jordan. She made him yearn for the white ways, even though it seemed an eternity since he'd lived among them and that experience had not been very pleasant. Yet if he thought about it, there had been good times— times when he'd envied the white men.

That evening as Gray Hawk sat to eat with the others, talk was rampant about the bounty of buffalo. All around him voices were raised in joy, and he tried earnestly to share their enthusiasm, but the truth was, he couldn't.

It was still early when he retired to his teepee. Ever since Jordan left, he had been incredibly lonely. He'd had plenty of opportunities to be with not just Running Deer, but other maidens. Yet no matter how much he yearned for a warm body, he could only be happy with one. His hand moved over the furs where Jordan once slept. Closing his eyes he saw her sweet face, her silky hair, her beautiful body.

He ran a fist into the furs. If what he feared about his peoples future did happen, then they would need him more than ever. He was wasting his time dreaming of a white woman that would never belong to him. He must forget about her.

"Gray Hawk?"

Gray Hawk glanced up to meet his father's obsidian stare, as he sat down on a fur. He was surprised by his father's visit, though it was not completely unexpected. He'd been aware of his father's watchful stare these last few days.

"You miss the white woman?"

"You know I do," Gray Hawk replied in frustration. The last few weeks had been hell. Every day it became harder to forget Jordan, when it should have been easier. The only time he had any peace at all was when he hunted, and if he kept at it, he'd supply the whole villages meat by himself in no time.

"My son, I know the secret war that is going on inside you, for I have fought those same emotions myself. Many say that you are not the same. That the white woman tainted you. They say that you have become cold, and you care nothing for your people...and I believe some of what they say."

Gray Hawk was shocked at his father's words. He had never turned his back on his people, nor would he. They were his family, but now, listening to his father, the only thing he'd managed to do was isolate himself and become unapproachable.

He was even more miserable than the day she left.

"I care little for what others think, father."

His father wrapped the blanket tighter around his frail body. "Tawanka said that she had a vision that you were going to leave us. That you would seek your own way...the white way."

Gray Hawk couldn't help but feel betrayed by the old woman, even though he had no right to. Tawanka loved him like a son, and had become like a mother to him when his own had left. She also knew him better than most. "I cannot read the future, nor do I believe anyone else can."

He'd angered his father, he could tell in the way that his back straightened, and the way his eyes turned dark.

"I realize that you are in pain, so I will disregard your words. Our people need you. I feel bad that you will have to carry the responsibility on your shoulders of what is to come. No one envies you that, but your people deserve to have your leadership. The battle you fight now is within yourself." His father studied him for a long moment, then said, "I've spoken with the council and they believe you need time to sort through your problems."

"Father—"

"Find your destiny, Gray Hawk. Discover what is truly in your heart. When that time comes, whether it is with The People or the white man, we will accept your decision. But in the meantime, I must insist you leave. It is the only way for you to be certain."

His father's words cut like a knife. He never dreamed that he would be sent away from the people he'd spent his entire life defending.

"What if I don't know what I'm looking for?" he asked in open defiance.

His father smiled slowly. "You will find it, my son."

The words were final. There would be no more discussion on the matter. Gray Hawk knew he would be leaving at dawn.

Chapter 14

JORDAN SAT back in the tub, sighing as the warm water eased her weary muscles. Having scrubbed pants, shirts and the socks of the Triple T ranch hands all day, she was ready for some rest and relaxation.

Though she and Kari had every intention of finding work in town, Shane had seen to it to keep them busy at the ranch. But she was grateful for her chores, because it kept her mind busy.

Every other night, she and Kari took turns trading off the kitchen duties so the other could relax. Thank goodness tonight it was her turn to take it easy.

She could hear Kari and Shane in the kitchen that was right next to the washroom, talking about their day. Jordan knew for certain that coming to Brogan was the best thing she and Kari could have done. Already they had made a good sum of money, but they also worked their fingers to the bone, and had the blisters to prove it.

As the water became cool, she stepped out, dried off, and put on her clean white cotton gown, embroidered with tiny rosebuds. It was soft and comfortable against her skin. Shane had been kind enough to take them to town and buy them dresses, but only with the condition that they repay him. However she noticed when she paid him for the clothing, her pay took a jump.

She glanced at her reflection in the mirror for a moment as she brushed out her long hair. In the month since leaving Gray Hawk, she had lost some weight, and it showed in her face. Her cheekbones were more pronounced, as were the hollows beneath her eyes—which were also attributed to lack of sleep. Something she hoped would remedy itself soon. One of the ranch hands offered her a solution, which she was told consisted of whiskey and a couple of ground up medicinal weeds. Maybe tonight, she thought, knowing she didn't want to lie awake again thinking of Gray Hawk again. Yet every night she lay in bed, her exhausted body begging to sleep, but instead of sleep, her mind would race with images of the handsome half-breed.

Hearing the scrape of boots on the floor, she quickly put on her stockings. When she heard more than one male voice, her brows furrowed into a frown. All the men ate outside, except for Shane, who would sit with them and the family at the table. Thinking that perhaps Hank had decided to join them, she tidied up the little room, opened the door, her gaze instantly coming to an abrupt halt on the broad shoulders of a guest.

Her heart thumped madly in her chest. Her eyes narrowed, knowing the width of those shoulders wasn't common. The man's black hair was shoulder length, and Jordan quickly let out the breath she'd unconsciously been holding. It was someone that looked remarkably like....

The man turned and she let out the breath she'd been holding. "Gray Hawk," she said in disbelief.

He stood, looking taller...and different than she remembered. Dressed in black pants and shirt, he looked like any other cowboy, but not like any other cowboy. His hair was no longer than Shane's, and he was even wearing boots.

"Hello, Jordan," he said, his voice sending a shiver down her spine.

Her hands trembled, and she quickly laced her fingers together in front of her. "Hello," she replied, nodding, willing her legs to move. She slowly strode toward the table, not once taking her eyes off him.

She sat across from Gray Hawk, who was once again seated. The children were eating in the other room, and she could hear Rebecca giggle.

Gray Hawk smiled. "She has done well."

Jordan nodded.

"How have you been, Gray Hawk?" Kari asked, pinching Jordan's leg under the table, while smiling pleasantly at their guest.

Jordan flinched from the pain, but sat up straighter and cleared her throat. She wanted to ask him why he had left his people, cut his hair, and was dressed like he was, but she said nothing, and instead stared, amazed at the change in him. He looked so different. There was so little of the warrior left in him, yet he still was so...dangerous.

"I've been fine. I've decided to leave the village for a while."

"Will you be staying long?" Kari asked, stepping on Jordan's foot.

"Shane has offered me work, and I would like to stay, but I think it's only fair to ask how you and Jordan feel about me staying."

"I think it's wonderful," Kari said with a wide smile. "Don't you think so, Jordan?"

Jordan swallowed past the lump in her throat. Everything was happening so fast. Weeks ago she had left him, never expecting to see him again, and now here he was sitting across from her, those gray eyes she had tried so hard to forget, boring into hers, obviously waiting for an answer.

"Yes, wonderful" she said, her voice coming out a squeak.

His grin was devastating, and instantly memories of what those lips felt like came to her. Her gaze moved to his hands. One was holding a knife, the other a fork, proving to her he wasn't as primitive as she would have liked to believe. As he cut the steak into bite-size pieces, she stared at his long, dark fingers, remembering how they had stroked her body.

Feeling her cheeks turn warm with the memory, she took a drink of water, and her eyes met Gray Hawk's over the rim of her glass. Those gray eyes were dark and sensual, as though telling her he hadn't forgotten either. Dropping her gaze, she set the glass down and picked up her fork with trembling fingers. She could feel him watch her every move. Forcing herself to concentrate, she managed to get a few bites down, though she had no appetite.

"You've lost weight," he said, and she glanced up.

She shrugged. "A little."

"That, and she never sleeps," Kari added. "She spends all day working her fingers to the bone, but at night she can't fall asleep...for some reason."

GRAY HAWK'S heart was pounding hard against his chest as he watched Jordan. Had he actually thought he could forget her? As he stared into her green eyes, he wondered why he had ever let her go. With the weight she had lost, she looked so fragile. Her hair was in a simple ribbon. How he longed to bury his face in the silkiness, to tell her how much he hated letting her go, and how much he still desired her.

"You cut your hair..."

Gray Hawk sensed regret in Jordan's voice, yet he could see the approval in her eyes as she stared at him. Not wanting to go into detail about his vision quest, he nodded.

"It's really nice to see you," she added, her voice soft.

"I've been thinking about you a lot," he said, feeling better than he had in weeks. For so long he'd waited to see her, and now it was as though it were just the two of them alone together.

It was the first time he'd seen her in white womens clothes. She was the picture of femininity. "You look good," he said, wanting to say so much more, but it was too soon and there were too many people in the room.

He concentrated on his food, though he wanted nothing more than to take her in his arms and make love to her.

Finishing with dinner, Jordan joined Rebecca and Tanner in the living room, trying earnestly to keep her attention on the game of cards, rather than the tall Indian who stepped into the room with Shane.

His gaze was like a hot caress that she could feel all the way to her soul. She yearned to spend time alone with him, but at the same time, she wondered if she could trust herself in the same room with him.

Trying to dredge up all the hurt feelings was impossible. She was just too happy to have him here at the ranch, especially when she didn't think she would ever see him again.

"Good night, Jordan," Gray Hawk said, reaching for the door.

"Good night," she replied, trying to keep the disappointment that he was leaving out of her voice.

"Good night, Gray Hawk," Rebecca said, running to him and hugging him. "I'll see you tomorrow."

Despite her efforts at remaining aloof, Jordan melted at the sight of Gray Hawk giving Rebecca a tight squeeze. "Sleep well, Little One."

He looked at Jordan with a soft smile before shutting the door behind him.

Everyone slowly went off to bed leaving her there to stare at the fire. She knew she should try and at least lay down, but now with Gray Hawk's arrival, there would be no way she could sleep. And she had no desire to lie in bed and stare at the ceiling.

She wished she would have had some time alone with Gray Hawk to ask him why he was here. Why had he cut his hair, and why was he taking a job at the Triple T? Subconsciously she had to think his decision had something to do with her, but maybe he had come because he needed help, and the only white man he knew was Shane Catalono. Plus, Shane had made it well known that he owed Gray Hawk a favor for saving Rebecca from the Crow.

A little while later the door opened and Shane stepped in. A pang of disappointment ran through her when he shut it behind him. Had Gray Hawk changed his mind and left? She wanted to ask, but couldn't get the question past her lips.

Shane looked exhausted, but he stopped when he saw her. "Not tired?"

"Not really," she replied too quickly. "Could I get you something?"

"No thanks. I've got to get some sleep," he said, heading for the stairs. "You should try and do the same. Maybe you should heat some milk. That always used to work for me when I couldn't sleep." He grinned boyishly. "Oh, just so you know, we'll have another hand around for a while, so you may want to make a little more for breakfast."

HANGING THE laundry on the line, Jordan kept looking over at the corral where the shirtless ranch hands were hard at work branding the cattle. It was a grueling process, each man with a specific task, sweat running down their bodies as the smoke swirled around them. The smell of burnt hair and flesh was enough to gag a person, but they went about it mechanically, intent on seeing it done down to the very last cow.

Gray Hawk had the arduous task of holding down the animal's hind legs, Hank held the front legs, while Shane did the actual branding. Nearby was another group of ranch hands busy at the same task.

But not one of those hands looked like Gray Hawk. Even from the distance, Jordan could see his muscles bulge beneath his dark skin. She was becoming accustomed to seeing him in ranch clothes instead of the once familiar leather breeches and vest. He was a man like any other...perhaps not like every other, she thought with a whimsical smile as her gaze slid to his firm backside that was clearly defined in snug black pants.

"Jordan Lee McGuire, if I didn't know better, I'd say you're staring somewhere you shouldn't be."

Jordan whirled at the sound of Kari's voice. A blush raced up her neck as she turned from her, making busy with the laundry that was taking her longer to hang than normal. "I was just watching the men work."

"You were distracted, and staring at his..." Kari cleared her throat, "his derriere."

Rather than deny it, Jordan shrugged, while clasping a clothespin over a sheet. "Ever since he's been here, I find it so hard to work. I'm all right when he's out in the pasture or out of sight, but when he's around, I can't seem to concentrate."

Jordan knew Kari heard little of what she said since she was busy staring at the men, or Shane in particular, who was holding the branding iron over the hot coals. Sweat streamed down his lean torso, disappearing into the band of his pants. Jordan could see the appreciation flare in her cousin's eyes. "Now who's staring?"

"Shush," Kari said, slipping behind the sheet, her gaze riveted on Shane.

Jordan laughed, loving the fact her cousin was going through the same emotions she was. How far they'd come from the young girls who had great aspirations; Kari of marrying a wealthy man and settling down to an easy life, and Jordan, who just wanted a man who loved to ranch as much as she did.

The cow let out a startled grunt as the brand found its mark.

"Oh no!"

Jordan glanced at Kari, who stared wide-eyed at Shane, who was coming toward them in long strides. "Well, what do you know. It looks like Shane needs something."

"Don't you think I know that?" Kari hissed.

Jordan smiled as Kari fumbled with a sheet, pretending to be busy hanging it.

"Ladies," Shane said, tipping his hat. "Dinner needs to be later tonight than usual. We've got a lot of cattle to brand," he said, motioning to the sea of cows corralled a short distance away.

Jordan noticed that for all Kari was pretending not to be affected by the cowboy, her bright pink cheeks were a dead give away, not to mention she was trying too hard to keep her gaze averted. A shame, since Shane was grinning boyishly, no doubt for Kari's benefit.

"Miss Kari, it looks as though you're allowing your cousin to do all the work," he said, with an arched brow that brought Kari's attention back to him.

Jordan had to bite the inside of her cheek as Kari's mouth opened. For a moment she looked ready to reprimand him, but a second later, she lifted her chin and asked, "What do you mean by that?"

He shrugged. "It just seems that every time I turn around, Jordan's doing the majority of the work, while you're daydreaming. If the chores are too difficult for you, then maybe we could find something else for you to do. There is no time to rest on our laurels around here. So let me know."

He turned on his heel so fast, Kari didn't see the satisfied smile on his face, but Jordan did.

"Well, that good for nothing—"

"Kari, he was just kidding."

Kari shook her head. "No, he wasn't. He was serious. His tone may have been playful, but his expression wasn't. Well, I'll show him!"

Jordan watched Kari stomp off toward the house. What was it between her and Shane anyway? The two loved goading each other. In fact, they seemed to go out of their way in order to irritate one another.

A smile came easily to her lips, because she knew exactly what was going on between them.

Hanging the rest of the laundry, Jordan decided the men probably could use a little refreshment. Going to the kitchen, she grabbed a few glasses and a pitcher of lemonade. Heading out to the corral, Jordan told herself she was only doing this for the men, and not just to be near Gray Hawk again.

Never mind she was taking special care on her appearance lately. Or the fact she suddenly looked forward to every meal, lingering longer at the dining hall when serving the hands and spending more time outdoors. Anything to see the tall, dark man who had come storming back into her life.

So many times she'd been tempted to sneak out and see him. But when he shared a bunkhouse with thirty other men, it was hard to be inconspicuous. She'd considered sending him a note, but thought of how embarrassing it would be if it landed in the wrong hands. No, the only way to get his attention was to become obvious.

Shoulders erect, a practiced smile on her face, Jordan marched out to the corral. The men were so intent on what they were doing, they didn't see her at first. For a second Jordan considered leaving, but she stayed and waited for one of them to notice her, preferably the tall half-breed, whose dark tan accented the solid muscles that played beneath his dark skin.

But since they weren't paying any attention to her, she used the opportunity to watch Gray Hawk when he wasn't aware of her scrutiny. Jordan knew of the strength it took to keep the cows from moving and kicking out when the hot iron scorched their flesh, yet he handled it with ease, as though he'd done it all his life.

Her heart swelled with pride.

Now that she had time to get used to it, she found she liked his hair shorter. He was so much more...civilized. Dressed as he was, he seemed like any other white man, except his skin and hair were a hint darker than most. He looked up abruptly meeting her stare. Her pulse skittered as his gray eyes bored into her. Slowly a smile came to his face, and she relaxed, smiling softly in return.

Lord, he was handsome.

Turning the calf loose, Gray Hawk said something to Shane, who glanced her way and smiled. She waited as the three came toward her and took the lemonade she offered.

"Thanks, we needed that right about now," Shane said, wiping a sheen of sweat from his forehead with a bandana. He handed Hank a glass, then drained his own, and setting it back on the tray, he headed back to work.

As Hank joined Shane, Gray Hawk took a little longer. He watched her over the rim of his glass, his eyes sparkling as though he knew exactly what it was she was thinking. Jordan glanced down at his hand on the fence rail. His long dark fingers were strong and callused, and she remembered for a moment what it felt like to have them on her body. How she yearned to have them there again.

She glanced up to find him grinning.

"You look nice," he said, looking over his shoulder at the men who were waiting for him. "Then again, you always do." He motioned to Shane and Hank that he'd be a minute more.

"Thanks," she said, overjoyed by his compliment, glad he noticed the efforts she went to.

Taking off his hat, he ran his fingers through his hair that was damp with sweat. The rock-hard muscles in his bicep rippled beneath his smooth, dark skin.

"I better get back," he said, his gray eyes pinning her to the spot. "Maybe I'll see you later." Perhaps she was only hearing things, but she could have sworn he'd asked it as a question.

The smoldering flame she saw in his eyes startled her, yet excited her at the same time. She ached for the fulfillment of his lovemaking, knowing it was the only way she would find peace again. "Maybe," she replied, her voice sounding huskier than normal.

"Okay," he said with a devastating smile that set her heart racing. She watched him walk away, then realizing she no longer had an excuse to be standing around and watching him, she headed back to the house.

Chapter 15

GRAY HAWK was tired and filthy. Many of the men ate their supper and passed out on their cots, exhausted from the long day of branding. Though his body yearned for sleep, he couldn't go to bed without a good scrubbing.

Grabbing clean clothes, he rolled them into a ball, and closed the door to the bunkhouse. It was a starry night, not a single cloud in the sky, the moon casting its glow upon the land.

Gray Hawk glanced at the large log home and the light that shined brightly. What he wouldn't give to walk up the steps, knock on the door, and see Jordan one last time before he closed his eyes this night.

Since he'd been at the Triple T, he had seen her every day, and each time she grew more daring. He noticed her smiles came quickly, and her gaze at times was down right seductive—seductive for an innocent.

He knew each time she stepped outside of the house, and was also aware of the way she watched him, even though she pretended not to. His heart pounded furiously seeing the blatant desire, knowing she wanted him.

Walking the familiar path to the pond, he let his mind wander, thinking of his family and the life that he had left. He thought about his father every day and worried about his failing health. Yet this new life was going well. He liked the long days in the saddle, the tending of the cattle, fixing fences—seeing Jordan.

He whistled, planning to make good use of the pond tonight. The sky was cloudless, the full moon bright, allowing him the opportunity to stay longer than usual. It would give him time to think about his future and what he planned to do. He knew he couldn't stay at the Triple T forever, living off of Shane's charity, but returning to his village wasn't an option now. His vision had told him to follow Jordan, and it was here he would stay, at least for awhile.

Hearing something, he stopped in mid-stride and listened. His eyes narrowed, his muscles tensed. He heard again the light rustling of meadow grass behind him—then it stopped.

He was being followed.

Instinctively his hand moved to the hilt of his knife as he continued toward the pond.

JORDAN QUESTIONED her motives. What was she doing following Gray Hawk into the trees in the middle of the night? What did she expect to say when he caught her following him? "Hi, I just wanted to talk," sounded completely ridiculous.

But she couldn't stop—not now. It was driving her crazy knowing he was around, but unable to share a moment alone with him. There was always someone around preventing them from having even a second to themselves. Sure, they shared some glances, a smile, or a nod, but she yearned for more. Exactly how much more, she couldn't quite decide. Letting him get a good distance ahead of her, she made sure to keep low just in case she lost her nerve and needed a quick escape.

At first Jordan thought maybe Gray Hawk had decided to leave the ranch without saying anything to anyone, until she recognized the trail that Rebecca and Tanner took when they went to the pond. Realization of why he was going there came slowly. Obviously he was going to bathe. What if she got there and he was naked? The thought of seeing Gray Hawk without a stitch of clothing on sent her heart racing with excitement. Then again, perhaps she should just turn back to the ranch.

She stopped as an owl hooted at the same time Gray Hawk disappeared into the trees. What would he think when he caught her watching him? But even as the thought crossed her mind, she continued, knowing she had to see him or spend another long night tossing and turning.

Hearing the splash of water, she considered waiting for him, but only for a moment before moving closer. Sinking down into the brush, she parted the shrub, and her mouth went dry as she watched him slicing through the water, his powerful arms stroking the water. He stopped and grabbed a bar of soap off the bank and began lathering his skin. Jordan stared as he ran the soap over his body, his hard chest, his muscular arms, and then down lower, his hand disappearing beneath the water. She swallowed hard, knowing she had made that very soap with her own hands.

Unable to continue hiding from him, she stood, ready to call out when he stepped from the water. The words died in her throat and her heart skipped a beat at the sight of all of him. She stood with mouth open, rooted to the spot, unable to move. Jordan had never seen a naked man before, except for an illustration in a medical book her uncle kept in his library.

Now her body tingled as her gaze fell past his massive chest to his hard stomach and lower still to his long, thick manhood.

He was not built like the man in the book. Not even close.

She swallowed past the lump in her throat, her gaze jerking back to his face to find him staring straight at her.

His eyes smoldered as they raked over her. He dried himself slowly, every move seemed calculated, and not once did she break eye contact. It was as though he dared her to look away. Well, she wouldn't disappoint him, since she couldn't stop staring to save her life. He was beautiful: long, lean, and powerful. A man any woman would like to call her own.

Throwing the towel aside, he took a step toward her.

Suddenly mortified at what she was doing, Jordan took a step back, and stumbled over a rock. Falling hard on her bottom, she quickly scrambled to her feet, grateful it was dark enough to hide her burning cheeks.

Rivulets of water clung to him, and she could see his skin was goose pimpled in the night air. A shiver raced up her spine that had nothing to do with the cold as his gaze slowly caressed her face with hot desire.

Opening her mouth, she found herself at a loss for words. Every line she'd memorized for days now faded away under his heated stare. He reached out in invitation. When she accepted and touched his fingers, sparks seemed to fly between them.

Then his hands moved to either side of her face, his thumbs lightly caressing her lips. In his eyes she could see the same longing that she felt. His fingers moved down her neck, stopping on the pulse beating wildly in her throat. He smiled softly, before continuing down along the swell of her breasts.

Her eyes closed, her head fell back on her shoulders as he teased her nipples, bringing them to hard peaks. Fire moved from her breasts, spreading toward the part of her that yearned most for his touch. It was almost like a pain, but such a sweet pain, and she knew that only he could ease the torment growing inside her.

He kissed her jaw, then her lips. Hungrily she accepted his kiss, pulling him tight against her, needing to feel his hard body against hers.

Gray Hawk was mad with desire. He wanted to take her to the ground, to make sweet passionate love to her right there, but a part of him resisted, wondering if she would hate him once it was over.

Jordan moaned low in her throat, and he smiled. This time there was no turning back. Her desire had gone too far. Putting her at arms length, he took a deep, steadying breath. Her face was flushed, her eyes dark with wanting as she stared at him with burning desire. Her nipples were pebble-hard against the thin material of her blouse. He'd never wanted anyone like he wanted her. Tonight would be a night neither one of them would forget.

"We'd better get back before someone notices we're missing," he said, knowing full well it would be morning before anyone would bother searching for him. Giving her a chance to back out before it was too late, he added, "I'll get dressed."

As he turned his back on her, Jordan felt many emotions; most of all rejection. Maybe he found her undesirable? Her body was trembling with the passion he had built within her. By his response, she knew he wanted her as much as she wanted him. His desire was all too evident. Maybe he was remembering the times before when they had come this far, and she had denied him. "Wait!"

He stopped and turned toward her, and she was there, her hand on his shoulder. "I..."

Gray Hawk felt his defenses weaken the moment her hand touched his flesh, but he would not take her, not unless she agreed. "Tell me what you want, Jordan?"

Biting her lip, she knew this was it. Now or never. "I want you," she blurted. The muscles under her hand stiffened, making her wonder if she was wrong by saying what she felt. But when he groaned and his lips found hers, she knew it was no mistake.

Her arms encircled his neck once again, pulling him toward her, pressing into him, needing to get closer. It seemed his hands were everywhere at once.

Gray Hawk lowered her to the soft grass, covering her with his naked body.

"Jordan," he whispered against her lips. "Are you sure this is what you want?"

She smiled up at him, never so sure of anything in her life. "Yes," she whispered against his lips. "I want you, Gray Hawk."

With a driving hunger, Gray Hawk kissed her with all the desire he had pent-up for far too long. His hands moved down her lithe body wanting to memorize every curve. He kissed her neck, her breasts, her flat stomach, and the tight curls nestled between her thighs.

Her pulse jolted as he pulled her hips up to meet his mouth. With an abrupt intake of breath, she squeezed her legs together, horrified at what he was doing.

"Relax. Let yourself feel how wonderful making love can be."

She did as he instructed, and the moment his mouth kissed the core of her desire, she moaned, the sound foreign to her own ears. Who would have thought that such a wicked thing could bring such wonderful pleasure.

Her fingers wove through his dark hair as she raised her hips off the ground. She knew it was sinful, but she couldn't help but watch him, entranced with what was happening between them. At that moment he looked up, his eyes burned with desire as he continued his wicked kiss. The momentum built like hot lava moving through her veins until she knew she would go mad. Then like a damn bursting, wave after wave of sensation flooded her, and she cried out, sure she would die from the pleasure.

With the last fluttering of her climax, Gray Hawk thrust deep within her silky warmth, plunging past the barrier that told him he was the first. His heart rejoiced to find her pure and he knew from that moment on she belonged to him alone.

He glanced down into her passion-flushed face. Her eyes were wide and dreamy, staring up at him. "Am I hurting you?" he asked, stilling within her.

Jordan looked up at him in wonder. How could a person feel so much pleasure? Already the sharp pain she had felt was waning, and in its place that wonderful stirring again. He filled her so completely, the sensation so wonderful, she lifted her hips against him. "Don't stop," she said, sighing as he moved again.

Lifting her hips, she urged him on. When he kissed her, she hesitated only a moment as she tasted herself on his tongue before giving herself to him fully and completely, the pleasure radiating outward until every nerve ending screamed for release.

Her response overwhelmed him as her hands moved down his back, pulling him to her urgently, her hips rising to meet him with every thrust.

In his dreams he had hoped it would be like this, and to have it happening was almost surreal.

Taking a nipple between his teeth, he teased it with the tip of his tongue. She arched against him, moaning with pleasure. He stilled within her again, wanting to savor every moment, wanting to love her so completely she would never forget it was he who had made her feel this way.

Her fingers wove through his hair, urging him closer to her breast. He could feel the mad thumping of her heart, matching his own as her tight sheath squeezed his hard length. When she lifted her hips to meet him, he pulled out only far enough that the tip of his manhood teased and kissed her hot desire.

She groaned, and as he plunged within her once again, she cried out, her hips moving furiously against his. He could no longer hold on, and as he felt the first fluttering of her climax, he soared with her in uncontrollable joy and ecstasy.

SHANE WALKED out of the house just as Kari was getting into the wagon. Rebecca and Tanner sat side by side, dressed in clean clothes, while Kari was wearing an attractive dress that he was seeing for the first time. His brow furrowed. What was she up to now? "Miss Hoffman, where you off to this morning?"

She turned to him, and breathing a heavy sigh, opened her parasol. "Into town. But first I'm dropping the children at school. There is a new schoolmarm in town who just arrived last week. She was kind enough to come by the house the other day and inquire if Tanner and Rebecca would be coming. Hank said Tanner used to attend, so I felt it would be all right with you."

"Still, don't you think you should have asked me first?"

Her chin lifted a full inch. "I tried, but you don't seem to have the time to listen. If memory serves, I was trying to gain your attention the other evening when we were interrupted by one of the ranch hands, who I might add, you always have time for."

"Please, Dad, we'll be late," Tanner cut in, his expression so earnest and hopeful, Shane didn't have the heart to deny him. Not that he would. He wanted his son and niece to have a good education.

Kari's expression was triumphant. "You needn't worry that it will interrupt your schedule. I will pick them up on my way home from work this afternoon."

Why, the little minx was gloating. The corner of his mouth lifted as his gaze slipped to her bosom that was amply displayed in her new gown. Then her words hit him. "Work?" he repeated. "But you have a job here."

"No, you were giving me charity, as you made it well known."

"I was only teasing you."

"Really?" Raising a tawny brow in his direction, she replied, "Well, I've got a *real* job, Mr. Catalono, and if I don't hurry, I'll be late." Flashing a blase' smile, she turned to Tanner. "Let's be on our way."

Shane scratched his head as the wagon left him in a cloud of dust. When had he lost control of his life? The women were taking over, giving him more time to spend in the fields with the men. And for all that he tried to tell himself the women were only staying temporarily, he had to admit that he liked them living with him. He woke in the morning and his breakfast was ready, the kids were bathed, the house was clean. Sure, Hank had done a fine job, but he lacked in a few areas—and it was nice to have female company. Plus, it was good for Rebecca to have the women's influence in her life—and it was good for Tanner as well. In fact, Tanner seemed rather fond of them.

But now Kari had got a job in town just to spite him. She had been a little bristly the other day when he made the comment about letting her cousin do all the work? He shook his head, that woman took everything literally.

Chapter 16

JORDAN HUMMED to herself as she rolled up the sleeves of her dress. Normally she dreaded wash day. But not today. Today was different. Today *she* was different.

Her whole life had changed last night. Her body was still humming from being in Gray Hawk's arms when he showed her how wonderful making love could be. Not once, but twice, and then they went for a swim in the pond. He had washed her tender flesh, bringing her to ecstasy once more. Never had she felt so loved—or so alive.

She'd slipped quietly into her bed late last night, and slept in this morning. She smiled as her stomach did a little flip, still finding it hard to believe that they had actually made love.

Grabbing a pair of black pants, she stopped before submerging them under the water. Gray Hawk had worn these very pants yesterday. She vividly remembered the way they clung to his sweaty body while branding. She glanced at the pile of clothes, his shirt was lying there on top. Putting the pants in the tub, she grabbed the shirt, looked around, then brought it to her face, rubbing the soft material against her cheek and smelling the masculine scent that still lingered on them.

"Jordan?"

Guiltily dropping the shirt in the tub, she turned to see Shane coming out the back door.

"There you are. Hey, I wanted to tell you that you may want to get an early start on dinner tonight. I gave the men the afternoon off after our long day yesterday."

"Thanks for the warning," she said, hoping he hadn't seen her smelling her lover's shirt. Lover—the word was so intimate, yet so right, because that's exactly what Gray Hawk was to her.

"Looks like you have your hands full, so I'll leave you to your washing."

She did no more than nod. Taking gentle care of the shirt, she lovingly rinsed out every speck of dirt. With careful fingers she hung it and his pants on the line to dry, her mouth curving into a grin.

As she walked up the back steps to the house, she rubbed her red, chapped hands together. She glanced down at her wet apron, and quickly changed into a fresh one. Wishing she had time to brush her hair, she instead used her fingers to rake through the curls. Already she missed Kari's help, who had taken a job in town at the dress shop. Jordan knew she'd done it to call Shane's bluff, but no doubt it would be Jordan who would pay for it.

An hour later, her exhaustion was forgotten as she took supper out to the men. Her heart began pumping within her chest having waited the entire day to see Gray Hawk. When she neared the door, the sounds of male voices filled the air. As she stepped inside the hall, she was met with smiles and praise on how great the food smelled. To her disappointment, Gray Hawk was not among the hands eagerly awaiting their dinner.

When she brought in the last of their meal, Gray Hawk still hadn't arrived. She lingered a few minutes, making sure everyone had what they needed. What if he'd left? Maybe she'd been a disappointment to him, and he was now headed back to Running Deer. Her heart lurched at the thought. Certainly he would have said something to her.

Suddenly depressed, she walked out the door and ran straight into a ranch hand. His hands went to her arms, steadying her.

"Hey."

Jordan looked up into Gray Hawk's gorgeous face and her hope was restored.

Closing the door behind them, Gray Hawk pulled her around the side of the bunkhouse and out of sight of the others. His arms encircled her waist, bringing her up against his hard length as his lips met hers feverishly.

"I missed you," he whispered against her lips.

"I missed you, too," she replied, leaning into him, savoring the feel of his strong arms around her. "I thought for a minute you had left."

His gray eyes were dark with passion as he kissed her again. "I would never leave you."

Laying her cheek against his chest, she closed her eyes savoring the moment.

"Meet me tonight?"

"Yes," she replied, before pulling his head down for one more kiss. "You better go before someone comes looking for you."

"All right, I'll see you later tonight."

She could feel his eyes on her all the way back to the house.

ALTHOUGH HER back ached like the dickens, Kari felt a sense of satisfaction. After six straight hours of sewing, she headed off in the direction of the schoolhouse where Tanner and Rebecca were at play with the other children. She smiled to herself knowing that a structured school day was exactly what both children needed. As she approached, they waved merrily, then after bidding their new friends goodbye, jumped aboard.

"How was your day?" Kari asked, as they rolled forward.

"Fun," Rebecca said with a wide smile. "We didn't have too much work, but we did play a lot, didn't we Tanner?"

Tanner nodded.

"How was your day?" Rebecca asked, sounding very much like an adult.

"I had a marvelous day. Mrs. Craven is the nicest woman to work for. She is very sweet and mild-mannered." So unlike Shane Catalono, she thought to herself.

They continued on in silence, the kids no doubt reliving their first day at school and Kari was exhausted, but elated she'd accomplished what she'd set out to do. Mrs. Craven hadn't asked many questions, but Kari noticed she mentioned renting the apartment above the shop to her and Jordan. She hadn't asked about their current living arrangements, but Kari had once again lied and said they were Hank's nieces from New York. Even though she detested telling the woman lies, it would be easier that way, less suspicious.

As they crested the hill overlooking the Triple T, Kari stopped so she could gaze at its sheer beauty. "Isn't it glorious children?" She took in a breath of fresh air. "*This* is what it's all about."

She realized Tanner was staring at her, and when she turned he looked away abruptly. He said so little around her, and was almost shy—though she'd seen him with the men and knew he was very outgoing. Obviously a sign of living with men all his life, without a mother's influence. His dark hair fell into his eyes, and she had to resist the urge to sweep the bangs back with her hand, uncertain of what his reaction would be. After all, he was only four years younger than herself. "It must be a good feeling to know that this will all be yours one day," she said instead.

He looked down at the ranch, his eyes so like his father's taking everything in. Then a small smile came to his lips before he nodded. "Yeah, it does feel good."

Kari's hands tightened on the reins as Shane stepped from the stables, his hand shaded his eyes as he looked in their direction. Seconds later he waved. Rebecca and Tanner waved exuberantly in return as she slapped the reins down sending the wagon lurching forward.

She could feel her carefree mood slipping away with every turn of the wagon wheel that brought her closer to Shane Catalono. He was so irritating! How she yearned to slap that sardonic smile from his face whenever she saw him.

"He says you're pretty?"

Kari turned to Rebecca who was grinning at her.

"Who said that?" Kari asked, her brow raised in question while trying to hide the excitement she felt even before Rebecca nodded in Shane's direction.

"Uncle Shane." Rebecca giggled. "He said you're ornery, too."

Kari's heart leapt in her chest. He thought she was pretty! She frowned. Clearly Rebecca had misunderstood him, for Shane Catalono certainly never looked at her with anything but a disapproving smirk. "You must have misunderstood him," she replied matter-of-factly. "He was probably talking about someone else—"

"No, she's right. I heard him," Tanner confirmed. "And he was talking about you. He said you had the face of an angel, hair like a field of wheat, and a smile that would make a priest blush."

Kari kept her eyes pinned on the man that was walking toward them in his long-legged stride. Obviously the children wouldn't lie, or come up with those phrases on their own. Did he really think those things about her? The thought warmed her insides as she stared at him. God broke the mold when He made Shane Catalono, Kari thought, for he was pure, unadulterated male. She swallowed the lump in her throat as she reined in beside him. To know he had said all those "nice" things about her was rather unsettling. For so long she'd built up a wall where he was concerned. A wall she meant to stay intact, she thought with firm resolve, as Shane looked right past her to Tanner and Rebecca.

"How was school?" he asked, helping Rebecca down.

As they rattled on excitedly about their day, he laughed. "Whoa, on second thought, tell me over supper. Go on, get yourselves cleaned up." He smiled after the two as they raced toward the house, and Kari stared at his strong profile. He was a handsome man, so masculine...and so sarcastic.

When he turned back to her, she immediately stood and went to step from the wagon, when he reached out and grabbed her. His large hands nearly spanned her waist as he let her down slowly, his blue eyes not once leaving hers. Once situated on the ground she resisted the urge to hold onto him to steady her wobbly knees. "Thank you," she muttered under her breath before she stepped past him.

"How was your first day on the job, Miss Hoffman?" he asked to her retreating back.

Turning, she found his eyes wandering down her body. Did he have any idea how wicked he looked when his gaze moved over her like that, or what he was doing to her pounding heart? "I had a very good day, thank you."

Shane watched as Kari turned toward the house again, enjoying the enticing sway of her hips as she walked with her chin held high and her back ramrod straight. As she jerked the door closed behind her, he swore under his breath. He had no business messing around with someone as young, and newly widowed as Kari Hoffman. Hoffman? His eyes narrowed, wondering why she didn't use the same name as her husband. Or perhaps she had been married to Jordan's brother—but they were cousins. Or maybe she just hadn't been married long enough to become accustomed to her married name. He wondered not for the first time what her husband had been like. He knew he had been twice her age. Had he been good to her? Did he love her and she him, the way that he and Lily had loved?

He was still pondering those same questions when he sat down to dinner.

Shane nodded as Kari passed him in a clean apron, her golden curls piled atop her head. He watched her as she moved around the kitchen methodically going through the motions, helping Jordan prepare the family's dinner, even though her cousin appeared to have everything under control.

She was at ease here. Familiar where everything was and where it went. Rebecca adored both she and Jordan, and Tanner had taken to the women better than he could have hoped. One day Kari would marry again and maybe even have children. The thought hit him like a fist to his gut. She would be a great mother. She proved that every day with Rebecca and Tanner.

As he stared, he noticed her skin turn a flattering shade of pink. Her back was ramrod straight, and her chin was tilted at that regal level he was becoming accustomed to. Only on rare occasions did she smile, and he realized how much he would love to see a grin right about now.

As Rebecca and Tanner took their seats, Jordan and Kari set the steaming roast on the table and sat down. Throughout the meal Kari kept her eyes on her plate, but she barely picked at her food. He wished they'd got off on the right foot, but it seemed from the first moment they met, theirs was going to be a different kind of relationship...he could only blame himself for starting it.

He ate, not really tasting the food as he tried to make sense of his emotions as far as Kari was concerned.

The physical attraction was obviously there from the very beginning, at least on his part, and he suspected she felt the same way if he wasn't misconstruing those tentative glances that were down right sizzling at times. He wasn't an arrogant man. It wasn't as though women were knocking down his door, but he wasn't a stranger to some of the women of Brogan. Once he even came close to settling down with one. Her name was Rose, a young lady with a quiet disposition and a love for painting. She would have made a good wife. Obedient, loyal, but she lacked a certain spark. Always she wanted what Shane wanted, never giving any thought to her own happiness. He broke things off, and within a year she married a preacher, and moved to a neaby town.

With most women, he made the mistake of comparing them to Lily. They didn't measure up, always lacking in some way. So why this attraction to Kari who was the complete opposite? He and Lily had similar upbringings. She had been content with her life on the ranch, but Kari...sure she had adapted, but what did he really know about her? Something about her and Jordan puzzled him. With their impeccable manners, and the way they carried themselves, made him wonder if they came from money. But if they had money, why did they work? There were a lot of questions where the two of them were concerned.

Why was he thinking about women anyway? He had his son and his ranch. He didn't have time for that kind of trouble. A woman who loved Tanner and Rebecca like her own, and who loved ranching and this country as much as he did. Would it be so bad? He thought to himself.

The children ate quickly, excusing themselves, anxious to play a game of cards.

"I'll be right there," he said, glad to get his thoughts off of Kari.

Jordan cleared the dishes from the table. "Kari, you don't have to help me. You've already worked a long day."

"I want to," she said quickly, her smile tight as she glanced in his direction. "Do you need something, Mr. Catalono?"

Shane's brows lifted at her question. "Can't a man sit and drink his coffee in his own kitchen?"

Kari turned her back on him and rinsed the dishes. Shane could see he wasn't wanted, so he left them.

Shane was sitting on a couch watching the kids play a game of cards, when Kari came into the living room a little while later. She took a seat nearby, avoiding his glance.

A warmth washed over him as she smiled down at the children, who had become so enamored of her. How often had he wanted a woman in his life? For so long he thought he would be alone, never imagining another taking Lily's place. Yet now he had hopes that perhaps this woman at his side could be a part of his life. He cleared his throat, bringing her attention to him. "Thanks for taking the children to school today. I think you're right, it is good for them to be around other kids their age."

Her eyes widened at the compliment, and she grinned. His heart skipped a beat, making him feel like a boy again.

"You're welcome," she replied, a soft blush creeping into her cheeks.

They sat in companionable silence for a while, content on watching the children. She sat forward, rubbing the muscles along the base of her neck.

Seeing her discomfort, Shane took the seat beside her. "Turn around," he said, brushing her hands away. His fingers gently kneaded the muscles along her neck and shoulders. The feel of her soft skin beneath his fingertips was wonderful as they moved up along the base of her neck, running along the silky tendrils that escaped from her bun. He yearned to bring the golden tresses to his face, to smell the sweetness, to feel the silkiness.

No matter how hard Kari tried to relax, she found it impossible. When Shane stood, she thought he was going to bed, but when his hands moved to her shoulders, she was more than surprised—she was terrified. Her heart was thumping so erratically she was sure he could hear it. But if he did, he wasn't letting her know it, for he continued his slow ministrations until she finally began to relax.

"Loosen up," he said against her ear. Rebecca glanced up at them, her face a sweet smile as she turned back to the game. Thank goodness someone else was in the room because if they weren't, Kari was afraid of the direction his assistance would take them.

Closing her eyes, allowing herself to enjoy what he was doing, Kari let her mind drift, imagining what it would be like to feel those hands on other parts of her body. Her wicked thoughts conjured up all kinds of images of the two of them together, much like all of her dreams lately.

His hands moved up either side of her neck. His fingers splayed, moving lightly over her ears. She swallowed hard as goose bumps covered her skin. His gentle touch was torture. A part of her wanted him to stop, and yet she dreaded the moment he would.

Shane glanced down at the beauty he was massaging. What had made him offer to ease her tight muscles? He was wishing he hadn't touched her, because now he wondered what it would be like to touch her entire body. It had been months since he last had a woman in his bed, and then it had been a prostitute he visited.

Kari sighed, making his thoughts turn even more vivid.

Why didn't he just admit it to himself? He was scared. Plain and simple. And he was terrified to give his heart to someone, only to lose that person again. Always he'd been so certain there was never anyone who could take Lily's place. Yet lately the thought of spending the rest of his life alone was bleak and desolate.

As his fingers brushed the soft curls at the nape of Kari's neck, he wondered if she wanted to find another husband. It had taken him a lot of years to get to this point, while it had only been months since she'd lost her husband.

Kari moaned softly, bringing his thoughts back to the present. "You've great hands, Mr. Catalono," she whispered in a low husky voice.

She has no idea how that sounds, he thought to himself, as his hands slipped down her neck, his fingers lightly grazing her collarbones before moving back to her shoulders. "Call me Shane."

Kari's heart leapt in her breast as his fingers lightly touched her collarbone, coming dangerously close to the swell of her breasts as his thumbs kneaded the knots from her neck. Her whole body was alive, and as his fingers lightly traced a path up nearly to her jawline, the innocent contact tugged at her innards. Surely this was wrong, and much too intimate. Feeling heat rise to her cheeks, Kari pulled away. "Thank you, Mr. Cat—Shane."

Thankfully, he stopped, his fingers lingering only a moment before he stepped back. Instantly she wished he was massaging her again, but as he sat beside her, she thought the best she could do right now was to go to her room, and try to gain control of her warring emotions again.

"My pleasure, Kari." His voice was soft and sensual.

"Well, I'd better be getting to bed now, I have an early morning." Not waiting for a reply, she jumped from the couch, hoping he didn't stop her, yet hoping he did.

Chapter 17

SITTING BESIDE the pond, Jordan held the flower to her nose. She put it behind her ear, her gaze returning to the spot where she and Gray Hawk had made love last night. A grin tugged at her lips, hoping she would experience the magic again.

When she heard someone approach, she quickly came to her feet. Her heart hammering, she brushed off her skirts, and looked up just as Gray Hawk stepped from the trees.

Her stomach flipped as Gray Hawk's eyes moved over her hungrily. Staring at his tall, lean frame, Jordan marveled at the strange new emotions that were rising to the surface as he came toward her in long strides. To think that she knew this man intimately, that he knew her like no one else did. His grin was boyish as he lifted her in his strong arms and kissed her soundly.

The smell of him, the taste of him, the feel of him was nothing short of exquisite, and as his arms tightened around her, she experienced none of the nervousness from the night before. Instead she shared his excitement, knowing what was to come.

With her arms locked around his neck, her breasts pressed tight against the hard wall of his chest, she marveled at his strength. He kissed the tip of her nose. "I thought about you all day."

"And I thought about you."

His hands moved to the buttons on the back of her dress, his excitement obvious as he quickly pulled it from her shoulders, until it pooled around her feet. She noticed his eyes darken as they moved down her body. With lithe fingers, he took off her chemise until she stood naked before him.

He kissed her, his hands moving down her bare back, splaying at her waist before moving over her hips. He stepped away and started shedding his clothes.

Jordan's heart hammered heavily as she stared at his beautiful body, and that part of him that had brought her to a pinnacle she'd never known possible. When she thought she could no longer stand the waiting, he pulled her down with him to the ground.

He wanted her to feel, to know the extent he cared for her, and he showed her with his hands, his lips, and his tongue, until Jordan's passion was at a fever pitch. "Please," she whispered as his mouth once again returned to her lips.

"What do you want?" he asked against her mouth, hovering, waiting for her answer as his rigid manhood pressed against her slippery warmth.

"I want you."

Gray Hawk hadn't intended to make love to her tonight, knowing that she was probably sore from the night before. He also didn't want her to think that this was all he cared about, because it wasn't. But when he saw her standing there, looking so beautiful, remembering the feel of her soft skin, he couldn't help himself. And her response to him made him realize that she wanted the same.

Kissing her softly, he reveled in the feel of her body at his side. His hands moved over her ripe young breasts, her nipples swelling under his touch.

When her fingers moved tentatively to his chest and further down, his breath caught in his throat. A second later she wrapped her fingers around his hard arousal. Covering her hand with his, he guided her, teaching her how to bring him to the edge of climax.

Jordan thrilled to the feel of his rock hard manhood in her grasp. Glancing up, she saw the fire in his eyes, could hear his ragged breathing and was awed that she could have such power over him.

His fingers moved down her ribs, past her belly, to the very core of her, playing with her until she writhed against his hand. His lips claimed hers, and then nudging her knees apart, he thrust within her.

Jordan wasn't sure if it was the anticipation she'd been feeling all day, or her need for him that sent her spiraling to climax so quickly. But soon the sensations began to build all over again, with even more power than moments ago. With a few quick thrusts, he took them both to the heights of passion.

Her fingers threaded through his hair, savoring the weight of his body on top of her. He kissed her neck, then pulled her to his side. She was so happy. She yearned to tell him exactly what she was feeling, but was afraid to share her thoughts so soon.

She smiled as his hand moved lazily up and down her back. Resting her head on his shoulder, she closed her eyes feeling more relaxed than she'd been in a long while. All the months of being scared and looking over her shoulder faded away like a morning mist as she lay in his strong arms.

That was her last thought before Gray Hawk woke her, telling her it was time to return to the ranch. "Why didn't you wake me?" she asked, as he helped her into her dress.

"I know you haven't been sleeping very well and you looked so content, I couldn't wake you. Plus, you felt so good in my arms, I didn't want to let you go."

Gray Hawk had enjoyed watching her the last hour. In sleep she looked so innocent and fragile, yet he knew the woman had nerves of steel. When she started talking in her sleep, he found it endearing, especially when she'd spoke his name and then whispered I love you. Though he knew it was only a dream, the words had a twofold effect on him. What they shared was more than just shared physical attraction. There was a bond between them that went beyond lovemaking—but was it love? The last time he had given his heart, it had been thrown back in his face. Samantha had loved him behind closed doors, telling him all her secret desires, promising him that she would leave her husband for him. Everything she said had been a lie. She never intended for anyone to ever find out about their affair. She had simply used him.

He knew he was Jordan's only lover, but would that still make a difference? And would she go with him to his village if he desired to return? Would his love be enough?

"What's the matter?"

He lifted a brow, not realizing his thoughts were clearly written on his face. "Nothing." He smiled reassuringly and she grinned, going into his outstretched arms.

"Tomorrow I have a day off. What do you say we spend it together?"

"I'd love that," she said, hugging him tighter. "I have to run into Brogan in the morning to pick up some supplies. Why don't you come with me?"

Since he'd been at the ranch, he'd never once ventured off Shane's property. The thought of seeing the town, and meeting other people made him hesitate, but seeing her wishful expression, he said yes.

GERALD KINCAIDE, Sheriff of Brogan, lounged against a post outside his office. Lately things had been awful slow, and he secretly yearned for some kind of argument to break out, maybe even a shooting.

He crushed his cigarette beneath the heel of his boot, watching with boredom as a rather large woman made her way into Mrs. Craven's dress shop across the street. He could see Kari Hoffman standing near the window. A bright smile lit her face as she talked with a customer.

For weeks now he'd been watching Kari, hoping that she would notice him. Unfortunately, aside from a friendly wave, she never spoke to him, and he still hadn't got up the nerve to ask her to lunch.

Kari Hoffman was by far the most beautiful woman he had ever seen, and he secretly yearned to make her his wife. He knew he wasn't handsome, but he did have a lot to offer a woman. For one, if she were married to him, she wouldn't be working as an apprentice in a dress shop. Instead, she'd keep his house and raise his children...their children. The thought of her round with child was heartening, and fire raced through his veins at the thought of bedding her. He would be the envy of every man in Brogan.

He'd asked Mrs. Craven questions about Kari, but she didn't know very much, aside from the fact that she was staying at the Triple T ranch, along with her family. He wondered where exactly she was sleeping. Surely she didn't sleep in the bunkhouse with all those men? It disturbed him to know she lived under the same roof with Shane Catalono. The rancher had been a confirmed bachelor since the death of his wife. He'd come close to marriage one time, but apparently had been spooked since the wedding was called off and his fiancée abruptly left town, a woman Gerald at one time coveted as his own. A fact that burned him to no end.

Nodding to a few passersby, he walked down the street toward the livery. Kari was coming out with her wagon just as he was heading in. Her smile was warm as she looked at him from the wagon where she was seated. "Sheriff Kincaide, how are you?"

He tipped his hat. "Just fine, Miss Hoffman. It's a beautiful day now, isn't it?" he said, staring at her delicate features, wanting desperately to touch her.

"Indeed," she replied, shifting the reins from one hand to the other. A few awkward moments of silence followed before she said, "Well, I really do need to get going."

"Oh, right." Stepping back from the wagon, he nodded as she circled around and headed down the dirt road. "Miss Hoffman," he yelled before he could stop himself.

She pulled upon the reins, stopping in the middle of the road. She turned toward him, her brows furrowed together. "Yes, Sheriff?"

Her face was pale despite the warm sun, which was odd, especially when he was sweating bullets. He approached her, wiping the sweat with his handkerchief before reaching her. "I was wanting to know." He ripped his hat from his head. Here he was thirty-two and acting like a schoolboy with his first crush. "Well, that is...would you have lunch with me tomorrow?"

Relief etched her features and she sat up straight. "Well, I sometimes don't get a chance to stop for lunch. I'll just have to see how busy we are tomorrow."

"Surely Mrs. Craven will allow you time to eat," he said, hoping his objections would spark an acceptance.

"We'll see," she repeated, before setting out again. "Good day, Sheriff."

A 'we'll see' was better than a flat out no. "I'll be waiting for your answer," he called after her. To his disappointment she didn't turn as she made her way out of town.

ALL THE WAY home Kari thought about the sheriff's offer, even after picking up the children. Though she made small talk with them, her mind was elsewhere. She'd managed up to this point to avoid the sheriff, yet today it had been impossible. It seemed every time she looked out the window, there he was watching her, making her wonder if he suspected that she and Jordan were on the run.

That evening she helped Jordan set the table, and when she couldn't hold it in any longer, she blurted, "The sheriff has asked me to lunch."

Jordan's brows shot up in surprise. "The sheriff?"

Kari nodded.

"What did you say?"

"I felt so pressured that I told him maybe."

Jordan ran a hand down her face. "Do you think he suspects something?"

"I don't know. He stopped me on my out of town. I've noticed him watching me a lot lately. His office is right across from the shop, and I swear every time I look up, there he is."

"Do you think he knows something?"

Kari shrugged. "I don't know."

Shane stepped into the kitchen, putting an abrupt end to the conversation, or so Kari thought.

"Good evening, ladies." He sounded jovial as he took a seat.

"Good evening," Kari replied at the same time as Jordan.

As they waited for the children to join them, silence filled the room until Jordan said, "Maybe you should ask Shane what he thinks?"

Kari stepped on her cousin's foot beneath the table, knowing exactly what she was trying to do. Jordan pinched her thigh in return.

"Ask me what?" he asked, looking from Jordan to Kari.

"Nothing," Kari said quickly, throwing Jordan a warning glance.

"What?" Shane asked, his expression suddenly serious as the children sat down.

"Sheriff Kincaide has asked Kari to lunch," Jordan offered much to Kari's dismay.

Kari dropped her gaze to her plate, but could feel Shane's stare.

"Dad doesn't care much for the sheriff, do ya, Dad?" Tanner said, joining in on the conversation.

"He must be a good man if he's the sheriff," Jordan added.

Shane snorted.

Kari felt like sliding underneath the table. Her appetite had vanished, but she pretended interest in the roast, which she took great pains to cut into minuscule pieces. Anything to keep from looking up.

"Well, are you going to have lunch with him?" Shane asked.

She looked up and found his piercing gaze on her.

Kari opened her mouth, ready to tell him no when Jordan said, "You may as well. After all, you wouldn't want to make an enemy of the sheriff."

"Could we drop the chatter," Shane said, his voice low and ominous.

"Geez, Dad, what's the matter?" Tanner asked, his eyes wide. "Your face is turning purple."

Shane ran a hand through his hair, then sat back in his chair. "I'm tired. It's been a long day." He stood up so fast the table rocked. Everyone grabbed their glasses before they overturned, all eyes fastened on him. "I'll eat with the men."

"Well, I wonder what's the matter with him?" Jordan asked innocently, hiding a mischievous smile behind her glass as their gazes locked.

Suddenly Kari's mood took a turn for the better.

SHANE STOPPED in mid-stride to the bunkhouse. He didn't want to eat with anyone. In fact, he wasn't even hungry. He backtracked to the house and set his plate on the porch rail. An image of Kari and the sheriff sitting at a little table in a quiet corner of *Oliver's Restaurant* tightened his gut into a tight knot. He should have known that once the men of Brogan saw her that she'd have them falling all over her, particularly Gerald Kincaide, a man he detested, who hated Shane just as much. He resisted the urge to slam his fist into the log columns.

Through the open window he could still hear Jordan and Kari talking about the sheriff. He listened as his son shifted the conversation to his day at school.

What did he expect from Kari? He'd been nothing but sarcastic since the day he'd met her. She was a beautiful woman that any man would desire. At least Gerald Kincaide was man enough to ask her out to lunch. It was more than he had ever tried to do.

He drowned out their voices and instead listened to the sounds of the night around him. The women's laughter filtered out to him from the window and blended with the men's loud chatter coming from the bunkhouse. Although he was surrounded by the people he cared about, Shane had never felt so alone.

His gaze moved past the bunkhouse to the small rise in the hill next to a cottonwood tree. Under the light of the moon, the white marble cross was clearly visible. "Lily, help me," he whispered, feeling a lump form in his throat. He stared for a long while, remembering all the good times they shared, as well as the bad. One moment he was on the verge of laughter, the next tears. He wasn't sure how long he'd sat there when a strange thing happened—a warmth filled him as though telling him everything would be all right.

Perhaps it was time to move on with his life.

Chapter 18

THE SKY was cloudless the following morning, adding to Jordan's good mood. Having slept eight hours, she woke refreshed and excited for the day ahead, knowing she was spending the entire day with Gray Hawk.

Being a workday for Kari, she'd already left for town and the children were staying on at the ranch to spend the day with Shane. Some of the other hands had already left for Brogan, but Jordan and Gray Hawk lingered a while longer, enjoying breakfast together for once.

Though she would have preferred to ride her horse into Brogan, she had a long list of supplies, and therefore opted to take the wagon. And she was glad when Gray Hawk joined her, their legs touching as the wagon rocked along the rutted roads.

She loved the possessive feel of his long fingers on her thigh, and the heat of his body as the wagon rolled along. Gray Hawk pointed out different types of flowers, trees and birds to her. She realized how much he respected the land. She listened intently as he talked, loving the sound of his voice, enjoying being able to stare at his strong profile without seeming obvious. It brought back memories of being with him at his village where it seemed they had much more time alone. There they had at least been able to sleep in the same quarters, within inches of the other. Here, that would be unthinkable.

With every mile she yearned to ask him if he intended to stay, or if one day he would return to his people. Yet every time she opened her mouth to ask, she became too frightened of what the answer might be, so she chose instead to remain silent.

When they arrived in Brogan, she stepped down from the wagon, deciding to leave it near the mercantile. "Do you want to join me, or would you rather see what the men are up to?" she asked, knowing what his answer would be. There wasn't a man around who would willingly want to go shopping.

"I'll see what the men are up to," he said with a boyish grin.

"I'll meet you in half an hour right here," she said, flashing a smile before heading off to do the shopping.

Gray Hawk could feel the stares of the townspeople all the way to his bones. As he walked along the dusty street, he heard a man whisper 'dirty breed', under his breath. A woman who had been walking toward him, saw him and crossed the street, her expression full of shock as though she couldn't believe he had the nerve to be in her town. Her young son buried his head into his mother's skirts as though he would shrivel into nothing if he were to look Gray Hawk in the eye.

Pretending not to notice, Gray Hawk moved in long strides toward the saloon, looking forward to spending a few minutes of idle time with the men of the Triple T, all of whom had become good friends.

Brogan would be like any other town. There would be those who feared him, and those who didn't—like Shane and his men, Kari, Rebecca, and of course, Jordan. She was the only thing that felt right these days. For all that he enjoyed his life now, he missed his father, and felt with every day he stayed away, he was betraying him and his people. He should return to them, yet he couldn't when he was so unsure of the future. Never had he been so torn as he was now. For all that he enjoyed ranching, he missed his friends and family, and the hunting.

Hearing the sound of the piano coming through the swinging doors across the street, he headed in that direction when a voice stopped him.

"Can I help you, partner?"

Gray Hawk turned to face a man, who was not much older than himself. His piercing blue eyes were not kind as he lifted his chin. There was an air of arrogance about the man that set Gray Hawk's teeth on edge.

"I'm just going to the saloon," Gray Hawk said, taking another step in that direction when the man lowered his rifle, blocking his way.

"What ya doing in Brogan, boy?"

Gray Hawk's shoulders stiffened, and when he met the man's lethal glare, he noticed his thumb inching the hammer of the gun back. "I work at the Triple T."

The sheriff lifted his brow. "The Triple T, huh? We don't get much of your kind around here?"

"And what kind would that be?" Gray Hawk fought to keep the rage he felt from his voice.

The man rolled back on his heels, the corners of his mouth lifted in a smirk. "Where exactly you from, boy?"

It was all Gray Hawk could do not to plant his fist in the man's face. "Who you calling boy?" Gray Hawk asked, taking the step that separated them until he could smell the strong scent of liquor on the man's stale breath.

"Are you trying to pick a fight with me, boy?"

Gray Hawk lifted a brow, but remained silent, holding onto what little patience he had left.

"I asked you a question."

"And I've answered it. Now I wish to be left alone."

"Listen, if you want trouble, you've came to the wrong town."

"I'm not making trouble. I'm just wanting to go into the saloon and have a beer with my friend."

The sheriff spit at his feet. "We don't want your kind here."

Gray Hawk shook his head. What a fool he was to think he would be accepted in this kind of society. He was different from them, not only by looks, but by cultures, and as they saw it, he was beneath them.

He glanced up to see a crowd had gathered around, obviously anticipating a fight. Women huddled together, their eyes wide with fear, while the men watched him with expectation, as though they knew it would end in a fight.

A wave of homesickness swept through Gray Hawk.

He had left his people for this?

HAVING COMPLETED her shopping early, Jordan crossed the street with the intention of visiting Kari at the dress shop before finding Gray Hawk and heading back to the ranch. She was so excited at the prospect of being with him the whole day, it took her a moment to realize that something was wrong.

Seeing a crowd forming in the street, Jordan felt a sense of foreboding when she saw Gray Hawk, his tall frame standing head and shoulders above the others. Her pulse skittered. If she wasn't mistaken, the sheriff was with him.

"He's a breed. Who does he think he is coming here? We don't want his kind," an old gentleman was saying, keeping a safe distance from the ensuing argument.

Another lady shuddered. "He scares me. He's so, so filthy."

Murmurs of agreement sounded by the others, then a gasp rang out over the crowd. "Look, the sheriff's going to fight him," another said, excitement lacing his voice. Jordan was horrified to see that Gray Hawk and the sheriff were arguing.

"They should hang him," one man said as they watched mesmerized.

"The sheriff's always hated breeds. Once heard his father had a soft spot in his heart for some squaw. I bet he puts a bullet in him."

Jordan's breath lodged in her throat, finding it hard to believe these people could be so callous. She was close enough to see the lethal expression on Gray Hawk's face, and knew if she didn't do something fast, things could turn deadly.

Wedging her way through the people, she went to Gray Hawk and took his hand. "Let's go," she said, ignoring the sheriff whose eyes rounded in disbelief.

"You with this man, Miss?" he asked, his words sounding more like a dare than a question.

"Yes, I'm with him. Is there a problem?"

"You work at the Triple T as well...with Miss Hoffman, is that right?"

Jordan met his gaze unflinchingly. "Yes, we're cousins."

The sheriff's smile was almost predatory as he stared at her, his gaze slipping down her body in disgust. "Well, I suggest you and your...friend here, head back to the Triple T, where you belong."

Unable to stand his horrible sneer any longer, Jordan, with Gray Hawk at her side, walked away from the sheriff and onlookers. His fingers were stiff beneath her hand. She could feel his hatred and humiliation.

"Don't pay any attention to them," she said, squeezing his hand tight. "They don't know anything about you."

Still, she could hear the gasps and outraged comments of the onlookers, but she didn't care. The only concern she had was for Gray Hawk. "I love you, Gray Hawk," she whispered, not sure if he heard her or not because he didn't respond.

But a moment later he stopped and looked down at her, his expression full of pain. "You don't have to do this. I can take care of myself." Even though he said the words matter-of-factly, there was pain in his eyes that contradicted his words.

She cocked a brow and grinned. "Are you saying you're embarrassed to be seen with me?"

His smile was slow in coming, but devastating when it did. "You know I'm not."

"Good, now let's get back to the ranch and have that picnic lunch by the pond."

Gray Hawk swept a wayward curl out of her eyes. Jordan wished people knew this man the way she did. He was compassionate, warm, sincere, and she loved him with all her soul.

"Injun whore!"

Jordan flinched as though struck. The word was said with such venomous loathing, she felt it all the way to her bones. She met Gray Hawk's tortured eyes and bit her bottom lip as she turned to her accuser, an older gentleman, who looked to have seen better days. But she didn't have time to respond, because Gray Hawk was in his face before she could blink.

"You owe the lady an apology," Gray Hawk said, his fury evident by the nerve ticking in his jaw.

The man was trembling, but he puckered his lips, then spit right in Gray Hawk's face.

Then to Jordan's horror, all hell broke loose.

"DAD, SOMETHING'S wrong."

Shane threw the shovel aside as he followed the direction of Tanner's gaze. Coming over the hill were twenty or more men on horseback, followed by a wagon, and if he wasn't mistaken, there was a person lying in the back.

"You and Rebecca go inside."

"But Dad—"

"Tanner, go," he said, grabbing his hat and running to meet the wagon.

His heart pounded in his chest the closer they came. He did a head count of his men, wondering which one was injured, or God forbid, dead. In all these years he'd been fortunate not to lose anyone, but he feared his luck had changed when he saw Jordan in the back of the wagon.

He knew then it had to be Gray Hawk.

"What happened?" he shouted, as the wagon came to a stop.

"He was shot," Hank said, anger lacing his words.

"Shot?"

"Boss, we were all in the tavern, when we heard this big ol' ruckus outside. That's when we saw Gray being beat up on by a whole group of men. We joined in, but the next thing we know is a shot's fired and Gray hits the ground. Think the sheriff did it, but the weasel says he's innocent and no one is talking."

"That son of a bitch," Shane said through clenched teeth, helping Jordan down.

Jordan's face was streaked with tears. Shane took her hand and squeezed it reassuringly. "It's going to be all right. We'll take care of him. Why don't you go in and have Tanner and Rebecca get the things we need to clean him up."

She nodded and raced up the stairs.

Gray Hawk's face was white, his once blue shirt stained red with blood. Shane had seen a man bleed to death before, and he knew the same could easily happen to Gray Hawk. As he helped his men pick him up, he thought back to the day when he had met the half-breed, a man who held a place of honor with his own. Here he'd come to Brogan wanting a chance at a different life, a life he was entitled to and look what the *good* people of Brogan had done to him.

"Boss, it was bad. You should have heard the things that they were saying."

Shane shook his head, disgusted at the people he had come to think of as friends. How dare they make Gray Hawk feel less than human? "What about the doctor?"

"He's out at the Carter's delivering a baby. Jake is headed there right now to tell him," Hank said, wincing under Gray Hawk's weight.

"We'll just have to do the best we can until he gets here. I'm glad you were all there to help. I'm proud that you stood up for him," Shane said, as they lay Gray Hawk on Shane's bed since it was the closest at hand. Shane closed the door and sat for a while at Gray Hawk's side as Jordan cleaned the wound as best she could. Gray Hawk opened his eyes once, his gaze fixing on Jordan before closing again.

"I'm so sorry," she whispered, taking Gray Hawk's hand in hers and bringing it to her lips.

Shane watched the unspoken emotions pass between the two. It had been obvious from the first time he'd met them that the two fancied each other, and now their feelings were out in the open for all to see. He respected Gray Hawk for facing people's hatred, yet he wished with all his heart he'd been there to help.

"Gray, who shot you?" he asked, not wanting to lose the only chance he may have at finding the killer, just in case the worst happened and he died from his wounds.

"The sheriff," he said, his voice weak and strained.

Shane nodded. The fury he felt making him shake with rage. "You hang in there, buddy. The doctor will be here soon."

Knowing Gray Hawk was in good hands, Shane patted Jordan's shoulder, went to his study, grabbed the rifle off the wall, shoved his pistol in the waist of his pants, and walked out the front door to the stables.

"Boss, where you going?" Hank asked, following close on his heels.

"To town."

"Not without us, you're not."

Shane turned to his foreman and put a firm hand on his shoulder. "I appreciate the offer, but this day has been a long time coming. Plus, I want you here protecting the children and the ranch just in case we have some unexpected visitors."

Hank nodded. "Okay, if you're sure."

"I'm sure."

"Good luck."

Shane's adrenaline raced through his body as he pushed his horse at a dangerous clip toward Brogan. How dare that arrogant son of bitch gang up on one of his own?

He had never got along with the wiry sheriff ever since they had both dated Rose, a woman who hadn't returned the sheriff's favor if she were to tell it. Whether the sheriff was angry about being jilted by a woman that neither one of them ended up with, it made no difference to Shane. There was nothing the man could say or do to make up for having shot Gray Hawk. And now Shane was resolved that he wouldn't get away with it.

As he rode into Brogan, people literally ran out of his way. Jumping off his horse while it was still in motion, he stormed into the sheriff's office only to find it empty, save for a drunk, who cursed at him and used his hands to shield the blinding sun from his eyes.

Having checked a few nearby establishments, Shane came to the conclusion that Kincaide had conveniently left town. In an effort to control his anger, Shane lit a cigarette. He saw a few townspeople watching him from nearby businesses, and he met their stares, daring them to say something to him.

He thought these were good people. God loving men and women who were beyond bigotry. From what he'd heard from his men, they hadn't given Gray Hawk a chance. They had judged on looks alone, not bothering to get to know the man behind the dark hair and gray eyes. He inhaled deeply of the smoke, blowing it out above his head as he shifted on his feet, wondering when the yellow-bellied sheriff would be returning.

The minutes ticked away, his temper died down, and his gaze kept straying to the dressmaker's shop across the street. So far he hadn't seen Kari, and up to this point, hadn't thought too much about her.

Before he knew what he was about, he was walking toward the dress shop in determined strides. Hesitating at the door, he took a deep breath, when the door was opened from the other side and Mrs. Craven welcomed him with a concerned smile. "Shane, we have only just heard—is your man all right?"

Removing his hat, he threaded his fingers through his hair, just as the back door opened and Kari came out, her face ashen and streaked with tears. "Shane, is he all right? I only just heard. I cannot believe it was Gray Hawk who was shot. A passerby said it was a drifter, and I just never imagined for a moment...if I had known it was him, I would have...how is Jordan...Mrs. Craven, I know that my cousin must need me."

Shane's heart lurched as tears streamed down Kari's cheeks, and she wiped them away with the back of her hand.

"Of course, dear. Go, your cousin and Gray Hawk need you far worse than I do."

"Thank you," Shane said, holding his arm out to Kari. She quickly took it, and he could feel her trembling.

When they were out of the store, she turned to him. "Tell me the truth, Shane. Will he live?"

She was watching him intently. He wanted so desperately to take away her pain and reassure her, knowing that she must be reliving the death of her husband. Gray Hawk had been a big part of her life since she had become a widow. He nodded. "I'm sure he will. He lost some blood, but God willing, the bullet will have missed any vital organs."

Glancing at the empty sheriff's office they passed by, Shane told himself there would be another time to deal with the sheriff.

Chapter 19

GRAY HAWK woke to a horrible ache in his left side. Trying to sit up, he sucked in a breath when another pain shot through him. Grimacing, he lay back against the pillows and opened his eyes slowly. Sunlight streamed through the open window, along with a cool breeze. He turned his head, and seeing Jordan asleep in a chair, he smiled.

It all came back to him: The sheriff, the townspeople, the crude names they had called Jordan, and then the searing pain as a bullet ripped through his side. For as long as he lived, he would never forget the look in the sheriff's eyes. The man had taken great pleasure in shooting him.

He just vaguely remembered Jordan crying out, coming to his side, holding his head in her lap as she smoothed his hair back off his forehead. Her voice had been strong for the both of them, telling him everything would be all right, despite the horrible taunts being yelled at her as she tried to comfort him.

But everything wasn't all right. He would recover from the gunshot. He'd been shot once before, so he knew the wound would heal, but it wouldn't be so easy to heal the wounds of his heart. The truth of the matter was he didn't belong here, and he never really would. For all that he had tried to become one of them, he wasn't—nor would he ever be. He wasn't white enough.

"Gray Hawk."

Jordan went to her knees beside the bed, and taking his hand within her own, she brought it to her lips. "I'm so glad you're awake. How do you feel?"

"I'm sore, but I'll be fine."

Her shoulders sagged with relief. "Do you remember what happened?"

He ran the backs of his fingers against her soft cheek. She looked so tired, so worried. "Yes, I remember how you stood up for me against all those people. You're a very brave woman."

"I love you."

Gray Hawk's breath lodged in his throat as he stared at her, watching the emotions flash across her face. He remembered her vaguely telling him that she loved him before, but now as she watched him so expectantly, he opened his mouth, but was unable to say the words, and not because he didn't feel them, but because he feared them. How many times had he loved, only to be hurt in the end?

He pulled her to him, kissing her softly, loving the feel of her. Though she tried to hide her disappointment, he could clearly see it in her eyes, and he knew she waited for him to profess his love to her.

As the silence lengthened, she pulled away, embarrassed. "Do you want something to eat?"

"No, I don't think so. Maybe in a little bit."

That seemed to satisfy her. Running her fingers down his arm, she pressed her lips together.

"How long have I been laying here?"

"About six days."

"Six days?" he said, sitting up, ignoring the pain that stabbed at his side. "I can't believe it."

"Well, believe it. And lay back down," she said, pushing him back into the pillows. "Thanks in large part to the laudanum."

He didn't fight her, but instead pulled her into his arms. "Gray Hawk, your side—"

"Is fine. I want to feel you, smell you, taste you."

She opened her mouth to protest, but he quickly kissed her, reveling in the feel of her silky tongue against his own. As she moaned and pressed her breasts against his chest, he groaned wanting so much more than just her kiss.

"Are you all right?" she asked against his lips.

"Yes, except I want you."

Gray Hawk lifted a brow as her gaze moved down the length of his body to the part of him that strained against the sheets. "I can see you're really hurting?"

"I want you," he repeated.

"Well, you'll have to wait," she said with a sigh.

He pretended to look hurt as she stood up and yanked the sheet up to his neck. "You need your sleep. And when you are well, then we will talk about—that." Her cheeks turned pink and there was a twinkle in her eye as she walked to the door. "I'll get you some Laudanum to help you sleep."

"I don't need any—"

"Don't argue with the nurse."

Standing there with hands on hips, looking beautiful as well as stubborn, he wasn't about to argue. "All right, nurse, I'll do anything you say. Just as long as you come back."

"Just try and keep me away," she said, then with a quick smile, she closed the door behind her.

But his grin quickly faded as he thought about what would happen next. A man shot him for no reason other than the fact he didn't like the color of his skin. The whole idea was absurd, yet from what he knew of whites thus far in his life, he shouldn't be surprised.

And now Jordan was part of the problem. Here she had come to Brogan to start a new life, and he had shown up and ruined everything. It had probably been just fine for her until he'd come. But now she would no longer be accepted by the townspeople. She would be shunned, labeled a whore, for no other reason than loving him.

Should he leave and go back to his people? He closed his eyes knowing that leaving Jordan would be the hardest thing he'd ever done. Because of her love for him she would suffer far worse then he ever had. He heard the names they yelled as they walked down the street together. *Squaw, Injun lover, whore.* And she faced them all with her head held high, not once letting his hand go.

Should he leave and hope she would be all right?

It wasn't a decision he wanted to make, but one that he must make—and soon.

TWO WEEKS after the day he'd been shot, Gray Hawk lay beside Jordan, his arms crossed beneath his head, looking as though he didn't have a care in the world.

She was so grateful to still have him with her, knowing how close she'd come to losing him forever. He had been up and around for a few days, and though she was reluctant to come to their place by the pond, she was glad when he insisted.

They hadn't talked about what happened in town, and Jordan wasn't sure if she really wanted to. Some things were better left forgotten and this was definitely one of them.

"What are you thinking about?" he asked, rolling to his side, pulling her against him.

I'm thinking how much I love you, and how much I want us to be together forever. She wanted so desperately to say the words out loud, but instead she kissed his chest, and lay her head on his shoulder. "I'm just so glad to have you back."

"I was never gone."

"You know what I mean."

He kissed her forehead. "Yes, I do."

As his fingers moved down her back, she wondered if they could ever truly be happy. When she lived with him and his people, she'd never been at peace, and now things had come full circle. Now it was he who was going through the same thing. People's reaction to him surprised her, and most of all, disappointed her. How could he ever be happy living with such bigotry?

And now they didn't only torment him, they tormented her. The man's harsh words came back to haunt her. Never in her life could she imagine that anyone could be so cruel. Now that she had been branded a whore by the entire town, she knew the humiliation Gray Hawk suffered firsthand. She hated every last one of those spiteful people for what they had said and done.

His hands moved to her skirt, and with one quick motion, he yanked it up around her hips. She smiled against his mouth as his fingers moved over that part of her that was already wet and hot with desire. How she had missed him.

Gray Hawk needed her desperately. For the last few weeks he'd seen the look on her face, the expressions of uncertainty. Did she doubt what they shared? Would she tell him to leave now that he had ruined her life?

Pushing the thoughts away, his fingers played along the dewy folds of her womanhood, against the tiny nub of pleasure. His lips kissed a path from her forehead to her breasts that were straining against the thin material of her blouse.

She quickly unbuttoned her shirt, then instantly freed him of his. Her head fell back as he kissed her collarbone, then took a nipple into his mouth, his teeth grazing it, sucking it as she writhed beneath him. A moment later he felt the flutter of her climax as her hips pressed against him.

Jordan's fingers threaded through his hair, pulling him close to her breasts as he suckled each while his fingers did delicious things to her. Feeling the sensations growing within her, Jordan cried out as he brought her to orgasm. And still he didn't stop. Again he brought her to climax using his fingers and tongue, but still she wanted desperately to feel his length inside her...only then would she have total release.

"Gray Hawk," she whispered. "Please."

Opening her eyes, he was gazing down at her, his gray eyes full of passion and wanting.

He pulled her hips up against him and slowly entered her from behind. Jordan's breath left her in a rush as the sensations washed over her. She felt him so completely, every hard inch of his erection stretching her.

His hands moved to her breasts, taking them within his palms, he rocked against her. It had been so long since the last time. Jordan had only dreamed that they would have another moment like this and as they climaxed simultaneously, she hoped that this was just the beginning of their days together.

KARI'S NAILS dug into her palms as the sheriff walked through the door of the dress shop.

"Miss Hoffman," he said, taking off his hat and running his hand through his thinning hair. "I've missed seeing your beautiful face since being away these last couple of weeks."

She smiled tightly. "Can I help you?"

His brow lifted. "I get the feeling you're mad at me." He leaned a hip against the counter. "Now, why would that be?"

How she wished Mrs. Craven was back from lunch. She didn't want to be alone, or even be having a conversation with this man. He was not to be trusted, and now as he watched her with those piercing eyes, she realized she was truly afraid of him.

"Mr. Kincaide, I have work to do. Did you wish to purchase something?"

"What I was wanting was a lunch date, like we planned before this...unfortunate accident occurred."

"An unfortunate accident?" she repeated. "Mr. Kincaide, you shot a man. A man who hasn't done a single thing to you."

He had the audacity to look shocked. "I didn't shoot no one. It was an accident, that's all. And to be honest, the breed had it coming. He would have killed ol' Curly if he hadn't been stopped."

"I refuse to argue about it, and I have no desire to have lunch with you today, or any other day for that matter." Thrusting her trembling hands in her skirt pockets, she lifted her chin. "Good day, Mr. Kincaide."

He shook his head in disgust. "What's going on with all of you out there at the Triple T? What is that breed to you and your cousin? Your lover? Do you take turns servicing him, or do the three of you—"

Kari slapped him soundly, her hand stinging from the contact. His expression was lethal as he grabbed her wrist, a vein standing out on his forehead. "Don't touch me, whore." Dropping her wrist as though it burnt his skin, he walked out the door, slamming it behind him.

Kari trembled, afraid that she had just made a grave mistake.

GERALD KINCAIDE opened and closed his jaw a couple of times, surprised that a slap could hurt so much. He was disappointed and angry with Kari Hoffman. He wouldn't have thought the woman would be loyal to a breed—but apparently she was. The question was why?

He grabbed the bottle of whiskey out of the bottom drawer of the nearby cabinet. Taking a deep swallow, he propped his feet on his desk and glanced at the wanted posters on his desk that had arrived earlier in the day. He skimmed through each, recognizing the same familiar faces of criminals who'd yet to be caught, while trying to memorize the new ones. He was ready to throw them back on his desk when a familiar depiction caught his eye. It was unusual, not because of the name, but because it was of a woman, and one he'd seen before.

Putting the bottle down, he leaned forward, squinting down at the poster. "Wanted for kidnapping, Jordan Lee McGuire, age 18. Armed and dangerous..." His voice leveled off as a smile came to his lips. "Why if it aint' the breed's whore." The word reward literally jumped off the page. "Ten thousand dollars if returned alive."

He whistled through his teeth. Ten thousand dollars! He'd be a rich man. He skimmed through the other images, but found none of Kari. Kidnapping? He'd always thought it was odd that all the sudden the two women and child had come into Catalono's life at the same time. He knew Shane Catalono's brother and wife had been killed in an ambush, and knew that Shane was out searching for the daughter. But that didn't explain Jordan and Kari's appearance. Sure, it was said they were Hank's nieces, but was that true? The women looked too much alike not to be related. He would just love to see the look on that little tease's face when he arrested her cousin. She wouldn't think she was so high follutin' then.

Even one better, he could finally have his revenge on Shane Catalono for harboring a fugitive of the law. He grinned having heard that the same day he'd shot Gray Hawk, the rancher had come busting into his office with his gun drawn. Well, that Indian lover would get his just rewards— the whole lot of them would.

Taking another long swig from the bottle, he leered at the picture. "You little whore, your days are numbered, and your breeds along with it."

Chapter 20

JORDAN LOOKED up from where she stood at the washtub and watched a dust plume rise on the horizon. Whoever it was, they were certainly in a hurry.

A sense of foreboding washed over her as five riders crested the hill within minutes. Shane came out of the stables, his hand resting casually on his hip, close to his Colt 45. As they came closer, Jordan recognized the sheriff, and several of the men from town.

Shane didn't move as the men reined in just a few feet from him. "Sheriff?" he said, trying to look at ease. But Jordan knew better. She recognized the hard edge to Shane's jaw, and the dangerous gleam in his eyes.

The sheriff moved his hat back on his head, his gaze roving over his surroundings. When he looked in her direction, she could clearly see the disdain in his eyes. "I'm here to talk to the breed."

Jordan's heart dropped to her feet at his words. Her first instinct was to cry out, to warn Gray Hawk.

"Kincaide, if you have a problem with Gray, I suggest you talk to me about it," Shane said, lighting a cigarette and blowing the smoke directly at the sheriff.

The sheriff sat forward in the saddle and crossed his arms over the saddle horn. "The Karlson's are missing some cattle. Some of the men are saying they saw that breed of yours in the vicinity."

Shane lifted a brow. "The only thing that separates my land from Karlson's is a fence, and Gray has been out fixing those fences, so it makes sense they've seen him. As far as stealing cattle, well, sorry boys, but I'm afraid you have the wrong man."

"He saw him last night, not long after dark."

Jordan flinched at the sheriff's words. Last night she and Gray Hawk had been together in their usual spot, which was close to Karlson's land.

"Gray was here last night, sleeping in the bunkhouse with the rest of the men," Shane replied, his voice clearly agitated.

"Do you know that for sure?"

Jordan was horrified at what was happening, but could do no more than stare numbly as Shane motioned one of the hands to get Gray Hawk.

Several of the men with the sheriff looked in her direction, and one man sneered, then spit on the ground not far from her feet. She recalled the man now. He'd been in town the first day she'd gone to Brogan with Kari and Shane to get dresses. Back then he'd been friendly, waving and smiling. Now he was letting her know he thought she was beneath them because of her relationship with Gray Hawk. He said something to the man beside him, and they both looked at her and laughed.

Though she felt like crying, she instead lifted her chin and met their cruel stares without blinking. She would not let them see her pain. After all, who were they to judge her?

Just then Gray Hawk stepped out of the stable, and all the attention was directed on him.

"Gray, were you here last night?" Shane asked.

"Yes," Gray Hawk replied, his gaze shifting from Shane to the sheriff.

"See, he was here all night," Shane said, his voice dangerously low. "Sheriff, you've wasted enough of my time. You've already shot this man as it is. If you've come looking to stir-up trouble, you can just turn around and head right back to town. Leave my property now, or you can get off that horse of yours and we can finish it right here."

Jordan's eyes widened in alarm, sure she was about to witness another brawl. The hands who were around the ranch came in, each one of them holding a rifle at the ready. Shane motioned he was all right, but few relaxed. "Well, what's it gonna be. I've been aching to have it out with you, and I can see no better time or place."

"You trust the breed's word?" the sheriff asked. It was obvious to everyone he wasn't about to get off his horse.

Shane's face was as unreadable as stone as he crushed his cigarette beneath his heel and his hand covered the butt of his gun. "I sure do."

The sheriff's Adam's-apple bobbed as he swallowed. "Well, I'll be doing some checking on my own, and if I find out different, I'll be coming back."

He glanced in her direction and smiled sardonically. His eyes sparkled, as though he knew something...Jordan's pulse leaped. Dear Lord, it couldn't be possible, could it? It had been months since they'd left Virginia. Her uncle probably hadn't even bothered to look for her...but what about Kari? Unable to meet his gaze for fear she was right, she quickly turned away.

GRAY HAWK listened to Shane as he tried his best to reassure him that everything was fine, when he knew that was not at all the case. Unfortunately, by coming to the Triple T, he'd brought trouble, not only for Jordan, but Shane Catalono as well.

He hated the sheriff and his men. It was all he could do not to snap the man's neck when he'd spit on the ground at Jordan's feet as though she were less of a person for loving him. Though she put on a brave front, Gray Hawk hadn't missed the horrified expression on Jordan's face.

He could handle the men. What enraged him more than anything was what they were doing to Jordan. He knew now his dream of their making a life together was unrealistic. Their cultures were too unforgiving of them to ever be together, and neither one of them wanted to give up their way of life.

The best thing he could do now would be to leave. To go back where he belonged, and leave Jordan here, where she belonged. Soon the people of Brogan would forget about this. Perhaps she'd find a husband, have her children, and her ranch.

But the thought of her with another man tore at his insides. She had given him her gift of purity. He had been the first, and he wanted to be the last. A blind hatred filled him at the thought of someone else's hands on her beautiful body.

"She'll be all right."

He turned to find Shane watching him. "She's a strong woman, Gray. She also loves you, and I think she'd like to see you." With a reassuring smile he continued toward the house.

Gray Hawk knew he had to leave. It was plain and simple.

He would tell her now, and whether she accepted it or not, he would leave by nightfall.

She stood over the wash bin, her hands vigorously scrubbing the shirt as she blew a tendril of hair out of her eyes. He stared, memorizing everything about her, her delicate features, her firm breasts, her tiny waist, her narrow hips. Her spirit, her love.

His heart already ached from the loss.

He was standing beside her before she noticed he was there. Looking up at him with a start, he could see the tears that stained her cheeks. She tried to smile, but it didn't reach her eyes.

"Come with me," he said, holding his hand out to her.

She looked around the yard. "I have work—"

"It's all right. Shane knows."

He pulled her along with him, down a trail, past some berry bushes to a secluded spot enclosed in the trees where they could talk privately.

He sat on the ground, leaning against a tree. Patting the ground beside him, she took a seat, her eyes wide in question. If only he could tell her that he would stay forever. That they would marry, have children, and share the ranch she'd always dreamed of. He'd give anything for that, pay any price to see the sweet smile on her face.

His fingers moved to the wayward curl that fluttered in the breeze. Rubbing the silky tresses between his fingers, he smiled sadly when her eyes darkened with passion. She was so innocent, and so easy to please. They could have been so happy.

He took a deep breath, and let it out slowly. "Jordan...I have to leave."

Her mouth dropped open. "What?"

"If I stay, I'll only cause more trouble for Shane and neither one of you deserves what's happening. Let's face it, I don't belong here."

"No," she said shaking her head adamantly. "Don't you see, this is exactly what they want? I don't want you to leave. They don't know anything about you. We want you here. We're the ones who should count, not them."

He pulled her into his arms, wanting to soothe the pain he was causing her, but she pushed against his chest and scrambled to her feet. He let her go, knowing nothing he could say would ease the hurt.

"I thought you cared for me."

"I do, Jordan."

"Then why would you leave?"

He wanted her in his arms, to feel her heart pumping against his own. He wanted to take her beneath him, to have her, to show her how much she meant to him. But it was not the time or the place, and it wouldn't change the outcome. "I know you don't realize it now, but I'm doing it for your own good. You were doing fine here until I came. Now they call you names, spit at your feet, treat you like—"

"They treat me the way they treat you." She lifted her chin. "Gray Hawk, I can handle it. I don't care what they think. I want you. I need you here."

He shook his head. "Jordan, I can't stay. I see the hurt in your eyes, the pain it's causing you—even if you won't admit it."

Closing her eyes, she let out an unsteady breath. "You would stay if you loved me."

He wanted to tell her just how much he loved her, but how could he? If he gave her his soul, he'd have no defense and it would only make their parting more difficult. "You have no idea how much I care for you. I'm leaving because you mean so much to me. One day you'll come to understand how much."

"What will you be going back to, Gray Hawk? You wanted to come, but now that you're here and have what you want, you're leaving. Will you go back to Running Deer?" She shook her head. "I don't understand you. I never thought you were a man who would run when trouble started, but that's exactly what you're doing. You don't care that you leave me here to pick up all the pieces, just as long as you have someone to keep your bed warm at night."

"I told you before that I haven't been with another woman since I met you."

He could tell by the expression on her face that she still didn't believe him.

She straightened her spine and lifted her chin. "I suppose this is goodbye then."

There was an awful finality in her words. She was resigning herself to the fact that they were to be apart forever. In that moment he wished he could take back his words. He wished that he could go on like they had been, not caring about what the town thought or felt, but he knew that he was being far too selfish. He could handle any kind of ridicule directed at him, but could she? Or would she in time begin to resent him for making her an outcast and learn to hate him? He couldn't bear it.

"When will you go?" she asked, her voice void of any emotion.

"Tonight."

Her response was a sharp intake of breath. And when he looked into her eyes, he was nearly undone by the agony he saw there.

Jordan stared at him in open-mouthed astonishment. This *isn't happening*, her mind kept screaming over and over again. Yet all she had to do was look into his eyes to know he spoke the truth. He was leaving tonight...forever.

She wavered on her feet and when he stood to steady her, she slapped his hand away. "Don't," she said, shaking her head, not wanting to do anything but feel the pain and anguish so she would forget that she even loved him.

"Jordan, please."

"Go away."

When his hand moved to her shoulder, she closed her eyes. How could she go on never to know his touch again? To never taste his lips on hers again, or to experience the joy of his lovemaking. As the tears slid down her face, she squeezed her lids even tighter. "Please, go," she whispered, unable to look at him, because if she did, she was afraid she'd lose what little pride and dignity she had left and beg him not to leave her.

His hand fell away and as she heard him leave, her heart shattered into a million pieces.

OPENING HER eyes to the first rays of a new day, Jordan sat up instantly in bed. Realization came fast, and with it, a sense of dread. Gray Hawk was gone.

He had left her.

The loss tore at her insides, choking her throat with tears that until now she'd been unwilling to shed. But with the dawning of a new day, her ache was so deep, she let the tears slip down her cheeks.

She cried silently. Not wanting to wake Kari, Jordan dressed and went downstairs. The rest of the household was still asleep, even Shane who was usually the first one up was still in bed. Not wasting any time on starting her chores, Jordan grabbed her basket and headed for the chicken coop. She needed to keep herself busy. She would not spend another minute thinking about Gray Hawk, or what her life would be like without him.

Yet as she stepped out into the cool morning, her gaze shifted to the bunkhouse. A sharp pain of regret lanced through her. He was gone, and oh, how her heart ached. Why did he have to come here, give her hope, only to leave again?

"Stop it," she said to herself. He didn't want her. It was obvious now. He had taken her virginity and used her, blaming the townspeople's bigotry for his excuse to leave. She'd given herself to him with all the love and trust in her heart. He took her most cherished prize for granted, then returned to his village—and Running Deer.

Though he had told her he hadn't been with the other woman, she didn't know if she could believe him or not. She shook her head. Why should she trust him?

But then again maybe there was nothing between he and the pretty Indian. Maybe his reasons for leaving the ranch were justified. Perhaps he realized how different they truly were, and knew a future together would not be easy. Perhaps he missed his home and his people, just as she had missed hers. Methodically she shooed away the chickens and picked up the eggs, wondering how and when, she would get over him.

It would do her no good to dwell on it. In fact, maybe it was for the best—she had been distracted since he'd come, not thinking about her ranch or her future. But not anymore. It was time to get refocused on her goals...starting now.

She was headed toward the house when a ranch hand stepped out of the bunkhouse. She glanced up, ready with a forced smile, then dropped the basket at her feet.

"Gray Hawk?"

The sight of her tall, dark lover was so unexpected, Jordan had to keep herself from running into his arms. But she held back, not sure why he was still here, or if he was just getting a late start. "I thought you were leaving?"

He walked toward her in long strides. Reaching out to her, he took her hand and brought it to his lips, kissing each knuckle.

Her blood warmed as she stared into his eyes that were so warm—with what? Love? Her pulse skittered. Was she seeing only what she wanted to see?

The backs of his fingers slid along her jaw. "I realized you were right. I was afraid I had ruined everything for you, but I know now that you took those risks for me. You stood up to everyone for me, and in return I almost walked away from you...the one person who means everything to me." His thumb moved gently over her bottom lip. "I'm sorry if I hurt you. I never meant to."

Her heart beat rapidly, not only from his declaration that he cared for her, but because he was staying. "Promise that you'll never leave me again."

He smiled softly. "I never left."

Chapter 21

"GIVE ME another."

With an uplifted brow, the bartender looked at Shane, and then at the nine empty glasses in front of him. "Ya' sure, Partner?"

Shane nodded in the bartender's direction. He used to be able to drink with the best of them, but now he wondered if he wasn't losing his touch when his vision blurred for a second.

Ignoring the beer the bartender sat before him, Shane turned to the room, meeting the stare of his ranch hands as they grinned at him. Very seldom did he come into town, and usually it was for one of two reasons; he needed some equipment, or he needed a woman. This time it was the latter.

The last few weeks had taken its toll on him. Between threats on his ranch, on Gray Hawk and Jordan's lives, and his attraction to Kari, he was in need of forgetting, if only for a little while.

The last of the threats came in the form of a note nailed on the wall of the horse stables, making him wonder if it was one of his own who plotted against Gray Hawk in order to carry out a vendetta against him.

Sure, he had enemies like the next man, but it seemed things had taken a turn for the worse when the women and Gray Hawk came to the Triple T. He considered talking to them about it, but every time he looked into Kari's innocent eyes, he remembered the hell she and Jordan had endured. And Gray Hawk—the man had been shot just because he was part Indian. Plus, he knew if he were to mention it, they would all leave and he didn't want that.

But what did he want?

He ran his hands down his face, feeling older than his thirty-six years. His gaze skid to a halt on a barmaid who was watching him from across the room. It wasn't China, his usual woman, who was already occupied upstairs. This gal was blonde, though it was obvious she wasn't born that way by the two slashing dark brows above her eyes. He sat mesmerized as she moved across the room toward him, her hips swaying provocatively in a tight, pink satin gown. Her breasts weren't large, but they looked enticing enough, the nipples barely covered by the faded pink lace of the bodice.

Her cheap perfume filled the air around him, and when she smiled, she displayed a row of tiny, slightly crooked, white teeth. She leaned forward, licking her lips, then made a great show of sitting on the stool beside him, making sure to bend over to give him a full view of her breasts.

"Hi there, cowboy," she said, her accent foreign. Her green eyes were painted with blue shadow, false eyelashes, and she wore too much rouge on her cheeks, but he didn't care. He needed a woman, and he needed one now. It had been a long time since he'd given into his body's urges.

Her pink tongue darted out to moisten her painted red lips. She put her hands on his thighs, leaning over to breathe a sexual innuendo in his ear that was rather lewd, even for a whore.

As she pulled him to his feet, he heard a couple of his boys whistle and yell suggestive remarks. "Give her a good one," Hank called from his place at the bar where he was busy fondling a voluptuous brunette.

Taking Shane by the hand, the woman led him to her room that was taken up mostly by a four-poster bed. The satin sheets were folded back invitingly, and for a minute Shane longed for the comfort of his own bed. Despite being the middle of the day, the room was cast in shadows, the window open, the breeze fluttering the heavy curtain. The smell of smoke, cheap perfume, and sex lingered heavily in the air. Even with nearly a dozen beers in him, misgivings began to plague Shane. After visiting China, he usually felt guilt, but it was always associated with Lily's memory and nothing else. Now he saw Kari's smiling face, even as the woman stripped her clothes off, leaving nothing but her black stockings on. She had a body ripe for loving, which bothered him because he waited for the stirring to come—the heaviness in his crotch that ached for a woman...one certain woman.

Shane moved toward her, determined to bring himself to life if it killed him. He was only a few steps away from the prostitute when he heard a familiar laugh come from the street below. He turned abruptly from the whore and went to the window. Pulling the curtain aside, he looked down at the street beneath him. There, like he knew she would be, was Kari. Her laughter reached him again, her beauty astounding as she talked with an old woman on the street below. The butter yellow dress was modest and simple, yet fit her innocence perfectly. Her hair was held up with pearl combs, and those gorgeous silky tresses hung down her back in soft, silky waves. She was so breathtaking, so angelic. What he wouldn't give to have her with him right now. Instantly blood raced to his groin, bringing that part of him to life.

He was quickly reminded of the woman with him when her breasts smashed against his back, and her hands cupped his now swollen manhood. She pulled the shirt from his pants, nearly tearing it in her haste. "Mmmm, you're a big one, aren't ya love?" she said in a husky whisper, while pulling his shirt off him.

As he looked down at Kari, the woman he truly wanted, he became instantly remorseful. This was wrong. He should leave. "I have to go," he said, pushing bills into the whore's hands.

When he turned abruptly, the plant on the windowsill fell from its perch and fell to the sidewalk below with a crash. He couldn't move fast enough, and he watched in slow motion as Kari turned at the sound of the shattering pottery directly behind her. Her gaze shifted from the broken bits of clay, dirt, and plant, to the window where Shane stood as still as a statue, too drunk to move.

The smile that had been on her beautiful mouth an instant before was quickly wiped clean as she spotted him. He knew the cause when he glanced beside him to see the naked whore had stepped out from behind him, in clear view of the street below, her hand possessively wrapped around his waist.

Infuriated gasps filled the air, and finally he found the sense to move away.

KARI WAS livid.

How dare the man publicly humiliate himself that way? It was bad enough to be caught with a whore, but in the middle of the afternoon, in plain sight of everyone, was downright disgusting.

Seeing the whore with her arm around Shane's waist haunted her as she made her way down the boardwalk. They were probably at that moment rolling around on that slut's bed, doing....
that. Tears burned the backs of her eyes, which only added to her fury.

Why did it hurt so bad to know he was with another woman? A whore at that! Her steps slowed. And why did she care so much? Shane Catalono was nothing to her except a landlord—a man who had taken them from an Indian village and given them a chance at building their lives. A man she truly did care about.

Kari swallowed the lump in her throat. The truth of the matter was the sight of Shane with that strumpet tore at her insides until she felt physically ill. She would have never imagined Shane the kind of man to pay a woman for sex. She shook her head of the horrible images that would no doubt stay with her forever.

Why did it have to hurt so bad?

Climbing into the wagon, Kari wondered how she could possibly face him again, knowing what she did now. Here he'd been acting as though he truly cared for her, and maybe even one day their friendship could become more. But not now. She would never forget the lustful look in his eyes, or the smirk on the whore's face, her naked body pressed wantonly against him as they looked down at her.

To think that all along he had only been kind to her, thinking she was a poor destitute widow who'd been captured by Indians. Perhaps that's why this was happening to her. She knew nothing good could come out of lying.

Thankful the kids were at home and she didn't have to pick them up at school, Kari headed out of town, her mind racing. Never had she wanted to leave a place so badly as she wanted to leave Brogan. She knew it had been a good step for both she and Jordan, but now it was simply time to move on. The problem was they didn't have enough money saved to pay the taxes on the ranch, and it would be at least another month or two before they had it all. But what if they got a loan? Who would she ask? The only person with that kind of money was Shane, and she absolutely refused to ask him for anything. Her fingers clenched the leather reins until her knuckles turned white.

Of course they could always just move out of the house. Mrs. Craven had offered to rent them the apartment above her shop, but that wouldn't help Jordan. She was happy working at the ranch, and it wouldn't be convenient for her to move into town. Plus, the kids depended on her to take them to school.

There was no choice...she would have to deal with it, no matter how difficult it proved to be.

Her thoughts were interrupted by the pounding of hooves against hard-packed ground. Sitting up straighter, she glanced over her shoulder to find Shane coming toward her like he was being chased by the devil himself. Her pulse skittered. She brought the reins down on the horses back, urging them to go faster.

But there was no way to outrun him, and she slowed as he came up along side her. Refusing to look at him, she kept her chin lifted high and her focus ahead. A moment later the wagon swayed under his weight, and he was sitting beside her, his hands moving to hers on the reins to stop the horses.

She dropped the reins as though the touch of his fingers burned her flesh. He brought the horses to a complete stop.

"What in the world do you think you're doing?" she hissed, hating him for the sole fact that despite the knowledge he'd been with another woman, she still wanted him.

"Kari, I know what it looked like, but I swear to you nothing happened." The smell of alcohol on his breath was so overpowering, it nearly knocked her from the seat.

He grasped her hand. When she tried to pull away, he held it firm. Glancing down, she was reminded that those same hands had been on a whore just moments before. "Please remove your hands."

"Kari—please, I want you to know nothing happened up there in that room. I mean I obviously went up there to—" He closed his eyes for a moment, and she stared at him, realizing how drawn his face was. Dark circles appeared like bruises beneath his eyes. He hadn't shaved for a few days, and to her dismay she found the growth of beard only added to his masculine appeal.

Long dark lashes framed his blue eyes that pleaded with her. It took Kari back for a moment. Always they'd been sarcastic with each other, but now there was no humor, just hope. "What I'm trying to say is that I made a mistake. Ever since I met you, I've been attracted to you, but I haven't wanted to do anything about it. I guess I became a little jealous when you started talking about the sheriff, and well—"

"I never had lunch with the sheriff. He knows how I feel about him, especially after he shot Gray Hawk. And even if I had gone to lunch with the sheriff, how can you justify that with visiting a whore? Having sex is quite different than having lunch, wouldn't you say!" She turned from him, and lifting her chin a notch, she continued, "I really don't want to hear anymore. Now, if you will please get out of the wagon, I would like to get hom—back to the ranch."

His gaze was surprisingly focused as he stared at her with what appeared regret. "All right," he said, his voice low and resigned before he stepped out of the wagon.

His horse had run ahead, but she didn't care if he had to walk a hundred miles as long as she didn't have to look at him. A whistle tore through the air and the horse spun and went running past her to his master. Kari rolled her eyes, distressed by how much power Shane Catalono had over so many people—and things.

GRAY HAWK woke to find a rifle pointed at his temple. Every muscle in his body tensed as he met Sheriff Kincaide's steely gaze.

"Care to tell me what you're doing?" Gray Hawk asked, knowing from his past experience with the man, that the words may well be his last.

"I'm taking you in, boy. We found the Karlson cattle on Triple T land with the brands switched. You're a sneaky one, now aren't you?"

When Gray Hawk tried to sit up, Kincaide tried to push him back down, but Gray Hawk grabbed his wrist and threw it back at him. "I have no idea what you're talking about. I haven't stolen any cattle, and the only cows I've branded have been those on Triple T land, so I suggest you get that gun out of my face."

The sound of a rifle being cocked behind the sheriff made Gray Hawk pause. A second later he heard Shane's voice, "Drop the gun, Kincaide—now!"

The sheriff did as Shane asked, his mouth lifted into a sinister smile as he turned to face him. "We found Karlson's cattle on your land. I can arrest the breed here for the stealing or I can arrest you, though I know it wasn't you, Catalono, since you're such an upstandin' citizen and all."

The nerve in Shane's jaw ticked double time as he lowered his gun. "Show me these cattle."

"All right, but just in case the breed gets any ideas of escape, I've enlisted one of my men to watch over him."

"Gray can come with us. After all, he's the one you're accusing—"

Following them, Gray Hawk knew he was being setup. The difficult part was that he was helpless to do anything about it. He could tell everyone around him that he was innocent of any wrong doing, but would they really believe him? After all, they had only known him for a short time.

As they stepped out into the daylight, he glanced up to see Jordan coming his way. He held up his hand telling her to stop, and tried to smile reassuringly, though he knew he failed by the concern on her face.

"See, right here's the proof," the sheriff said, pointing to a makeshift pen where five cows stood, each displaying a Triple T brand burnt over the brand of Karlson's K within a circle.

Shane lifted a brow. "Well now, looks like someone branded right over Karlson's brand. If a person went to all the trouble of stealing the cattle, why in the world would they do such a shoddy job of branding?"

The sheriff met Shane's accusing stare, then looked past him to Gray Hawk. "Probably cause the breed don't know better. Who knows, Catalono, he was probably staking you out, too. Within days he could have been gone, that is after cleaning you out."

Shane took the step that separated him from the sheriff. "I think he was set up. In fact, I bet you know who it is that did this."

Gray Hawk watched the sheriff intently, noticing how the man's beady eyes narrowed and his face turned red. With chest puffed out, he took a step back. "All I know is that Karlson wants retribution by way of having this man arrested, and I'm meaning to do that."

The sheriff moved to grab Gray Hawk's hand, but Shane shoved him away. "You can't just come in here and take my man, especially when it's your word against Gray's."

Shane turned to Gray Hawk, his expression almost apologetic as he asked, "Did you steal Karlson's cattle?"

"No," Gray Hawk replied, every muscle in his body tense.

Shane faced the sheriff. "There, you see, he didn't do it. Now take your cattle back to Karlson. Tell him he's got the wrong man."

The sheriff's mirthless laughter set Gray Hawk's nerves on edge.

"Karlson wants the breed and that's all there is to it. Now, I'm taking him in. Scotty, you see to handcuffing that boy up now, will ya?"

The sheriff's young deputy cautiously approached Gray Hawk. Staring the boy down, Gray Hawk didn't even resist arrest, knowing the hot-headed sheriff wouldn't hesitate to put a bullet in him.

Why hadn't he left Brogan when he had the chance? Instinctively he glanced toward Jordan, who was standing on the porch one minute, the next she was running toward him.

Throwing her arms around him, she kissed his neck, his jaw, then his mouth. "Don't worry, we'll get you out of this." She tried to smile, but failed, her lips trembling.

"We have to go," the sheriff said, moving past Jordan with a look of disgust.

Gray Hawk was shoved into the front of the wagon. Sitting in back of him was the young deputy and a couple of other goons, while the sheriff rode at Gray Hawk's side, a rifle trained on him.

JORDAN STARED after the wagon with a feeling of helplessness.

"We'll get him out, Jordan. Don't worry," Shane said, determination in his voice as he strode toward the stables. A few minutes later he was off like a bolt of lightning.

The day was the longest of Jordan's life. Not even her chores could take her mind off Gray Hawk's plight. It was obvious the sheriff had a vendetta against Gray Hawk from the moment they'd met, and as if shooting him hadn't been enough, now he was intent on seeing him hang.

Later, when Shane rode in looking defeated, Jordan waited for the worst, knowing that whatever happened, she would have to stay strong for Gray Hawk.

Shane ran a hand through his hair in frustration. "I wish I had good news, but I don't. It appears that Karlson has a half dozen men who say they saw Gray on his land the same night the cattle were stolen. What we need to do is talk with our men and have them account for Gray that night."

Jordan's pulse skittered with alarm. She thought of the many nights she and Gray Hawk spent together by the pond. All she had to do was tell the sheriff that she was with Gray Hawk. But knowing the man, he wouldn't believe her—or just wouldn't care.

Knowing she shouldn't borrow trouble, she decided to wait, but that evening after dinner, Jordan realized how perilous the situation was when Shane hit his fist on the table. "I don't know what to do. The men say Gray Hawk took off every night at the same time and would come back real late. He always said he went to the pond to bathe, but why then would he spend so much time there? Someone tell me I'm not wrong...I want to believe he's innocent."

Kari shook her head. "It doesn't make sense. Gray Hawk is an honorable man. I know that. We all do."

Jordan felt heat race up her neck and stain her cheeks pink. Her lover's life depended on her, and she knew she had to stand up for him. Glancing at the children, she said, "Shane, could I talk to you in the other room?"

Avoiding Kari's questioning glance, Jordan went to the Living room and waited for Shane. When he walked in a moment later, she took a deep breath and blurted, "Gray Hawk was with me that night—and all those other nights."

Comprehension softened his features. "You were together?"

Jordan bit her lip and nodded.

His relief was evident.

"You have to speak on his behalf. It's his only chance."

She nodded. "I'll do anything."

"You're a strong woman, Jordan. You've proven it before, but even more so now. To stand up against ridicule is a tough thing for anyone."

His words somehow made it easier, and she agreed to go with him into town the following morning.

Dressed in her best gown, she took special care with her appearance. As the wagon rolled through Brogan, people on the street stopped to stare. Refusing to meet anyone's gaze, she took Shane's hand and stepped down from the wagon. She marched straight into the sheriff's office, determined to free Gray Hawk.

The room was filled with cigar smoke and the smell of unwashed bodies. Jordan looked past the sheriff to the cell where Gray Hawk lay on a cot. Seeing her, he came to his feet, and she rushed toward him. Taking his hands in hers, she brought them to her lips and kissed each palm. "You'll be out soon, I promise," she whispered.

Shane stepped in and nodded to Gray Hawk before turning his

attention to the sheriff. "Kincaide, we have a witness who says she was with Gray the night he supposedly stole the cattle from Karlson."

The sheriff leaned one hip against his desk. "Is that so?" His gaze shifted over Jordan quickly, his lip lifted in disgust. "What were you all doing out in the dark that late at night?"

Despite her effort not to, Jordan felt her cheeks grow hot under the sheriff's cruel stare. He was baiting her, knowing full well what it was she and Gray Hawk had been doing.

She lifted her chin. "We were making love."

The sheriff lifted his brow, his lips thinned. "Are you married, Miss Hoffman?"

Jordan shook her head. "No."

His laughter vibrated in her ears. How she longed to slap his insolent face.

"How old are you, Miss Hoffman?"

"Eighteen."

"Did this injun rape you?" he asked, pointing to Gray Hawk.

Jordan's gaze swiveled from Gray Hawk back to the sheriff. She frowned. "What?"

"You heard me. I asked if this man here, this Gray Hawk as you call him, if he raped you?"

The room was so quiet Jordan could hear the pounding of her heart. "No, he did *not* rape me. I made love to Gray Hawk of my own free will. I love him."

The sheriff rolled his eyes dramatically. "You love him? Miss Hoffman, you shame all white women."

"You're pushing it, Kincaide," Shane said, stepping forward, his fists clenched at his sides. "We've provided proof that Gray was not alone that night, and now we're asking you to let him go."

"Can't do that."

"What?"

"It's her word against six of Karlson's men. Let's look a little closer at this situation, shall we. We have an eighteen-year-old woman who is sleeping with the breed. A woman we know nothing about. Where does she come from...what do we really know about any of them?"

Shane's jaw hardened as he grabbed Kincaide by the shirtfront and brought him inches from his face. "You're going too far and you damn well know it."

The sheriff pushed Shane off. "No, Catalono, you're going too far. The breed stays here until Karlson drops the charges. Miss Hoffman's word isn't enough for me to let him go. He's the one who pressed charges, and the only one who can drop them."

Shane's eyes narrowed as he stared long and hard at the arrogant sheriff. "You son of a bitch. You called Karlson in on a favor, didn't you? This couldn't have anything to do with you dropping the charges on his son that was caught stealing last fall, now would it?"

Kincaide's smile was cruel and mocking. "Watch it Catalono, or you could find yourself behind those bars alongside your friend, here."

Jordan grabbed Shane's arm and steered him toward the door. "Gray Hawk needs your help now, Shane, and I don't need to be trying to get both of you out."

"Gray, we'll be back," Shane said, slamming the door behind him.

GRAY HAWK lay back on the cot waiting for something to happen. He knew the sheriff wasn't about to go down without a fight, and he was ready.

It had been twenty-four hours since he'd been arrested and not once had the man asked him if he wanted food or drink. Though his stomach grumbled, Gray Hawk would be damned if he'd ask the man for anything.

The sheriff lifted a bottle to his lips, spilling some of the liquor on his shirtfront. He'd been drinking since noon, right after Shane and Jordan left, and he hadn't stopped since. With every hour that crawled by, he became more inebriated, and crueler, calling him every deplorable name known to man.

When Kincaide stood abruptly, sending the chair toppling to the hard floor, Gray Hawk sat up on the cot.

Bracing himself against the bars, the sheriff held the bottle out to him. "How bout a drink?"

Gray Hawk shook his head.

The sheriff lifted his brow. "What, ya' too good to drink with the likes of me?" he asked in a slurred voice.

Gray Hawk remained silent, knowing the man was looking for any reason to start a fight. He glanced down at the keys hanging from his waist. It would be so easy to get them. All he would have to do is snap his neck and take the key, leave and never look back. But at what price?

He'd be a man on the run, who was not only wanted for cattle rustling, but for murder as well. Every bounty hunter from a hundred miles and beyond would be after him—and wouldn't stop searching until he was dead.

"How was that *Hoffman* woman?" the sheriff asked with raised brow. "I often thought of her and her pretty little cousin. Tell me, did she part those lovely white thighs for you whenever you asked? Did she stir beneath you all hot and bothered, or does she just lay there like a rag doll?"

Gray Hawk's adrenaline raced through his veins. How dare he make Jordan sound like a whore? She was a beautiful woman who had given herself to him without remorse, who loved him for who he was, and not what others saw him as. What he wouldn't give to stop the man's verbal abuse forever.

"Oh yeah, I bet she's real good. And her cousin, now there's a real lady. Don't you ever wonder exactly where they came from? I mean, doesn't it seem a little odd to you that they just appeared out of nowhere. But you probably know all about them, don't ya? Especially since you appeared out of nowhere at about the same time." He chuckled, the sound making the hair on the back of Gray Hawk's neck stand on end. "Let me show you a little something before you're strung up, breed."

He stumbled toward his desk, opened a drawer, and pulled out a rolled up piece of paper. He took another swig off his bottle, then chuckled as he threw it in the cell.

Gray Hawk picked up the paper and unrolled it. His gut clenched into a tight knot seeing a drawing of a woman, who looked a lot like Jordan. He kept his surprise in check as he read the caption.

Wanted for kidnapping, Jordan Lee McGuire, age 18. Auburn hair, green eyes, slight build. Considered armed and dangerous. Ten thousand dollar reward if found alive.

His brow furrowed into a frown. *McGuire?*

"Since ya can't read, let me tell ya what it says," the sheriff said, an arrogant smile on his face. "You see, she's not who she claims to be. She's not a Hoffman at all, but a McGuire. Do ya know who the McGuire's are?" The sheriff laughed again. "Hell, of course ya don't. Why would ya? Just let me tell ya, they are well-known. A bunch of Eastern snobs who have lots and lots of money because of some invention. People who can do whatever they please, that's who."

Gray Hawk's mind was churning like a swollen river.

Although he knew little about Jordan, he couldn't imagine why she would have lied to him about who she was—unless she had good cause. But what was the kidnapping charge about? Who had been kidnapped, and why wasn't there a poster of Kari? Unless it was Kari who had been kidnapped. Which made no sense. The girls looked too much alike not to be related. Not to mention the close bond they shared.

"Why show this to me now?" Gray Hawk asked, keeping his voice level.

"Cause, my friend, I thought you'd like to know you was poking a real lady. And since we're gonna have us an old fashion hanging party, I thought you'd like to take that bit of news to your grave. It's probably the only thing ya ever really accomplished."

The minute the sheriff produced a length of rope and pulled a chair up to the bars, Gray Hawk stood up, every muscle tense.

The sheriff walked slowly across the room and closed the door to his office. He threw the bolt, locking it, the sound echoing against concrete walls. Pulling the blinds down, he came toward Gray Hawk with a menacing smile. Taking the rope, he strung it through the bars.

When the sheriff met Gray Hawk's gaze, his eyes were bright with excitement. "This is the end of life as you know it, Injun."

Gray Hawk thought it was too bad the man was so excited at the prospect of killing him, because he was about to be mighty disappointed.

Chapter 22

FREDERICK McGuire looked up from his newspaper, his gaze falling on the endless countryside where trees were becoming fewer, and the land stretched out in all directions. He shook his head, wondering why in the world anyone in their right mind would want to live in the West.

Despite the gloomy locale, Frederick was pleased since receiving word from Brogan, a small town smack dab in the middle of Wyoming territory. The sender had been a sheriff who knew the whereabouts of Jordan McGuire—alias Jordan Hoffman.

For months now he had been waiting for this news.

Especially after the men he'd employed to track the girls had come up missing without a trace after having received a large retainer from him. He should have known better than to pay them so much up front, but he wouldn't make the same mistake twice.

Jordan's intended, Marvin, was still waiting patiently, thinking his lovely young bride-to-be was on a trip to Europe with her cousin. He was suspicious at first, which was expected. But Patricia finally explained to the older man that Jordan and Kari had left suddenly to visit an ailing friend in London. If Marvin or anyone else knew the girls had runaway, it would ruin future chances of marrying either one of them off. But he was certain he'd find them, and Jordan would marry Marvin as planned. He would deal with his daughter later.

He had expected Jordan to rebel against him about her impending marriage but he was actually shocked she had gone so far as to leave Virginia in order to get out of it. The ultimate blow came when she took his daughter on her wild escapade. Well, she would lose her wild ways soon. Marvin had a way of breaking a woman. It would do her good. She was much too strong-willed, just like her father had been.

He shook his head, remembering when his brother had built the rustic home out in the wilderness, turning his back on a dynasty their parents had built for them. Of course, it ultimately worked to Frederick's benefit, leaving him in control of the company. In his opinion, his brother deserved the horrifying death he'd experienced at the hands of savages. It was just grossly unfair that he was left to raise his brother's brat.

Jordan had come to live with him and his family, and in the process had led his beautiful daughter astray. Before she arrived, Kari had been a manageable child, who did everything he and his beloved Patricia asked of her. But Jordan's influence began to rub off on Kari, and soon she took up some of her cousin's traits that no tutor could reverse, no matter how hard they tried.

And now she was costing him a fortune. In the last month his debts were piling up, to where he had people knocking on his door asking for payment. He had a lot of investments, but his young wife had a tendency to spend more than he could make, and he knew if he didn't find his niece soon and marry her off to Marvin, that he would be in even more dire straights.

Patricia had warned him just a few weeks before, she would leave him if he didn't save their London home, a place she visited perhaps one month out of the year. He'd invested heavily in a new company that had yet to show a profit, and until it did, the purse strings had to tighten. But his wife was being difficult. She didn't want to hear they were in financial trouble, so therefore she ignored him, and continued spending money like it grew on trees.

He knew if Jordan had any clue as to how much she was worth, she would run, which meant he had to keep her inheritance a secret until the ring was on her finger and she was Marvin's wife.

The stage driver knocked three times on the top of the coach. "Brogan's straight ahead, sir."

Frederick smiled. The day of reckoning was at hand.

JORDAN WAS leading her mare from the stable when she saw a lone rider coming hell-bent for leather over the hill toward the Triple T. Her heart hammered recognizing the man's broad shoulders and black hair. "Gray Hawk," she whispered, squinting against the sun, wondering if her mind was playing tricks on her.

The past twenty-four hours had been hell. Sleep had been impossible, and several times she had to talk herself into staying in bed. She wanted to be with Gray Hawk—needed to be with him. She didn't trust the sheriff. If his earlier behavior was any indication, he was going to be nothing but trouble until Gray Hawk left Brogan.

She could see Gray Hawk clearly now, and her breath caught in her throat seeing a gash on his forehead and a rope burn around his neck.

He jumped off the horse that was still moving, and came toward her in determined strides. Reaching out to him, he took her into his embrace, pulling her tightly to him, stealing the breath from her lungs.

She buried her face in his shirtfront, kissing his chest. "What did he do to you?"

He put her from him, his face strained. "The bastard tried to hang me. He'll be coming for me shortly."

"Where's the sheriff now?"

"Hopefully still laying unconscious in a locked cell."

"What will you do?"

"I have to go...I can't stay here."

"We can hide you," Shane said, stepping down off the porch. "Kincaide's not going to move too fast, especially since you got the best of him. He'll get as many men together as possible before heading this way, and since I talked with some of the townspeople, I believe he'll have a hard time getting any help."

Jordan knew by the look in his eyes that he was leaving. There was nothing she could do to stop him. Even with the suspicion she carried his child, she couldn't use that to keep him with her, no matter how bad she wanted to. They had been together for weeks now without a single declaration of love from him. Obviously he didn't return her sentiment.

"Gray, if you need anything." Shane grasped his hand. "You know where we are."

"Thanks, I appreciate it."

They were silent until Shane disappeared in the house and closed the door.

"When I was in jail, the sheriff showed me something I think you might be interested in."

Jordan's brow furrowed into a frown. Nothing the sheriff could do or say would interest her, or so she'd thought until Gray Hawk pulled out a piece of paper and unrolled it. The breath left her lungs in a rush. "Oh my God," she said, her voice sounded hollow to her ears as she stared at the picture of herself—a wanted poster. Her worst nightmare had finally come true.

Gray Hawk had obviously gotten it from the sheriff. So why hadn't Kincaide arrested her? "Did he wire the law in Virginia?" she asked, her mind scrambling, thinking what she should do next.

"I don't know. I just need the truth, Jordan. Just tell me the truth."

Her gaze shifted to the hill, waiting for the sheriff, or even worse— her uncle, to come and take her away. If Frederick were to come, there would be nothing she could do but leave with him. Her stomach sank like a stone. She was desperate for a solution, yet no matter how much she wanted it, she couldn't ask Gray Hawk to marry her, especially when he didn't even love her.

"Kari and I left Virginia when my uncle was going to marry me off to a seventy year-old man." She took a deep breath, hoping he understood.

"All my life I wanted to come back to Wyoming to claim my ranch and spend the rest of my days raising horses. When I told my uncle that, he said the ranch was gone, that the taxes hadn't been paid. I couldn't stay knowing I would marry Marvin Johnson, so I left, and brought Kari with me. We've been working to get enough money to pay for the taxes, so it will be mine again."

He watched her intently, and she knew he was searching for the truth.

"I hated Mr. Johnson so much, I would have rather died than marry him, and if my uncle comes here, Gray Hawk, he'll make me return to Virginia and marry."

He pulled her against him, comforting her. "He's not taking you anywhere, because we won't be here for him to take you."

Her pulse skittered, fear working its way up her spine. She put him at arms length. "Where will we go?"

"We can return to my village...we'd be safe there."

A thousand emotions ran through her. To return to Gray Hawk's village would be difficult, but with her uncle breathing down her neck, she had little choice.

FREDERICK McGuire straightened his tie and headed toward the sheriff's office, grimacing at the grime that covered his Italian shoes. He was filthy from head to toe. What he needed was a hot bath, a change of clothes, and a stiff drink. But first he needed to check with the sheriff to make sure his niece and daughter were still in town.

The door to the sheriff's office was locked. He frowned, jerking the door handle. He was ready to turn away when he heard a muffled cry from the other side. Peering into the dark office, he saw a man in a cell, his fingers wrapped around the iron bars yelling for someone to let him out. The law in the west was definitely different than in the east, Frederick thought, lifting a brow, deciding it was best to come back later rather than deal with a drunk prisoner.

Crossing the street to the only hotel in town, Frederick took the best room they had, which ended up being a chamber no larger than his sitting room back in Virginia, and a bed that was as hard as a board.

Having ordered a bath to be brought up directly, he lay back on the uncomfortable bed smoking a cigar. Half-an-hour later a knock on his door provided a tub, servants with buckets of steaming water, and a bottle of the best brandy the cow town had to offer.

After the servants had seen to his every whim, he dismissed them and sank low in the tub, letting the stress of the long trip dwindle away with the dirt. He poured himself a drink and didn't pause when he heard the door open, then close.

He smiled hearing the sound of high heels clicking against the wood floor a second before he opened his eyes to find a blonde, complete with a gaudy purple satin dress, sitting on the bed in a very unladylike position.

Instantly he was surprised that a place like Brogan would have a whore who looked as good as this little peach before him. He smiled like a cat ready to pounce on a mouse as she began to slowly undress, her gaze not once leaving his. His hand moved to his erection, gripping it with a firm hold as the prostitute began a nasty striptease. It had been too long since he'd slept with his wife, a woman known for her theatrics in bed, as well as her abstinence when she wanted her way. But even when they did make love, Patricia was no whore, and he was in the mood to make love until he could scarcely stand.

The blood gorged in his manhood as the prostitute flung the remainder of her dress at his head. She giggled as she sank down in the bath, the water lapping at her creamy thighs as she sat directly on his erection. Groaning with delight, she let her head fall back on her shoulders, her fingers teasing her nipples until they were as hard as diamonds.

She bounced up and down, sending water over the edge of the tub, onto the floor. Her cries of passion were so loud he was sure servants would come running, but he didn't care. He was in the middle of this god-forsaken country, and his wife was a whole world away. He could have his way with this great piece every day if he wanted, until it was time to head back to Virginia, to his wife, who would never be the wiser.

JORDAN'S HEART lurched seeing the tears that stained Rebecca's cheeks.

"Honey, we'll be back soon."

Rebecca squeezed her eyes tight. The trio that stood on the porch looked dismal at best. Shane's face was expressionless, but she saw the tension around his eyes. Even Tanner, who usually was so animated, said nothing as he stared straight ahead.

"We'd better go," Gray Hawk said, his voice urgent.

"Wait!" Shane said, coming toward them in long strides. "Wouldn't it be better if Kari stayed here? If the women were in different places, it would complicate things somewhat. I mean, he wouldn't leave one of you behind."

Kari looked stricken, glancing from Shane to Jordan.

"She can't go into Brogan," Jordan said, hating the thought of separation.

"She doesn't have to. She can stay here. I need the help, especially now that Rebecca's with us. For all that Hank says he enjoys cooking, he'd rather be out roping cattle. And as far as her safety is concerned, I have a lot of men that live on this land. Nothing will happen to her, I promise."

He turned to Kari, his expression imploring. "I know that at times you feel I've been unjust, and you'd be right in that," he said smiling softly. "But I want you to stay. I think it would be easier on everyone that way, especially the kids...and myself."

Jordan looked at her cousin. She saw the indecision in her eyes. "I think he has a point, Kari. Gray Hawk and I will be fine. Shane can protect you, and it's not you they're after anyway."

"Are you sure, Jordan? I mean if you want—"

Jordan leaned over and hugged her. "I've never been more certain of anything." Tears burned her eyes, but she blinked them back and looked down at Shane. "I trust you to do as you say. Watch her as though your life depended on it."

He nodded. "You can count on it."

She managed a small smile. "I will."

WITH THE whore asleep in his bed, Frederick left the hotel having given explicit orders not to disturb his room while he was gone.

With a clean set of clothes and a new disposition, he set out once again for the sheriff's office. This time the door was wide open, and the man sitting at the desk looked remarkably like the man who'd been locked in the cell earlier.

"Mr. Kincaide?"

The man sat up taller in his chair, muttering something under his breath to the young man who stood at his side. To Frederick they appeared like a couple of dimwitted brothers, but he had expected little better from a small town like this. Apparently it was hard to get anything of quality...except for that little piece lying snug in his bed, he thought with a smug smile.

"I'd be Kincaide, and who might you be?" the man asked, his gaze shifting up and down Frederick's form.

"I'm Frederick McGuire."

As comprehension set in, the sheriff's face split into an immediate smile, and he stood up, nearly upsetting his chair. "Well, Mr. McGuire, I'm mighty pleased to meet you. I wasn't expecting you until tomorrow though."

Ignoring the man's hand, Frederick nodded toward a chair. "May I?"

"Sure, go right ahead."

"I received the message from you in regards to my niece, Jordan. Tell me, is she still here?"

The man sat down once again, leaning forward in his seat. "Yes, she's at a ranch not far from here."

"And is there another woman with her?"

"You mean, Kari?"

Frederick nodded at the mention of his daughter, surprised the man would use her given name. "Yes, Miss McGuire."

"Oh yes, Kari—I mean Miss McGuire lives there at the ranch as well, but you know what, she works right here in town."

"Works?" Frederick repeated, unable to believe what he'd just heard. His daughter *worked* for a living? The very idea was ludicrous. Kari was not a commoner, but a lady who was used to being waited on by servants. In fact, once she saw him, she may very well beg him to take her back to Virginia.

The sheriff looked confused. "Yes, she works at the dress shop. She sews clothes, and does a mighty good job, if I should say so myself. I own a shirt she made."

Frederick eyed the man's ripped shirt and too small breeches. "Really?" he said, trying to at least sound surprised. "Is she working today?"

The sheriff's brows furrowed together as though concentrating took all his energy. "Well, let me see. Naw, since today's a Saturday, she'd be off. Just comes in during the weekdays when there's school."

"School?"

"Yeah, the Catalono children attend the school just outside of town. Kari, I mean Miss McGuire, drops them off and picks them up every day." The sheriff lit a cigarette and exhaled. "So when do I get my reward."

Frederick waved the smoke out of his face and watched the sheriff for a long moment. The blankness in his eyes indicated he wouldn't care if and when he took the women out of his jurisdiction.

"Soon enough. I would like my visit to my niece and daughter to be a surprise. You see...I don't want Jordan arrested, I simply want her and Kari back home. Mind you, if she doesn't cooperate, then I'll take her by force, and I would appreciate your help if that's the case. When I have them in my carriage headed for Virginia, you'll see your money."

"Yes, sir." The sheriff hesitated, glancing up at his deputy, before turning back to Frederick. "Oh, and just so you know, she's been hanging out with a breed."

Frederick's eyes narrowed. "Breed? As in a half-breed—an Indian?" The blood roared in Frederick's ears as one side of the sheriff's mouth tipped into a confirming smile.

"Yeah, and they've been." He wiggled his brows. "You know."

He needed no affirmation as to what the sheriff meant. The innuendo was quite clear, and startling. "You do mean Jordan, and *not* my daughter?"

When the sheriff nodded, Frederick felt vast relief, knowing it wasn't his daughter. But that did cause a problem. If Jordan wasn't a virgin...he closed his eyes. The girl had left his side no more than seven months ago and already she was spreading her legs for an Indian. Her father was no doubt rolling over in his grave. Had he taught her nothing? Then a horrible thought raced through his mind. "What about Kari? Does she have a...beau?"

The sheriff shook his head. "No, she's a lady through and through. I kind of even liked her. Wouldn't mind her being my bride one day, but that damn Catalono—"

"Over my dead body," Frederick said under his breath as he stood, not wanting to hear another word out of the man's mouth. Even in his worst nightmare things hadn't been this dire. "I'll be staying over at the hotel in room twenty-one. Should you need me, knock twice, then three times fast."

He rolled his eyes when the man quickly wrote the instructions down on a piece of paper.

"I've had a trying day, so I'm going to head back to my hotel room and have a nice dinner before retiring. I would ask that you not disturb me tonight under any circumstance. I have business to attend to." Without another word, he left the two men staring after him.

His steps were light as he walked across the muddy road, not caring he was ruining his most expensive pair of shoes. His mind raced with his next plan of action. Hopefully, Jordan's lover was away when he visited the ranch. Having never seen an Indian firsthand, he decided he'd rather keep it that way.

As he climbed the steps to the hotel, he felt like a young man, his blood pumping in his veins as he marched down the hall to his room. Unlocking the door, he closed it slowly behind him, smiling to see the whore was still asleep in his bed.

Chapter 23

JORDAN'S HEART sank with every mile she put between her and Kari. After spending so many years together, being away from her cousin for any amount of time was difficult, but now it was necessary.

And just maybe the time apart would do them both some good, give them time to think about their futures now that they both had men in their lives.

Jordan turned to Gray Hawk, who stared straight ahead, quiet, just as he'd been since leaving the ranch. She knew he was feeling guilty for having brought so much trouble to Shane, but she also worried that he was mad at her for not telling her the truth about who she was from the beginning.

Or maybe his silence was because of the ridicule he'd experienced in Brogan—or maybe because he was returning home.

They had talked little about the past, aside from the fact he had been asked to leave the village, to go on a vision quest. The farther they traveled, the more silent he became.

Despite Gray Hawk's present mood, Jordan tried to tell herself she didn't want to go back to the village, she was actually looking forward to seeing the Cheyenne again, except for one.

But she put Running Deer far from her mind, and instead focused on her future, which she could only hope included the man at her side. He was her lover now. He'd proven that he cared, and she had to believe that he loved her—even if he refused to say it.

Making camp, Jordan sat down next to him as he skewered a rabbit and set it over the roaring flame. She loved to just watch him, his concentration so complete as he went about any given task.

He glanced up at her, his smile soft. "You hungry?"

She shrugged.

"We haven't eaten for hours."

She sighed. "I am hungry...but not for food."

His smile widened as he kissed her, and with a moan, took her to the ground, kissing her, his hands pulling up her dress as she fumbled with his breeches.

"It seems like so long—"

"It seems like forever," he said against her lips, rubbing his rigid length against her. Without bothering to undress completely, he thrust within her.

Gray Hawk slowly moved within her, wanting to prolong the ecstasy. For days now he'd kept his hands off her, telling himself that putting some distance between them would be for the best, but it had been torture, and he was pleased she felt the same need as he did.

Her hands moved under his shirt, gripping his back, and moving lower over his buttocks as she pulled her hips up against him. Would he always feel this way with her?

Feeling the fluttering of her climax, Gray Hawk could no longer hold himself in check and with a satisfied groan, spent himself, collapsing on her, smiling as she kissed his shoulder.

KARI TOOK Shane's advice to heart and never strayed from the ranch. Every day that passed she waited for the sheriff to arrive and start asking questions about Jordan.

Having put her mind at ease for the time being, Kari watched as Shane took off on his horse. The last week he had been incredibly sensitive and kind, going out of his way to make her feel wanted and safe.

And she enjoyed it. She liked being at the ranch, cooking, cleaning, washing...taking care of he and the kids. It was almost like having a family of her own. The kids were great, asking her to tuck them in at night, and even read a bedtime story. Tanner, though hesitant at first, seemed genuinely happy to have her at the ranch, and even told her once.

Without Jordan around there was a lot to be done, but it was better than having too much time on her hands. With all the chores, including mending the men's clothes, she didn't get a chance to miss her job as a seamstress.

Sometimes her mind would wander and she'd worry about Jordan, wondering if she and Gray Hawk had made it back to the village by now. A part of her wished she had gone with them, yet every night when she stared across the table at Shane, she was glad she'd stayed. She belonged here for now. Along the way, something had changed in their relationship. There was no sarcasm, just warmth that radiated from him, making her feel wanted.

Last night he'd asked her about her father and Jordan's engagement to Marvin. He also asked about her husband, and she felt her cheeks burn having to tell him she had lied to him. "When I told you that story, I hadn't realized you'd lost your wife," she said, and the sweet smile on his face said he already forgave her.

Having come clean with the truth was a huge relief, because now there was nothing standing between them. He had yet to kiss her, or even touch her for that matter, but she could see the look in his eye when he watched her. How soft his face became. She smiled to herself. He was coming around. It was just going to take awhile.

The sounds of pounding hooves on hard ground interrupted her thoughts. Seeing her father through the window, Kari's breath caught in her throat, and she ducked, hoping he hadn't seen her. There were a few men with him, among them was the sheriff.

"I'll get it!"

Before Kari could stop Tanner, she heard the door open and the sheriff say, "Hey there, boy, could you tell me if Jordan and Kari are here?"

Kari's heart lurched in her chest, her mind racing, wondering what she would do. Shane was off in the fields along with the other hands. Rebecca was over at a friend's house, leaving she and Tanner alone.

"No, she's not here?" Tanner replied in a steady voice.

"Which one?" the sheriff asked, exasperation obvious in his voice.

"They're both gone. They don't live here anymore."

The sheriff cursed.

"What about the breed—Gray or whatever it is they call him?"

"He's gone, too."

Dropping down to the floor, she crawled on her hands and knees toward the back door, the blood pounding in her ears. She stopped where she was, just shy of escape. She couldn't leave Tanner here alone.

"Do you know when they'll be back?"

"Nope."

"Can I help you gentlemen?"

Kari almost collapsed with relief hearing Hank's firm voice from outside. Prying the back door open, she looked around and seeing it clear, she darted for the brush.

She ran for what seemed forever, her heart hammering heavily in her ears, her stomach clenched in a tight knot, sure that any minute the sheriff would step out, or even worse, her father. Just the thought of him taking her away from Brogan and back to Virginia made her run faster. Knowing her father, he probably had a double wedding planned.

After all this time she couldn't imagine facing him. She'd always considered him a decent person, but she knew now what a horrible man he was. He hadn't always been so mean. When her mother was alive, he had been easy-going and affectionate. But when her mother died, part of her father died too, and when Patricia came along, the Frederick McGuire she had known and loved no longer existed.

Patricia took control of every facet of his life. The house and everything in it belonged to her now, and no matter what anyone said, they were wrong—Patricia was right. How Kari hated the woman, almost as much as she hated her stepsisters who acted like pampered princesses.

After running for what seemed like hours, Kari collapsed in the meadow grass trying to regain her breath. Lying back on her elbows, she looked up at the sky. "Lord, I knew this day would come, but I beg you to help me...to help us." How desperately she wished Jordan was with her now—her cousin always knew what to do.

She looked in all directions, and her heart plummeted to her toes. Everything was unfamiliar. She had never been any good at direction, and being in such a state of panic, she hadn't thought to pay any attention to which way she was headed. Now all she knew was that she was a long ways from the ranch, and the sun was close to setting. If she didn't find her way back soon, she'd be spending the night out here in the open. It wasn't something she hadn't done before, but this would be the first time she was alone and unprepared.

Blinking back tears, telling herself not to panic, she started walking again, focusing her mind on all the things that had happened to her and Jordan in the last seven months. She laughed, smiled, and even cried thinking that for all the hell and torment, it was without a doubt the most exciting time of her life. She wouldn't trade a moment of it for anything. Not even the time in the village, for there she had learned a truly valuable lesson. Everyone was equal, no matter what race or creed. A fact she'd been oblivious of living in her father's household, where the rich white man ruled supreme.

She stopped abruptly, listening carefully. Dropping down behind a large rock, she waited for the horse and rider that was coming her way. From the sounds of it, it was only one horse, making her think of the sheriff, a man she despised, and quite frankly, was terrified of. Daring a peek, her heart skipped a beat when she recognized the familiar figure. She stood and yelled, "Shane!"

Relief etched his handsome face as he raced toward her. He jumped from the saddle even before the horse had stopped. Taking her up in his arms, he squeezed her tight, nearly taking all her breath. "You scared me to death," he said against her forehead. "I thought...never mind, I'm just glad to find you."

Her heart hammered heavily against his chest as her arms encircled his neck. For so long she'd wanted this, to be in his arms, to kiss him. As she stared up at him, he bent his head, his lips just inches from her.

Sighing, she leaned into him, accepting his kiss, opening her mouth to him when his tongue traced the seam of her lips.

It was all Shane could do not to take her to the ground and make sweet, passionate love to her. But now was not the time. With Kari he needed to take it slow. He broke the kiss and put her at arms length. "We should get you back now."

"That's a good idea," she said, shifting on her feet, reminding him that she was a lot younger than he was. He traced the line of her jaw with his thumb, and couldn't help but kiss her once more, but this time a chaste kiss that promised more was ahead.

FROM THE moment they entered the village, Jordan knew they would be safe. For the first time in a good many days she wasn't looking over her shoulder, as though expecting the sheriff or her uncle to be there.

Yet misgivings began to plague her just within hours of their arrival, for soon Gray Hawk shed his ranch attire for his leather breeches and vest. He was once more transformed into the Indian, and gone was the cowboy she'd known at the Triple T.

That evening he spent a long time in his father's teepee. Tawanka told Jordan that soon Three Moons would die and Gray Hawk would be Chief.

"He will lead our people," she said, taking Jordan's hand into her own. "Gray Hawk is a strong man, who can lead us against our enemies, against our foes."

She didn't mention whites, though Jordan knew it was the issue that concerned them most. As it should be. On her journey West she'd heard enough about the gold rush in California, and knew that the whites were coming in record numbers. It only made sense that the Indians should fear them.

That evening while sitting across the fire from the others, she noticed a few of the cool glares she received. It wasn't until Running Deer approached her, an icy glare on her face, did Jordan realize that she wasn't welcome. "You should leave here. You do not belong, and you will only bring hardship on my people."

"I came with Gray Hawk."

"Gray Hawk belongs with us now. You have steered him away from his purpose. We need him. Go back to your own kind and leave him to us."

Jordan swallowed the lump in her throat. "He is not yours to have. He is a grown man who will make his own decisions."

"Do you not see that you have bewitched him?" Running Deer went down on her haunches in front of Jordan, to where her face was mere inches away. "Release him. If you care for him at all, leave here and never look back."

There was something in the other woman's eyes that made Jordan stop and think about what she was saying, but for all that she understood it, she was too selfish to give him up. "I love him."

Running Deer's jaw clenched tight. "I love him, too."

"He loves me," Jordan replied just above a whisper.

"He has told you this?"

Jordan paused for a moment. Gray Hawk had never told her he loved her, and now that she faced her foe, saw the pleased expression on the other woman's face, she realized it didn't make sense to love a man who didn't love her back. It would only give her more heartache.

"If you do in fact love him, then leave him." Without another word, she stood and left Jordan watching the fire silently. Tawanka said nothing, but her presence was soothing none-the-less, and Jordan felt like she was her only friend in the village.

Jordan's gaze shifted to Three Moons' teepee. What should she do? It was obvious she wasn't wanted. Just like Gray Hawk hadn't been wanted in Brogan. Neither one of them would be accepted by the others world.

Therefore there was nothing more to think about.

Tawanka took her hand and squeezed it tight. "Follow your heart, child. Do what it tells you." Without another word, Jordan was left alone, a solitary figure by the fire.

GRAY HAWK touched his father's forehead. How thin his skin was, and how very old he looked—how very tired.

Three Moons opened his eyes. He blinked a few times, then a soft smile came to his face. "My son, you have returned to us."

Seeing the hope in his father's eyes, Gray Hawk smiled warmly. "Yes father, I've returned."

"I knew you'd come back to us. I knew it."

The words were like a double-edged sword. For every mile of the journey that had led him back to his people, Gray Hawk had tried to convince himself that this is where he belonged; that his people needed him just as much as he needed them.

"You will lead our people." Though he didn't state it as a question, Gray Hawk knew it was indeed one. A question he wasn't ready to answer, yet as he stared into his father's eyes, he knew he could not deny him.

He nodded. "Yes father, I will lead our people."

A shadow fell over him. Gray Hawk turned to find Iron Bear standing behind him.

"So, you've come back."

Gray Hawk nodded. "Yes."

The displeasure on his brother's face hurt far more than Gray Hawk would ever admit.

"He will be Chief," Three Moons said, closing his eyes.

Iron Bear's jaw clenched tight, but he remained silent.

"You need your rest, Father," Gray Hawk said, resting his hand on his father's head. In all his years he'd never told his father how much he loved or respected him. Now with Iron Bear present, he could not form the words.

Gray Hawk walked past his brother out into the night. He looked for Jordan, and saw her heading back toward the teepee. He needed her companionship desperately.

"How dare you bring that woman back to our village."

Gray Hawk turned at the sound of his brother's voice, who approached him in long strides.

"How dare you bring that woman back into our camp."

Every nerve in Gray Hawk's body tensed. "She has brought no harm to any of us."

"Our father is ailing, he will die because of her."

Gray Hawk shook his head. "Our father is dying because he is ill. Jordan's presence won't change the inevitable."

"Will she stay with you? When you become Chief, will she remain?"

"I hope so."

Iron Bear took the step that separated them. "If she stays, I will leave here, and I will take our people with me."

It was a threat, and one that Iron Bear obviously intended to uphold. Gray Hawk didn't doubt it for a minute. "Do what you feel you must do."

WITH EVERY day that passed, there was a distance growing between Jordan and Gray Hawk, one that made her increasingly uneasy.

The hostility toward her was increasing, to the point that now she was isolated, though a few took pity on her and would sit beside her at the fire, while Gray Hawk kept vigil over his father. Three Moons was getting worse. The women chanted constantly, and the mood around the camp was growing grimmer. She had noted a few of the women had made marks on their bodies, as though knowing their Chief would not live to see another day.

Her stomach churned realizing what it meant.

Three Moons would die, and Gray Hawk would become Chief. He would never leave his people. He would not be returning to the ranch with her, of that she was certain.

Jordan's hand rested on her stomach. She knew for certain that she was pregnant. For days now she'd been ill, and at first she'd thought perhaps it had been the journey, but now she knew that wasn't the case.

She would have Gray Hawk's baby.

And Gray Hawk would stay with his people. It was his destiny, and though Jordan wanted desperately to tell him about the baby, she couldn't bring herself to ask him about the future, afraid of what his reaction would be. Would he insist she stay if he knew she was to have his child? Chances were, he would, and she couldn't stay where she wasn't wanted. Nor did she even want to.

She would have to leave. Their baby would be born back at her ranch and he would never find out. Her child would grow up without the love of its father—and they both would survive. But even as she thought it, she had to fight back the tears that threatened.

Conscious they wouldn't have a future together, Jordan wanted to leave right away. After the long ride here, combined with morning sickness, she had little choice but to stay a while longer. Plus, she needed to allow enough time for things to die down in Brogan. Then she would go back to the Triple T, begin her future by facing her past, and namely her uncle. She wouldn't keep running. What was the worse thing that could happen? Sure, her uncle could arrest her for kidnapping, but if Kari told him she had come with Jordan willingly, he really had no case against her.

Knowing her uncle as she did, he probably came solely for the reason of bringing them back to Virginia—back to Marvin. In all these months she began to wonder what kind of a deal her uncle had made with the equally rich man. There had to be more going on than what met the eye. Her uncle was too shrewd a businessman to let any money slip through his greedy fingers.

But he wouldn't get anything out of her, especially once she told him she was pregnant. She almost laughed out loud, imagining his face when she told him she was going to have a half-breed's child.

Pulling a fur tighter around her shoulders, she shivered as a cold breeze entered the teepee followed by Gray Hawk, reminding her that fall was on the way and with every day the weather would get harsher, making travel difficult. He sat down near the fire and watched her. She met his stare but said nothing. He looked so tortured and sad. His father was dying, and soon all the responsibility would fall on his shoulders.

He already had too much to handle. Knowing about the child she carried would only make things worse for him. Or would it? She opened her mouth to tell him, then quickly shut it. She didn't want to burden him further.

"You rarely go outside anymore."

She shrugged. "I don't feel that I'm very good company."

He frowned. "I want you to be happy here, Jordan."

She stared at him, waiting for him to continue, but he didn't. Maybe it was better they didn't discuss the future.

I'm pregnant with your child she wanted to shout into the silence, but the words wouldn't form on her tongue.

"I must stay and take care of my people. Tell me that you'll stay with me," he said, taking her hand in his.

She looked down at her lap where their fingers lay entwined. "How can I stay where I'm not wanted? They have isolated me. I don't belong, and I know they blame me for your father's failing health."

"That's ridiculous."

"But it's the truth."

He didn't deny it, confirming what she already knew. "Jordan, I need you with me."

His words were like a sharp stab to the heart. As he reached to touch her, his fingers lingering on her jaw, she felt her resolve weakening, but knew she must remain strong.

"I want you, Jordan. I need you desperately," he said, leaning toward her.

Needing him as much as he needed her, she gave herself over to him. He crushed her in his strong, powerful embrace, bringing her to the furs, his hands roaming every inch of her. He sat up abruptly, stripped off his shirt, and then his breeches. She stared unabashedly, taking in every inch of his strong, hard body, knowing it would be for the last time.

"Do you know that the first time I saw you, I was absolutely terrified of you." As he lay next to her, she snuggled against him, loving his strength and the comfort he gave. Always she felt safe in his arms, as though the rest of the world didn't matter.

He kissed her forehead. "You know what I thought when I first saw you? I remember thinking what a pretty face you had for a boy."

She hit him in the arm.

"Well, I wasn't sure you were a woman until you opened your mouth. I knew at that moment no man would have such a voice. Not to mention your lovely breasts." His fingers moved over her sensitive flesh. "You have no idea how much I wanted you."

"Not in the beginning," she said with a frown, knowing he had felt anything but desire.

"You were stubborn," he admitted, "But that didn't stop me from craving you."

His words excited her, and now her body trembled with the need that raced through her. Her hands greedily splayed over the hard muscles of his chest and abdomen, going lower to that part of him that could bring her such pleasure. Her fingers gripped his rock-hard manhood, loving the feel of satin over steel. Her breathing became labored as his fingers worked their magic, trailing over her nipples, down her stomach, slipping between her legs.

He shifted, grabbing her by the waist, guiding her until she straddled him. His smile was sinful as he sat her down on his thick erection. She gasped as he filled her completely.

His hands were braced on either side of her hips. He kept his gaze locked with hers, straining to keep control when she moved the slightest bit. Her movements were tentative at first, then she gained confidence as her own needs began to build. Soon she rode him with wild abandon. He smiled up at her, filling his palms with her firm breasts. Sitting up, he took a nipple inside his mouth as she continued rocking against him, her moans and cries warning him of her coming release.

Her tight sheath pulsated around his shaft, pulling every ounce of his seed from him. She collapsed on him, her breathing coming in deep gasps. He could feel her heart pounding beneath his fingers as he ran them along her spine. How she wished they could stay like this forever.

Jordan's breathing was barely back to normal when Gray Hawk hands began to wander again, bringing back to life the familiar stirring. He began to grow inside of her, filling her completely, and when she glanced at him, his smile was nothing short of predatory.

It was the early morning hours before she finally closed her eyes. For hours they had made love, taking time to learn what each other liked and wanted. She smiled down at her exhausted lover. His features were softened in sleep, making him look so young, almost boyish.

In her heart she didn't want to leave him, but she had to. There was no other choice. He belonged to his people, and she belonged with hers.

Chapter 24

FREDERICK was getting tired of the obnoxious sheriff. Since arriving in Brogan the man had become his bonafide shadow. With every day that passed, Frederick seriously considered eliminating the man from his plans. He was prepared to pay the reward money just to get rid of him...that was when the women were here in Brogan. But now that they had left, he had to come up with a new game plan.

"Darling, come to bed."

Smoking his pipe, Frederick glanced over at the bed where China, his sweet little whore lay naked on a pair of clean sheets. He smiled softly, hating to admit to himself how attached he was getting to the woman. Every day he called for her, and every night she satisfied him to no end. Finally, he agreed to pay for all her time until he left. An arrangement which pleased him immensely.

Just this morning he had received a telegraph from Patricia saying she missed him and was waiting for his safe return. In essence, the bitch was wanting to know if the money was coming to keep her in diamonds and gowns, as well as her cherished homes in London and Paris.

Then there was China. Sweet, China. Not once did she ask him for anything. Instead, she was committed solely to his pleasure, doing whatever he desired and more. He bought her a few new gowns, having been unable to stand the sight of the hideous satin ones that were much too small and far too gaudy for his tastes. She deserved to be clothed in the finest silks and lace, and what a little beauty she was when she was all cleaned up.

He crossed the room and lay down beside her, taking her in his arms. She cuddled up to him, pressing herself into his body as though she'd been made just for him.

He knew his business would soon be concluded, and he wondered if China would have any interest in going to Virginia. Never in his life had he thought of keeping a mistress, knowing if Patricia were to find out, she would see to his ruin, yet he wasn't sure if he could give China up. He was so relaxed when he was with her, reminding him of the days when his work wasn't everything.

"Have you ever been to the East coast, my love?" he asked, keeping any pretense out of his voice.

She kissed his neck softly. "I lived in New York for a while, but I wanted to come west. Is that where you're from?"

"No, Virginia," he said, pulling her on top of him. The woman brought his blood to a boil every time he even looked at her. "Have you ever been there?"

She licked her bottom lip, and instead of answering him, she slid down his body, proving to him she was worth every cent he'd paid.

GRAY HAWK reached for Jordan, but came up empty-handed. He turned and finding her gone, sat up, his heart thumping madly. He frowned while running his fingers through his hair. Last night they'd spent little time talking, yet now that he looked back, he knew by the urgency of her lovemaking that she was saying goodbye.

But why?

Even as he wondered, he knew why...his people's hatred had been too much. She would not stay with him, even though he wished she would.

Now she was alone, traveling by herself in dangerous territory. Any number of tribes could take her captive, but despite that threat, she had left.

The anger he felt toward his people was enough to choke him. He dressed quickly, his heart pounding, his anger growing with every second. He would go after her, but only after he had his say. His people would feel his wrath.

He stepped from the teepee, and stopped, noticing many of his people crowded around the campfire. Muffled cries filled the air, and all talking came to an abrupt stop as Iron Bear turned to him, his gaze scathing as Gray Hawk approached.

All the mens hair had been unbraided. The womens wailing grew with every step that brought him closer.

His father was dead.

Tears burned the back of his eyes as his gaze shifted to Three Moons' teepee, then back to his brother.

All his life he had prepared for this moment. His father had spent endless time telling him what he expected of him as chief of their people. Yet now as he looked at every face, each bringing a memory, he felt incapable of the task set before him.

The silence was deafening. His gaze found Running Deer standing not far from his brother, her smile triumphant, and he had to wonder why she was so happy. His father was dead.

He stopped before his brother. Iron Bear's eyes were cold and penetrating, his jaw tight, the nerve pulsing there. Gray Hawk stared at him for a long moment. "You will make a fine chief, Iron Bear," he said. "You deserve the honor much more than I do."

A gasp rang out over the crowd, and Gray Hawk saw the look of disbelief on his brother's face. He turned and addressed his people. "Iron Bear is now your chief. I would ask that you join me this night in celebrating the passing of a father's legacy to his son." Tears welled in his eyes, and Gray Hawk had to blink them back. "He will be a fine chief and lead you well."

As he walked toward Three Moons' teepee, he passed by Tawanka, whose smile was wide, telling him he had done the right thing.

A fire was lit in his father's tipi, taking the chill off the morning. Three Moons lay with his arms crossed over his chest, looking more peaceful than Gray Hawk had ever seen him. The tears that had been threatening flowed freely, and though he knew his father had always told him tears were a sign of weakness, he was helpless to stop them, nor did he want to.

Last night he should have told his father how much he loved him, how proud he was to have called him his father. Now he would never have that chance.

"I don't understand," Iron Bear's voice reached him.

Every muscle in Gray Hawk's body tensed. He wiped the tears with the back of his hand and turned. "You are better suited to be their leader than I am. You were right all along, I don't deserve to be their chief...but you do."

"But our father—"

"Wanted the best person to take over for our people. You've reminded me too many times in the past that I yearn to be other than what I am. I think you're right, and what's even worse is that now, when I've been treated terribly by the whites, I still would live among them, take their hate and their bigotry as long as I had Jordan."

"She left this morning."

"I know."

"Will you go after her?" Iron Bear asked, his voice softer than Gray Hawk had ever heard it.

"Soon, but first I will say goodbye to our father and to my people, for I don't know when I'll see you again."

Iron Bear nodded and put a hand on Gray Hawk's shoulder. It was the first time in their lives he'd shown any emotion other than hatred. "For all my life I lived in your shadow. When you were a child, I hated the way our father spent most of his time with you. And always you could do no wrong. No matter what I did, how hard I tried, he would never look at me the way he looked at you. In time I felt the only way to try and best you was to hurt you, but now I realize how wrong I've been. You've only wanted the best for me, when in turn I wanted the worst for you. Now, after all I've done to you, you are giving me what I've wanted most of all." He shook his head. "How can I take it, Gray Hawk? How can I when I know in my heart, it is not me who deserves it, but you. Our father wanted you—"

Gray Hawk shook his head. "That's where you're wrong. Our father wants the man who can lead our tribe against our enemies. He loved you Iron Bear, you just chose not to see it. He often talked of your bravery." He smiled softly. "As well as the unnecessary chances you would take, but he also respected that, knowing you would go to any lengths for your people. If you think of this as a gift, then so be it. I look at it as your right—a right you deserve and one you have proven yourself worthy of." He took a long, unsteady breath. "Now, your people are waiting for you."

Iron Bear took the step that separated them and hugged him tightly. For the first time that he could remember, Gray Hawk felt he truly had a brother again, and he knew for certain he had done the right thing.

KARI HELD her hands over the stove, trying to get warm. The days were getting more frigid, and just this morning Shane mentioned a chance of snow.

Jordan and Gray Hawk had been gone for weeks now, and though Kari knew her cousin might be gone until spring, she already missed her horribly, and secretly prayed for her return.

Her father hadn't come around since that day, and word had it he had left town, along with a young prostitute who he never let out of his sight. Kari shook her head. If Patricia only knew, she would kill him.

It was too much to hope that he had gone back to Virginia. She suspected he was just waiting for the moment when Jordan showed her face.

Well, he would have a long wait then.

She was grateful for Shane Catalono's protection. In a lot of ways she felt guilty, knowing that she brought all this on him, putting him and his family in danger. Had she and Jordan just left for Fife, none of this would have happened. But then again, Gray Hawk wouldn't have taken Rebecca from the Crow, and knowing the dreaded tribe, Shane probably wouldn't have made it out alive.

All things happened for a reason, and fate had seen to it to bring Shane Catalono into her life.

Just the sight of the handsome rancher made her heart skitter. She feared she was in love with Shane, but didn't know how to go about gaining his attention more than what she was already doing, which was little more than stealing quick glances, or sharing a quick word.

She knew Shane was twice her age, but she didn't care. There wasn't a man around who made her feel the way he did. And when he looked at her with those blue eyes, her stomach turned inside out.

Hearing the sound of his boots on the front porch, she quickly ran her fingers through her hair, straightened her apron, and returned to frosting the cake she had made that afternoon.

"Mmm, smells great," he said from the other room.

She smiled at the compliment. Less than a year ago she couldn't even bake a cake, or do any of the domestic things that now came like second nature to her. Sure, she did burn things on occasion, but it was rare. Strange that a woman who had grown up expecting to have a team of servants to see to her every need, had come to realize she could do all those things herself, and actually enjoyed doing it.

Shane walked into the room, making her thoughts scatter. As she watched him she noticed his hair was getting longer, and she had to admit that she kind of liked the way it curled up at his shirt collar. And there was something very appealing about his unshaved jaw that gave him an almost dangerous appearance.

He came up beside her and took a finger full of frosting. "Shane!"

"What?" he asked, grinning from ear to ear.

Licking the frosting off his finger, he leaned his hip against the counter, watching her with those beautiful eyes of his. He grinned. "It's the best frosting I've ever had." Was it her imagination or were his eyes darker now than they had been a minute before?

The way he was watching her gave Kari the impression he was about to kiss her. Her lips parted, waiting.

Then the front door opened, then slammed, and Rebecca and Tanner came running in, nearly knocking Kari over in their haste to get to the cake.

Shane closed his eyes and took a deep breath before he turned to the kids who were already fighting over who would get to lick the spoons.

"Later," he said just low enough for her to hear. Her pulse skittered as his eyes held hers, promising her he would finish what he started.

Throughout dinner, Kari could sense his gaze on her. Feeling like a schoolgirl, she couldn't keep the smile off her face, or the blush from her cheeks.

Then a loud knock pounded on the door, ending her joyful mood. Shane stood up and motioned for them to be quiet.

Kari waited, listening intently as Shane opened the door. Several moments passed without anyone speaking. Then she heard voices, and then footsteps coming toward the kitchen. With her gaze riveted on the kitchen entrance, she waited nervously, holding her breath, half-expecting her father to come around the corner.

She let out her breath in a rush as Jordan walked in.

"Jordan!" Kari cried, standing so fast, she knocked her chair over in her haste as she threw her arms around her cousin. "I didn't expect you back this soon. But look at you, you're so cold and I'll bet you're exhausted."

Kari put her at arms length and though Jordan had a smile for her, she saw sadness in her eyes. "Where's Gray Hawk?"

Jordan averted her gaze. "He's staying with his people."

"Why did you come back?"

She met her gaze once again, and Kari clearly saw the pain there. "We need to talk."

It wasn't only the way she said it, but how she looked when she said it that worried Kari. "Alright, but why don't you eat first."

Jordan accepted the hugs from the kids, then took a seat.

After eating a few bites, she pushed her plate back, rested her arms on the table, and waited for Tanner and Rebecca to leave the room before saying, "I've given it a lot of thought, and I think it's best to turn myself in."

"Jordan, no."

"We can't keep on running for the rest of our lives. I want my ranch, Kari. I'd rather spend time in jail than return to Virginia and marry Marvin. I'd die first."

"He'll insist we go back to Virginia. How can we stop him?" Kari asked, sending Shane a worried look, not liking the idea of facing her father after all this time.

"By telling him the truth. That I love someone else, and that I'm...pregnant."

Kari sat back in her chair, her breath leaving her in a rush. "You're pregnant?" she gasped in disbelief.

"Does Gray Hawk know?" Shane cut in.

She shook her head. "No, but it doesn't matter."

"Jordan, if you're carrying his child, he has every right to know."

Jordan smiled tightly at Shane. "I understand what you're trying to say, and I wanted to tell him, I truly did, but when we returned to his village, his father was dying. In fact, he's probably already dead."

"And Gray Hawk is chief," Kari said, her voice little more than a whisper.

Jordan nodded.

Kari ran her hands down her face, her heart aching for her cousin. "Jordan, I'm so sorry."

"Don't be. It was a mistake. I should have known better, but now I'm going to have a child, and I plan to raise that child on my ranch. I'll give him or her a good life."

Shane patted Jordan's hand and smiled reassuringly.

"Well, since you have your mind made up, I guess the next step is to invite your uncle here to the ranch."

Jordan shook her head. "We've already involved you—"

"You did no such thing. I offered you to come in gratitude for taking care of Rebecca. I'll send word to your uncle that he can come here to the ranch."

Chapter 25

JORDAN RECOILED at the sight of her uncle who stood on the porch of the Triple T, looking completely out of place in his three-piece designer suit, custom-made shoes, and bowler hat.

His thin-lipped smile told her he was as happy to see her, as she was him.

He gave her the once over, but said nothing, his gaze then turned to Kari. Disappointment clearly marked his features.

"Mr. Catalono, I presume," he said, extending his hand toward Shane, who greeted him with a handshake.

"I'm sure you are as surprised as I am to find that you have my niece, who is wanted for kidnapping, sleeping under your roof. I must tell you, however, that I do not hold you responsible for harboring a fugitive of the law, though I have every right to bring charges against you."

Jordan had to refrain from lashing out at her uncle. His insolence absolutely amazed her.

Shane stepped in front of Jordan. "From what I understand, the women left your home with good cause. Jordan didn't want to marry the man who you thought suitable."

Frederick threw back his head and chuckled without mirth. "Oh, dear sir, you live a different life out here in the sticks." He lifted his brows. "In Virginia it is the guardian's responsibility to find a suitable groom for their ward. I have seen to that in Jordan's betrothed. He's a man of great wealth and power—"

"Who's old enough to be her grandfather."

Frederick cleared his throat abruptly, obviously irritated he was being questioned by a mere cowboy. "Within a few years she may be a very young, very wealthy widow."

Shane frowned. "I come from a place where people are given a choice as to how they live their lives and who they live it with. If I'm not mistaken, Jordan prefers to stay here. Being that she's old enough to make her own decisions."

"Well, it doesn't really matter what she wants, because her husband-to-be is awaiting her arrival in Richmond by the end of the month." He turned to Jordan and Kari. "I'll expect you two to get whatever belongings you may have. We'll be leaving now."

"I'm not going anywhere with you," Jordan said, lifting her chin a notch. Her uncle's piercing eyes stared her down, as he had done so often through the years. But she was no longer a child, and instead of being intimidated by the man, she felt resentful of the hell he had put her through.

"You will get your things, now."

Jordan shook her head. "No, I will not. I'm staying here. I want to raise my child in Wyoming, on my ranch."

Frederick's eyes widened, his gaze slipping to her stomach. "You little slut. You're no better than a whore, spreading your legs for every man who comes along."

Kari gasped beside her, but said nothing.

"You're pregnant with an Indian's baby. Have you no shame?"

Jordan ignored his cruel words, knowing it didn't matter what he thought. He'd never approved of anything she did, and he never would.

"I'm tired of your insults. Just leave me in peace."

"I will not leave you here. You will return with me, we'll see that the baby is aborted. I know a doctor who handles such things."

Shane drew his gun and leveled it at Frederick's head. "Sir, you go too far."

"I would rather die than harm my child," Jordan hissed, hating him with all her heart.

"Marvin will never accept a breed's baby," Frederick said menacingly, ignoring Shane who had since lowered his gun.

"Good, then it's settled. I'll stay here."

"The ranch will never be yours. It's already been sold."

Jordan's heart died a little at his words, and as he patted his vest pocket and the papers within, she began to tremble. His thin lips curved up in the corners.

"You're lying."

Her uncle leaned toward her with victory in his eyes. "It's sold now. It will never be yours."

Shane cleared his throat. "You mister, are a heartless cad. What reason would you have to deny your niece her childhood home?"

"It is nothing but a shack," Frederick said with distaste. "Plus, it doesn't matter to me. As far as I'm concerned, she can live in a teepee for the rest of her life, along with the Indian and his brat. You're no good to me anymore as it is."

So many words were on the tip of Jordan's tongue, all words that would only make things worse. Shaking her head, she took Kari's hand and walked toward the front door when her uncle's voice stopped her.

"I may be leaving you here to rot in hell, but my daughter is coming with me."

Kari's fingernails bit into Jordan's arm. Her back straightened, and she went white as a sheet.

Frederick cleared his throat. "Marvin will be just as happy with you, my love."

"You're bluffing," Kari said, turning white under her father's cruel stare.

Frederick lifted a brow, reminding Jordan of the devil himself. "You know I don't bluff."

Jordan stepped in front of Kari protectively. "She can't go."

"Of course she can! I am her father, and I am taking her back to our home in Virginia."

"I'm afraid that's impossible, sir," Shane cut-in.

A nerve ticked in Frederick's jaw. "And pray tell, why is that impossible?"

"Because she's marrying me," Shane said, his expression set in stone.

Frederick flinched. "That's absurd!"

"No, it's a fact, isn't it, darling?" Shane asked, looking at Kari as though he was very much in love, which Jordan realized with a start was not conjured. He loved Kari—and had for some time.

"Well, as her father, I say the engagement is broken, and she will return to Virginia, where she will live the way she is accustomed."

"That's impossible," Shane said, a satisfied smile on his face.

Frederick frowned. "How so?"

"She is no longer a virgin. I've compromised your daughter." Shane said the words with conviction. "In fact, she may very well be carrying my child as we speak."

Jordan heard Kari's quick intake of breath, making her wonder if Shane lied, though he seemed pretty convincing as he held out his arms to Kari. Her cousin wrapped her arms around his waist, and looked completely at ease as she rested her cheek against his chest.

Frederick's face became flushed, and beads of perspiration dripped from his forehead as he threw a hostile glare at his daughter. "You're no better than that whore," he hissed, nodding in Jordan's direction. "You're both nothing but lying little sluts."

"I'm tired of you speaking to your daughter and niece this way. Especially when your own morals have to be questioned, considering the hundreds of dollars you've spent to entertain a whore in your hotel room since the day you arrived in Brogan." Shane smiled, though it didn't quite reach his eyes. "You see, in small towns everybody knows everyone else, making it hard for certain things to go unnoticed."

Jordan could have laughed out loud at the expression on her uncle's face. Shane's statement had taken her by surprise, but she knew it was the truth, especially when Frederick retreated to the elaborate carriage that looked grossly out of place in this part of the country.

"We won," Kari said, smiling up at Shane.

Jordan wasn't so sure. As the carriage disappeared out of sight, she felt defeated. She'd lost Gray Hawk and now her ranch; the two things that meant everything.

THOUGH KARI may have thought Shane had been bluffing about marrying her, he proved that very evening that he meant it. By that weekend they stood on the steps of the small white church in Brogan and took their vows in front of a few friends, and of course, all the ranch hands at the Triple T, who welcomed the new addition to the Catalono family with open arms.

It was a bittersweet moment for Jordan, who knew that her cousin and Shane truly loved one another. Though she was thrilled for Kari, Jordan was also sad, knowing if things had worked out differently with she and Gray Hawk, that she too would be happy and in love, starting a new life with a wonderful man.

Hank agreed to watch Tanner and Rebecca for the weekend while Kari and Shane honeymooned in a nearby county, giving Jordan the opportunity to head to her ranch, to start thinking about her future.

FREDERICK McGuire started packing his bags, his gaze continually returned to the woman standing at the window, her back rigid, her chin held high as though she were a princess, and not a prostitute.

This past month she had been a constant in his life, and though he mentioned her coming to Virginia with him before, he had never really asked her.

"China?"

She turned to him, her beautiful green eyes misty with tears. She was only twenty-nine, so she said, and without makeup she looked even younger. He knew for certain her life had been a tough one, she'd told him everything, holding nothing back. The abuse she suffered as a child by the hand of a stepfather who hated her, selling her to the highest bidder at the tender age of thirteen. He cringed, realizing how it was almost as if she were talking about him and the way he had been so willing to sell his eldest daughter or his brother's only child to a man who was unworthy.

Granted it was a marriage, but was it so different? He tried to think back, wondering when it was things had gone so wrong. When had he become the man he was now?

China came to him, her eyes focused on his chest, a habit she had of not meeting his eyes. A habit he hated.

"Look at me."

She glanced up and flinched. His fingers touched the soft skin of her cheek, then trailed down her neck. Pulling her to him he kissed her. He knew after today she would be back in the brothel, spreading her legs for other patrons. The thought tore at his insides.

"I need to return to Virginia, but before I go, I want to ask you if you would come with me."

She pressed her cheek against his chest.

"Would you come with me?" he asked again.

"You're married."

He nodded. "I am."

Her smile was sad, and he knew the answer before she replied, "I will not break up a marriage, and if I return with you, it could destroy you...I would never do that...not ever."

"But it kills me to leave you here."

She shrugged indifferently. "You'll survive, and I'll survive."

"What are you saying?" he asked, fear eating at his insides.

"I'll be the first to admit I'm a whore. At least I'm honest with myself and everyone else. But I have to be honest with you, Freddy. I can't be someone's wife, or even a mistress to someone who would hurt and destroy their own family for his own gain. Especially his daughter and niece, a girl who was entrusted into your care by your own brother."

He realized now that he'd told her more than he probably should have. "I'll give you a life you could otherwise only dream of," he said desperately, hating the thought of a future without her.

The silence was too final. Dropping to the edge of the bed in defeat, he stared at her in shock.

"Please don't misunderstand me," she said, kneeling in front of him. "I love you, Freddy. But despite my profession, I do have my pride. Wife, or no wife, I couldn't live with a man who only thinks of himself. What if one day you decided to use me in one of your schemes, the same way you've used your daughter and niece? And they're your family." She shook her head, disapproval of what he'd done evident in her eyes. "No Freddy, I could never stand for that."

He flinched as though she'd struck him. Never in his life had anyone talked to him the way she had and lived to tell about it. Yet as he stared at her, he found it impossible to be angry. With gentle fingers he traced the soft skin of her cheek. "Please reconsider," he whispered.

"Oh, Frederick." It was the first time she had used his given name. "I *feel* sorry for you. You're filled with so much greed and hate."

As she stood and walked away from him, he felt the loss like a fist to his gut.

She was to the door when she turned to him, a soft smile on her lips. "Thank you for this last month. They've been the best days of my life. I'll never forget you." Then she closed the door behind her.

He sagged against the bedpost, knowing she was right.

How ironic that it took being rejected by a whore to make him see the kind of man he'd become. Patricia would have no doubt applauded his behavior of late, encouraging him to ruin his own daughter and niece.

China. It would never work bringing her back to Virginia with him, and if Patricia ever found out...thinking of his wife, he flinched. For far too long she held a power over him that was quickly slipping away. He had changed since she came into his life, letting her mold him into something he despised.

His mind raced, realizing how horrible he had been in the past. He grabbed the whiskey bottle off the night stand and took a long drink, enjoying the burning sensation as it raced to his gut.

As he left the hotel, he left two letters, and paid a young man to carry them out to the Triple T.

Later that day when he left Brogan, he left behind a little piece of his heart.

KARI TREMBLED as Shane helped her out of her dress. His fingers seemed to burn through the material, scorching her skin, much as his eyes were doing to her body as he slipped the garment down her arms and hips, letting it pool around her feet.

All day she'd been anticipating this moment, knowing that after tonight she would be a woman.

Shane kissed her, first softly, then with more urgency, until she felt her knees go weak. He smiled against her lips and picked her up, placing her with gentle care on the bed before standing back to look at her.

Instinctively her hands went up to shield herself from his gaze, but the soft expression on his face made her relax and she dropped her arms back at her sides, watching as he undressed. He removed his pants and she could feel her cheeks burn as his long, hard manhood was exposed to her devouring gaze. She talked to Jordan about what to expect on her wedding night, but still she was nervous. And it must have shown on her face because Shane smiled reassuringly.

He joined her on the bed, his tall lean frame stretching out beside her as he pulled her against him. He kissed her again, his fingers moving to her breast, skimming over her nipple that went hard beneath his ministrations. "You're so beautiful," he said against her lips. She wanted to please him, and she let her hands wander over the hard planes of his shoulders, his chest, down his abdomen where his manhood jutted out. With tentative fingers she touched him.

A dark brow lifted as her fingers skimmed the silky, hard surface. "You're so big," she said in awe.

His laughter brought her gaze back to his face, afraid that she had said something wrong. "And you always know what to say."

She relaxed as he kissed her and his fingers moved down her belly to the triangle of hair between her legs. Her insides pulsated as a finger slipped inside her, moving in and out, a moment later his thumb played over sensitive flesh. She felt as though she were being unwound nerve by pulsating nerve.

Pushing her legs apart with his knee, Shane slowly inched his way into his new bride. Her eyes were wide, staring at him, biting into her bottom lip. She was so tight, so sweet. Sweat began to bead on his brow, and as he came up against the proof of her virginity, he kissed her and plunged. She gasped against his mouth, and he stilled, letting her get used to the size of him.

But it was torture. Her tight sheath was so hot and slick he couldn't wait any longer and finally began to move, and with every thrust he felt her relax a little more until she matched his rhythm.

With great restraint he held himself back and was greatly relieved when he began to feel the soft flutters of her climax. Her eyes closed, her head fell back against the soft pillows, her mouth opened as she cried out, and a moment later he followed her.

As he lay with his wife at his side, he pulled her to him, kissing the tip of her nose. "I love you, Mrs. Catalono."

Her eyes so soft, looked misty with tears, and for a moment he thought he had hurt her, but her fingers moved along his jaw, and then without lifting her head off the pillow she kissed the air. "I love you, too, but I'm so tired I can't even lift my head."

He laughed then, and cradling her head on his shoulder, wrapped his arms around her, content to stay that way for the rest of the night.

Chapter 26

IT HAD been over eleven years.

Eleven long years since she last stood at this spot, looking at the slain bodies of her parents as four Indians rode away, never to be found and convicted of the crime.

Jordan stood at the front door of her ranch, fighting back emotions that had been long hidden away. But as the front door of the cabin creaked open, so did the memories, and along with it tears that slipped down her cheeks unchecked.

Swallowing the lump in her throat, she stepped inside the small room that at one time had seemed so large. White sheets that covered furniture were covered with dust and grime. The curtains her mother had spent days crocheting were now yellowed and brittle.

Her small chair sat by the fire, beside it, one of the dolls her mother had made. When they had left for Virginia, she'd only taken one with her, and the twins had destroyed it, cutting off its golden hair and pulling the arms off its body. Picking the doll up, she squeezed it tight. She would keep it for the daughter she would have one day, even if that child was not the one she now carried in her womb.

She moved to the kitchen, thoughts of her mother humming as she made dinner, mingled with memories of the sound of her father's greeting when he came home after a long day out in the pasture, taming wild horses. The feel of his strong arms as they lifted her high and held him to her, telling him how much he loved her. And then she had watched her parents kiss and hug. They had truly loved one another. As a child Jordan hadn't realized to what extent, but now as an adult, having loved herself, she knew what they had shared.

The bedrooms were the hardest, because things were still as they had been when she'd left all those years ago. Her mother's brush and comb sat on the dresser. Her father's pocketwatch sat on the table by the door. As usual he had forgotten to take it with him, as he did most every day.

Shutting the door behind her, she went to her room and sat down on the small bed. It was strange how everything now seemed so small. From the eyes of a seven-year-old, it had all appeared so much larger.

By the time she stepped back into the Living room she was both physically and emotionally exhausted. Lighting a candle, she sat down in her mother's rocking chair and waited for dark.

A feeling of total peace came over her as she thought about the future.

This is what she wanted. This is what she needed. This was her dream, and she would have it, and have it soon.

She was nearly to sleep when she heard the pounding of hooves outside. Her heart skittered remembering the day eleven years ago when her life had been upended. She came to her feet just as footsteps fell on the front porch. She froze, unable to do anything but stare at the door.

A moment later it opened and she nearly fell to her knees, for standing before her was no enemy, but the man she loved more than life.

Gray Hawk's face was drawn. He looked so tired, and almost—angry.

"You left me," he said, his voice harsh.

"How could I stay, Gray Hawk? No one wanted me there."

He frowned. "I wanted you there."

How could she tell him that from the minute she'd left the village, she almost turned back a thousand times, knowing that a life without him would be unfathomable. Yet she'd been unable to return, knowing she could not turn her back on her dream, and she wouldn't take him away from his.

Silence filled the small room, and it seemed for a minute that he was about to leave, but he had only turned to shut the door behind him. He leaned back against it. "My father died the morning you left."

His grief was obvious and she wanted desperately to comfort, but couldn't find any words other than to say, "I'm so sorry."

"I once thought being chief was all I would ever want, yet I found when I was given the opportunity it meant nothing, because I didn't have you."

Her heart lurched.

"I know you would never be happy in the village. When we went there, I hoped that you would change your mind."

"I belong here, Gray Hawk. This is my home, this is my dream. I know we come from different places, and I knew it would one day come to this. I cannot return with you, no matter how much you want it."

He walked toward her in slow strides, his gaze shifting over her in a way that made her heart race and long for things that could not be. How desperate she was to have him take her in his arms and tell her everything would be all right. How she longed at this moment for him to make love to her.

He stopped before her and took her hands in his. "Marry me,

Jordan."

"What?"

"Marry me. Be my wife."

"But I can't leave my ranch."

His lips curved into a smile. "I never asked you to."

As comprehension set in, her heart swelled. "You would stay with me? You would give up being chief?"

"Iron Bear will lead our people. He is their chief."

She threw her arms around him, holding him close. "Yes, I will marry you."

Lifting her chin with his fingers, he kissed her softly. "I know I don't have much to give, but I promise you I'll work endlessly to make this ranch prosperous."

"And I'll work endlessly to make you happy."

His face softened as he stared at her. "You've already made me the happiest man alive."

She shifted on her feet, uncertain whether to tell the news that soon they would be parents. Knowing there was no better time to be honest, she took a deep breath and blurted, "I'm pregnant, Gray Hawk. We're going to have a baby."

His gaze left hers to settle on the soft swell of her belly, which his hand moved to, splaying there. When he looked at her again, there were tears in his eyes. He opened his mouth, and without saying a word, he hugged her tightly to him.

Never in her life had she known such happiness.

A BLISSFUL two weeks had passed for Jordan. In that time, she and Gray Hawk had been married by the minister of the small church in Fife. He had been a kind man, who didn't question the differences between she and Gray Hawk. The man's wife had served as the only other witness.

They returned to their ranch that same day, where they celebrated by having a quiet meal out by the creek that ran in back of their home. There they had made love under a starry sky, promising each other the world.

Jordan felt like the luckiest woman alive.

Yet the next afternoon a young man rode up to the property, and her heart lurched in her breast, even though she knew she was beyond her uncle's touch now that she was married. Yet fear for her ranch made her call out to Gray Hawk, who was nearby working on a corral.

"Are you Jordan McGuire?" the young man asked, taking the hat from his head and running a hand through his sweaty hair.

Gray Hawk put his hand out toward the man in greeting. "She is, and

I'm her husband, Gray. Can I help you?"

"I've a letter for you."

He handed Jordan the envelope, and instantly her heart sank recognizing her uncle's penmanship. "Thank you," she replied to the young man, who left as quickly as he arrived.

"Are you alright?" Gray Hawk asked, watching her intently.

"It's from my uncle." She took a deep breath and with trembling hands, opened the letter and read it out loud.

"Dearest Jordan, I fear I have done you a great injustice. Not only have I behaved horribly toward you all these years when you needed my love the most, I have also betrayed you to which lengths you cannot imagine. That is why I write this letter to you. Your father was a very wealthy man, and when he died he left you the ranch, and a considerable sum of money which was left in a disclosed location. Your father was never one to trust banks, and therefore, saw to it to hide the money on your land, in your home. He entrusted me with this information, so I in turn would tell you.

In the homestead, at the base of the stove there are bricks lining the floor. Toward the back you will find several that give way. Therein you will find a steel box, which was opened before your arrival—there you will find the deed to your ranch, along with enough money to buy those horses you always talked about as a child. Oh, Jordan, I cannot take back all the years of ill that I caused, but I do hope in my heart that you will one day forgive me. I am on my way back to Virginia, and if God wills it, I shall see you again one day. Until then I remain, your Uncle Frederick.

She looked up at Gray Hawk, whose wide smile mirrored her own feelings. "I don't believe it."

"It's yours, Jordan. No one will take it away."

"I have my ranch," Jordan said, tears stinging her eyes. "And we have money, which means we can buy lots of horses and make this ranch one of the largest in the region."

Gray Hawk pulled her into his arms and kissed her soundly. "I'm so happy for you."

"I'm happy for us. This is *our* money, Gray Hawk. This is *our* ranch. And what are we waiting for?" she asked, as she ran for the house, stopping just short of the stove.

She turned to Gray Hawk. "Do you want me to do it?" he asked, motioning toward the stove.

"No, I'll do it," she said, and with shaking hands she unearthed the steel box.

"You open it," she said, trembling with excitement and a sense of fear, as she handed it to Gray Hawk, hoping it wasn't a cruel joke.

Taking his knife, he pried the lock off and opened it up. Her breath caught in her throat at the sight that met her. Never in all her years could she have imagined that this kind of money existed in her family. Hers had been a simple upbringing with little in the way of frivolous things. But her parents had obviously put away for a rainy day, not realizing their own lives would be cut short.

"Do you know what we can do with this money?" she asked, meeting Gray Hawk's stare.

"I have a feeling you're about to tell me."

"We can build onto the house, make more rooms for our children."

"Our children." He smiled. "I like the sound of that." His eyes darkened and he tossed the box aside as though it were loose change.

Jordan laughed, knowing that money was the last thing on his mind.

Epilogue

JORDAN AND Kari sat on the porch swing, watching their husbands as they tried to tame the wild mustang.

Kari laughed under her breath as Shane was thrown yet again. Grimacing, he stood and rubbed his worn-out backside.

Though Jordan was content with the life she and Gray Hawk had made before she'd discovered the money, there was no question it had made a huge difference, enabling them to start their ranch sooner than expected.

Already they had an impressive selection of horseflesh, and they had queries from people in nearby counties who had heard the McGuire Horse Ranch was up and running again.

The only distressing thing for Jordan was that Gray Hawk didn't allow her to lift a finger, afraid that it would harm the baby. So she was resigned to doing the housework and tending the garden, while he and Jake, a young hand from Shane's spread, worked on breaking the wild horses they had acquired.

"He's so happy," Kari said, bringing Jordan out of her revelry.

Kari and Shane had arrived early last evening. They'd spent the entire night catching up on the months that had passed. Jordan squeezed Kari's hand. There was no denying how good it felt to have Kari with her.

Jordan smiled as Shane attempted to mount the spirited mare without success. Her gaze shifted to her husband, who laughed and stepping into the corral, soothed the horse, talking to it in low tones. He moved to its side, then mounted with an ease that surprised all of them. The horse bucked a few times, but Gray Hawk held on, and as though realizing the man on his back wasn't about to give up, it calmed down and pranced around the corral.

"Show off," Shane said with a defeated smirk, while sitting on the rail, shaking his head.

Gray Hawk's grin stole the breath from Jordan's lungs. He winked, and jumped from the horse, laughing at something Shane said.

With a smile Jordan turned to Kari, whose hand rested on her protruding stomach. Though her cousin was due two months after her, she was almost as big. Just last month the doctor had told her he'd heard two heartbeats. Kari at first had been frightened by the news she was having twins, but Shane had been thrilled.

Kari took her hand in hers and squeezed it tight. "We got everything we ever dreamed of it, didn't we?"

Jordan looked from her to Gray Hwak, who was now patting Shane on the back. Her heart filled with love for the man who had stolen her heart. "Yes, we certainly did."

~ * ~

Julia Templeton

An avid reader all her life, Julia discovered historical romance when she was nineteen, and to this day she still gets excited when she walks into a bookstore. She is a member of Romance Writers of America: National, Rose City Writers, and Hearts through History Chapters.

SURRENDER TO LOVE is her second historical romance to be published. Julia loves reading all sub-genres of romance, as well as all time periods.

Julia lives in Brush Prairie, Washington, with her husband and their two teenagers She is currently at work on her next historical romance. She loves to hear from her readers. Please feel free to email her at jtempleton9@attbi.com.

Printed in the United States
24752LVS00001B/95